NOTHING TO US

SCARLETT FINN

Also by Scarlett Finn

GO NOVELS
GO WITH IT
GO IT ALONE
GO ALL OUT
GO ALL IN
GO FULL CIRCLE

EXILE
HIDE & SEEK
KISS CHASE

WRECK & RUIN
RUIN ME
RUIN HIM

**THE BRANDED
SERIES**
BRANDED
SCARRED
MARKED

**FORBIDDEN
PREQUEL DUET**
ALL. ONLY.
ONLY YOURS

THE FORBIDDEN NOVELS
FORBIDDEN DESIRE
FORBIDDEN WANT
FORBIDDEN WISH
FORBIDDEN NEED
FORBIDDEN BOND

**BOMBSHELLS & BILLIONAIRES
(ROXIVERSE)**
NOTHING TO HIDE
NOTHING TO LOSE
NOTHING IN BETWEEN: ONE
NOTHING TO DECLARE
NOTHING TO US
NOTHING IN BETWEEN: TWO
NOTHING TO SAY
NOTHING TO GAIN
NOTHING IN BETWEEN: THREE
NOTHING TO YOU
NOTHING TO THIS PREQUEL: ONE WILD NIGHT
NOTHING TO THIS
NOTHING IN BETWEEN: FOUR
NOTHING TO DO
NOTHING TO NO ONE
NOTHING TO FEAR
NOTHING TO DENY
NOTHING TO BEAT
NOTHING TO THE WEDDING
NOTHING TO TELL
NOTHING TO IT
NOTHING TO SEE
NOTHING TO WIN
NOTHING TO OFFER
NOTHING TO PROVE

**LOVE AGAINST THE ODDS
STANDALONE COLLECTION**
SWEET SEAS
HEIR'S AFFAIR
RESCUED
MAESTRO'S MUSE
GETTING TRICKY
THIRTEEN
REMEMBER WHEN...
RELUCTANT SUSPICION
XY FACTOR

KINDRED SERIES
RAVEN
SWALLOW
CUCKOO
SWIFT
FALCON
FINCH

MISTAKE DUET
MISTAKE ME NOT
SLEIGHT MISTAKE

LOST & FOUND
LOST
FOUND

**THE EXPLICIT
SERIES**
EXPLICIT INSTRUCTION
EXPLICIT DETAIL
EXPLICIT MEMORY

TO DIE FOR...
TO DIE FOR TRUTH
TO DIE FOR HONOR
TO DIE FOR VIRTUE
TO DIE FOR DUTY
TO DIE FOR LOVE

**RISQUÉ & HARROW
INTERTWINED**
TAKE A RISK
FIGHTING FATE
RISK IT ALL
FIGHTING BACK
GAME OF RISK

ONE

"YOU'LL BE OKAY, Jane, honey," Toria said, giving her a hug.

"Are you sure you want to party with… rock stars?"

Her friend was too excited to contain her glee. "Oh, God, yes!"

Crimson LA. One of Zairn Lomond's exclusive nightclubs. As if just being there wasn't enough, they'd spent most of their evening in a central private pod. A restricted room in the middle of the VIP area that could only be accessed by appointment or certain individuals. Exclusive within exclusive. Their roommate Roxie Kyst was their "in" because Zairn spent most of his time *in* Roxie… and he'd put a ring on their best friend's finger.

Their engaged friends had departed not long ago. Obviously, the allure of alone time outweighed the couple's interest in being social.

Now her other best friend, Toria, was running out of the private pod to go party with rock star, Logan Lowe, and his entourage at someone's "crib." Was there a more terrifying prospect? Not many. Nope, not for her. Such an event went way far beyond her comfort zone. Way far, like light years beyond her comfort zone. Maybe if she had more liquor in her system. Only then did her confidence rear its head… and her stupidity.

"Just be careful."

"You can come if you want," Toria said. "He said you can."

Jane was already shaking her head. "No. That's a hard no."

"Okay," Toria said, laughing as she gave her another quick hug. When they parted, Toria leaned sideways to look around her at the only other remaining member of their group. "You make sure she gets home safe, Knox."

The billionaire media mogul offered a two-fingered salute in reply. His opposite fingertips rested on the rim of the glass on the wide arm of his leather chair perpendicular to the couch. Toria kissed her cheek and dashed out, leaving her and Knox alone in the enclosed space.

This was it. The moment she'd have to face what she'd done with him. *To* him.

A whole nightclub of people danced and drank beyond the exit in front of her. Escape was right there. If she just reached out and took the handle… she could save herself more humiliation. Except it would always be there. Her audacity. She could run but hiding from it forever was out of the question.

Damnit.

In the private pod, she and Knox were cut off from everyone else. Cut off from distractions that might prevent her from doing something stupid. Something like she'd done the only other time they'd been alone. Why had she done it? Since when was she so brazen?

The transparent walls of the private pod were great until she was by herself with one of the world's most eligible bachelors. What would the ogling Crimson patrons think? They'd wonder why she was with him. Not that she was with him, they were just—

"You going to stand over there all night?" Knox asked.

If it was that or turn and face him, the former was preferable. Women across the world would fall over themselves for the chance to be alone with Knox, middle Collier son, heir to more than half the planet's media corporations if the internet was to be believed.

Knox was one of Zairn's best friends. Roxie was one of hers. If the two were to be married, she and Knox would be spending more time together. That meant one thing…

Swallowing her pride and shame, it was time to apologize.

She took a deep breath and spun on the spot, forcing herself to look at him before releasing the air from her lungs. "I'm sorry."

He frowned. "It's okay, take your time."

"No, I…" Pursing her lips, she took tentative steps toward the seating area. "For the other night… the night Roxie was missing."

Roxie and Zairn had broken up three nights ago. On the back of that, Roxie vanished, freaking everyone out. And it was that night, in her fear and grief that she'd lost her mind, grabbed Knox, and kissed the bejesus out of him in a hotel suite restroom. They barely knew each other. No, actually, they didn't know each other at all. And she'd taken serious liberties, which was not like her.

"In the restroom."

"Right," she said, gliding down to sit at the far end of the couch. Far, far from him. Out of kissing radius. "I was worried and you… You just wanted to use the bathroom and found me in there… I was a mess. You were trying to comfort me, being nice. I took advantage of—"

"It was a kiss," he said, an almost snicker in his words. "We were talking, and we kissed."

This guy was a gentleman. "I kissed you. You came into the restroom and… I have to apologize. Please let me apologize."

"Don't worry about it," he said, raising his glass from the arm of the chair to drink the liquid within.

"I'm not that type of woman. I don't… I'm never bold, and I shouldn't have… I'm sorry."

He put his glass on the end table. "My family pays a lot of money for security to protect us from threats. Enough that we could wage war against a small foreign nation." That was probably a joke, but she was wound too tight to laugh. "You're not a threat, Jane."

His cool smile soothed some of her guilt. When their friends were present, it was easier to relax. With Roxie, Zairn, and Toria around, she'd avoided looking at him, pretending, probably, that he wasn't there at all. But alone, there was no escape. The glow in his receptive eyes drew her in. Just like that night in the restroom. What had he been saying? Had she heard his words?

Her lips parted, her breathing slowed and grew deeper at the same time. Geez, he was hot… the square jaw, the almost dimple… the severity, the unbreakable shell. Every part of him was loose in its confidence. What was it like to exist with such certainty? Could a woman ever break through? Maybe she'd be around to see it.

Her mind was wandering, her imagination too. Somehow, he enraptured her. What was it about the allure of his mystery that transfixed her?

Even as she stared, his smile faded to something much more intense. Something harder yet just as tempting. It was insane. She was insane. Without a touch or word passing between them, warmth gathered within, her sense and hormones reacted all on their own.

Tingling swept across her, beneath her clothes, in every most intimate part of herself. Her breasts grew heavier, her nipples tightened, sweet stimulation woke between her thighs.

Gorgeous. Could a person really be that attractive? Grabbing him and kissing him in that restroom had set her into a spiral of insanity. And it was still going. The crazy was rising, volatile and eager within her.

"Would you like another drink?" he asked.

If only the words were enough to break the spell. "No, that's not a good idea."

"Then I should apologize to you."

Confused, she asked, "Why?"

"Can't have been that great a kiss."

If only he knew… "It wasn't," she said, startling him, which startled her. "I mean it… it wasn't a great kiss."

"You've had better?"

"Never," she said on a lustful sigh. "It wasn't a great kiss. It was an epic kiss. An incredible, unreal, completely panty-melting kiss."

Her jaw moved, but the words had stopped. Her mouth watered as she replayed how it felt to grab his face, pull him down, and plant her mouth on his. Their forbidden kiss in a secret corner. It was so out of character. So wild. So bizarre. So incredible. In that second, she'd needed his kiss. Needed it like the blood in her veins.

Her friend had been missing. Being carnally overcome in such an intense moment was so inappropriate, which may be why she hadn't told a soul. She, Roxie, and Toria had lived together for years, and usually told each other everything. But she'd kept her shame to herself. The guy just needed to pee. It wasn't like he'd sought her out. Their paths crossed by chance, and she'd assaulted him. She was an assaulter.

"Okay," he said, clearing his throat as he shifted to retrieve his phone from his inside pocket.

"Oh, God, I'm sorry…" Her palm rose to her forehead. "That was inappropriate too. I'm sorry. Maybe I'm sick."

"I don't think you're sick," he said, typing into his phone, then slipping it back into his jacket. "Let's get out of here."

What did that mean? She didn't have time to ask because he stood up and came over, holding a hand toward her. Should she…? He wasn't even looking at her, he was intent on the door. Her hand met his, and he swept her up into his momentum. On the approach to the pod door, a guy in a black suit opened it for them and stayed close as another appeared in front, leading the way from the club down into an underground parking garage she hadn't known existed.

The first guy opened the front passenger door, and Knox guided her inside. The hotel was close by, if she could keep her mouth shut long enough—Knox got in beside her.

The rumble of the engine was… arousing. As she processed the vibration rumbling through her, he gunned it, grabbing her attention.

His smile slid into view. "You're hot."

What did that…? He revved the engine again before speeding out onto the LA streets.

Breathing in, she was enlivened just by the freedom of living to feel. To experience each moment. Each second. Sometimes she'd been terrified of him, but when she let herself just be around him, liberation infused her.

"Was that inappropriate?" he asked.

Being so caught up in her own fantasy, she hadn't even heard him. "Hmm?"

He flashed her another dazzling smile. "I said you're not sick, you're hot."

"Like attractive?"

"Like turned on," he said. "But you're that kinda hot too."

Flattered, she smiled, but he was only being polite. "You have excellent manners."

"My parents thrashed them into me." Horror hit her, but he laughed. "I'm kidding, relax."

"You must get women throwing themselves at you all the time," she said, figuring that was why he was so casual about it. "Do women line up outside your house? Do you have a house of your own? Do you and your brothers stay with your parents in a big mansion somewhere?"

"I'm thirty-five," he said. "There isn't a house big enough to contain the Colliers… not that any of us could survive in together for more than a day. Sometimes just getting through a meal is touch and go."

From the curl of his lips, she guessed he was kidding with her. Was he kidding with her? "I don't have brothers and sisters… Well, not blood anyway. Rox and Toria are my sisters."

"I get that. I have friends I consider brothers. We don't see each other every day, but if the shit hits the fan, we're there."

"Like Zairn," she said, clasping her clutch in both hands on her lap. "I don't think he has a house. He has a building, so I guess that's… I've never been in a billionaire's house."

"Until tonight."

"Zairn's apartment is lovely, New York is amazing but—what did you say?"

"We're going to my place," he said. Glancing around, she didn't see anything familiar. Not that she was an LA aficionado. "Unless you have any objection."

"I…" She should object. Cool air crossed her tongue, a shiver of excitement joined the vibration in her belly. "Rox and Toria will be out all night." She'd only worry about them. "I'd rather not be alone."

"Not something you have to worry about in this city."

"I don't want to impose. Maybe I take a peek and call a cab?"

"You're a real delicate thing, always worrying about something," he said, picking up speed. "Tonight, you get whatever you want."

Whatever she wanted. She shouldn't want. Shouldn't be thinking about satisfying her curiosity. Shouldn't be letting her imagination creep into inappropriate territory… again.

"Do you know Logan Lowe?"

"We run in different circles, but there's no report he's dangerous," he said, his brow hardening as he pressed a button on his steering wheel.

"Boss?" a disembodied voice echoed from the speakers.

"Put a couple of our paps on Toria Lovell."

"Boss."

He pressed the button again. "She'll be looked after."

"What does that mean? Paps?" She gasped. "You don't mean paparazzi! Don't they hunt people down and cause accidents?"

"Sometimes," he said. "But these are our paps. They only look like paps, they won't hurt her, and they won't let anyone else hurt her either. The only person they report to is me."

"And you'll print details of what she does to the world?"

He laughed. "What do you think of me, Jane? No, no reporting. Logan Lowe's antics are below my paygrade. Unless you want me to ruin him." She gasped again. "That I can do in a heartbeat."

Indignation faltered in the face of the truth. "You really could…"

"If you want me to."

She wasn't the type of person to make that sort of request. Maybe Toria and Logan would hit it off, or maybe… "If he hurts her," she said, relaxing. "Maybe then."

When he glanced at her smile, his grew again. "I don't believe you'd ask even if he did."

"No," she said and laughed. "But Roxie will."

"Maybe I wouldn't do it for Roxie."

Why would he say that? Why wouldn't he? He'd do it for Zairn. Maybe that's what he meant. There would be no need for Roxie to ask, or for her to ask. Zairn would take care of it. Thank goodness they didn't run in the same circles as Logan Lowe. It didn't bear thinking about how they'd deal with one of their posse hurting someone Roxie loved. That could cause real problems.

Which brought her up short.

What was she thinking about kissing one of Zairn's best friends? Going home with him? They weren't going home for anything that was… nothing intimate, it was just… Unless he thought different. Maybe Knox believed she was the kind of woman to go home with a strange guy. But, uh… that's sort of exactly what she was doing.

They slowed at a pair of huge wooden gates that were already opening. If this was it, if they were there, she had no time to figure out how to tell him she wasn't one of those women.

On the other side of the gates, they drove up a curved, gleaming driveway. How did they get the road so white and shining even in the night? The moment the beautiful house came into view, she forgot everything else. Two floors, maybe three, maybe more if there was a basement.

Glass and white concrete, it was modern, and the roof tilted various different ways. She hadn't taken it all in when they stopped just beyond the front door.

"Stay there," he said as he got out.

She wasn't sure where she'd go. It didn't seem right to approach something so magnificent without a guide.

Knox opened her door and reached in to take her hand from her purse. Had she been resisting? Maybe that was why he was laughing as she stood.

"I don't think this is a good idea," she said as he guided her up the shallow slate stairs toward the full-height glass frontage showcasing the front door.

"I disagree," he said without disguising his amusement.

"You'll have expensive things in here, what if I break something?"

"I'll replace it."

"What if you can't? What if it's irreplaceable?"

He touched a panel and the door opened. Her heels clacked on the marble floor inside. The door closed, distracting her, so when she turned back and he gave her a tug, she fell against him.

"There's only one thing in this house that's irreplaceable," he said, coiling their joined hands around her to hold her tight against him as he descended. "That's you, delicate blossom."

"I'm not so delicate," she panted in a whisper, mesmerized by his mouth.

"No? Let's find out."

"I didn't think this through," her words came out in one breath.

"Thinking is overrated," he said, tilting his head to press his lips to hers.

Shit.

Her purse fell from her fingers as he boosted her up to wrap her legs around him. She wasn't aware of much but the slick heat of his talented tongue corrupting hers. But it wasn't his fault. Her hoochie body wanted him to take her upstairs. Her hormones craved satisfaction that could only come from him. The guy had a hundred percent success rate. Each time they kissed, every part of her responded.

The pulse between her legs screamed for completion. The void within her prepared for him as she tightened the circle of her legs, rubbing herself against his impressive body.

When they dropped and she landed in what had to be his bed, he broke their kiss to fight with his jacket.

"Knox," she whispered as he freed his arms and tossed the fabric away. She grabbed for his shoulders and was delighted by their resistance. Solid, unyielding, the rest of him beneath that shirt was just as formidable. "You work out."

"I'm about to."

She'd known he was fit. That was obvious from looking at him across the room… and yes, she might have seen a picture or two of him online, sometimes he and Zairn hung out.

As he ripped open his shirt, he ducked to kiss her again, consuming her with a hunger that couldn't match hers.

"Knox," she gasped as his mouth dropped to her throat.

His lips trailed to the side of her neck, up into her hair, kissing behind her ear, down around her hairline, sending her senses into laser mode. Not that she'd experienced anything like it before. How did he do that? Know exactly the right pressure to use, when to kiss, when to lick, when to just breathe against her.

"Oh, my… Knox," she whimpered. "That's amazing… I can't…" the build of pressure in her hips was something new too. The threatening climax was coming from somewhere untouched deep within her. "I can't breathe."

He rose, his heavy eyes seeking hers through the shadows. "What do you need, beautiful blossom?"

"To… be here…" Her palms skimmed across his bare shoulders and around to the back of his arms. "With you."

"What else?"

"Nothing," she said, languishing in the liberation of being under him, stroking his toned body. A laugh came out with her smile. "This is everything I need."

TWO

EVERYTHING SHE NEEDED? What the hell was that? What a stupid thing to say.

Light threatened the sky when she woke in his bed. One-night stands weren't her thing and there was no excuse. She hadn't been that drunk. Hadn't drunk that much. She slipped into her dress and found her scattered shoes. It was a blessing he was still asleep. Shameful morning afters weren't in her comfort zone either.

Sometime in the wee hours, he'd left her in bed to take a call. She should've snuck out then instead of waiting for him to come back and ravish her again. None of her decisions around him were sound. Speaking to him would threaten her sanity. She had to get out while he slept. Had to. It wasn't rude, it was self-preservation.

Tiptoeing down the stairs, she swept her hair up, holding it on her head as she sought her purse. There on the floor at the foot of the stairs, it was impossible to pick it up without replaying their arrival. His hold. His kiss. His…

What was wrong with her brain?

The front door opened behind her, shattering her imaginings.

She shot to her feet as another gorgeous guy entered. All of LA seemed to be filled with handsome suited men.

"Morning," he said, the door closing on its own behind him. One look at her put a twitch of a smile on his face. "Not many women sneak out on a Collier." Stunned, her senses were playing possum. "You want a cup of coffee?" Her head moved in a loose shake.   His smile grew unashamed. "Eggs? Pancakes?" Another shake. "Steak?" He laughed. "You're not making this easy on a guy who's been up all night… Want to tell me your name?" When she didn't respond, his ease began to ebb. "I'm Zach Kintyre, one of Knox's oldest friends, you don't have to sneak out or be afraid. Did you and Knox argue?"

"No," came Knox's voice from the top of the stairs.

"Shit, you took your time," Zach said. "Thought you were going to leave me vamping down here all day." He passed her as Knox descended the stairs. "It was a pleasure to meet you. There's a car in the driveway that will take you anywhere you want to go… whenever you're ready."

His smile was genuine, but it dropped fast. Zach went up the stairs, muttering something at Knox as he passed.

By the time Knox got to her, Zach had disappeared. "Sneaking out on me?"

What was she supposed to say? Her mind didn't want to play ball, not at all. Her shock wasn't made any easier by her ripped lover wearing nothing more than a pair of black boxer-briefs. Saliva gathered at the corner of her mouth. She swept it away with her tongue, forcing her lips to part.

"I didn't want it to be weird."

"Okay," he said, stepping backward. "Let's have breakfast."

Shaking her head, she retreated. "We can't."

"We can have sex, but we can't have breakfast?"

"We shouldn't have had sex," she said. "Last night was amazing, but you're the best friend of my best friend's fiancé. This is their love. Roxie's great love. I won't do anything that might hurt her happily ever after."

Though it could easily be argued she'd done that by falling into bed with Knox.

"This will not break their… relationship."

"You don't know that. We don't know that and… Roxie can't ever be in a position where she has to pick between her friend and her man."

He chuckled. "No one's asking her to choose."

"Not now, but… This is a bad idea." Because, unlike Roxie, she'd never stayed friends with an ex. Never had to see them every time there was an event, or her friend celebrated some milestone. "We have to forget this ever happened. We can't ever tell anyone—"

"I'm not ashamed of my attraction to you," he said, anger strengthening his brow. "And I don't apologize to anyone for my choices. I won't apologize for acting on this."

"I don't want you to apologize," she said, as much to blame for what happened between them. In truth, her burden of guilt was greater. "I kissed you. I started this… that was my mistake."

"This your MO?" he asked, glaring. "Get a guy on the hook then shut him down? The whole innocent thing an act?"

"What?" she asked, alarmed. "No! I don't—I wouldn't… I never have one-night stands, I didn't want us to be… This is my fault… all my fault."

The heat of tears gathered in her eyes. She wanted to flee but couldn't, not until he understood.

His glare relaxed. "Jane," he said, coming closer to rest a hand on her shoulder. "Nothing is your fault. This was your personal choice, our choice. Roxie shouldn't expect you to grovel. We're consenting adults, we did nothing wrong."

"Roxie's an amazing person," she said, moisture dropping from her lashes. "She wouldn't ever ask me to apologize for anything, she accepts everyone, but… She's always the one looking out for me. Protecting me. Standing up for me. If we tried to pursue this, it would put pressure on all of us. On our bonds to each other… Long distance relationships never work. We'd break up and then it would get difficult… No one can know about this. About any of what we did. It's my turn to protect her. I want her and Zairn to work, she loves him so much. Do you want to sabotage Zairn's happiness?"

His hand slid off her shoulder. "No. The way he is with Rox… I've never seen anything so right. He believes in it. Loves her more than I've seen him love anyone."

Relief came with a smile though another tear fell. "So we agree. We tell no one. No one can know about this. We have to forget it ever happened." A thread of panic tensed her. "Your friend Zach—"

"I'll talk to him," he said. "He's going through his own shit. I doubt he knows Rox's roommates' names, let alone what they look like." Good point. "He won't say anything."

"Thank you," she said, relaxing into a smile. "Thank you, Knox."

She started to turn, but he caught hold of her arm to pull her back. "I can't put a lid on what I feel."

"I won't play with you. You won't hear from me. And if we end up in the same room…" Which they would for Roxie and Zairn's wedding at least. "We'll say hello, be polite, but that's it."

"I don't know if I like that idea," he said, searching her. "You're really sure this is for the best?"

"I'm really sure." Though keeping secrets from her best friends was unheard of. "We can't be selfish for sex. That's it. Done."

THREE

BACK IN CHICAGO four days later, she couldn't exactly claim to have found her sanity, but at least there was some semblance of normality.

Toria was still working on edits in LA and Roxie was in New York dealing with some issue for Zairn and his buddy who'd just got engaged. Everyone was making commitments, planning a future, and she was working notice at her job without any idea of what came next.

Her company had offered to let her transfer to New York. While she hadn't completely discounted that option, it wouldn't be a good idea. Graham, a guy from their London office, traveled to New York sometimes. One of those times, they'd met for a date after an extended long-distance flirtation.

It was a bust.

Completely.

She'd expected him to be her forever guy yet had zero chemistry with him. How was it she could be sure of their compatibility when they were apart and so against it when they were together?

She was back at zero.

Lower than zero.

Without a job, she was relying on Roxie's goodwill to support her in New York, one of the most expensive cities in the world to live in. Zairn was based in the Big Apple. Without her friends' support, and agreement they'd move from Chicago with her, Roxie may not have taken the leap into the engagement. Toria was sure happy futures awaited them all. If only optimism would get them through.

Her measly emergency savings wouldn't last long in New York. Roxie would look after them. Zairn would look after them because they meant so much to the woman he loved. It was romantic, swoon-worthy.

Unless you were the friend without a job, boyfriend, or future up ahead.

Sitting on the floor, alone in her apartment, she distracted herself filling boxes, packing up their lives. It should be exciting. It was exciting. Moving to New York, her best friend in love, there was so much to be happy about. But what the hell was she doing?

Exhaling, she sank back on her knees to sit on her feet. Thank God for wine. The glass on the floor next to her had been filled more than once, maybe more than twice, since she got back from work. Yes, it was Sunday, but she'd taken time off for the LA trips and, well, she wasn't that good at saying no. Her colleagues had her for another month and, apparently, planned to make the most of that time by requiring her to work weekends in addition to extended hours during the week.

Someone knocked on the door.

Her phone was somewhere, maybe Roxie was trying to get in touch and she'd missed a call.

The only people allowed anywhere near her door were those approved by Trevor and his security team. The bodyguards lived in the apartment next door after being installed by Zairn for Roxie's benefit. Although her friend wasn't home, they were still around and vetted anyone who wanted to come inside. They also followed her to work every day, probably because they had little else to do. That and her friends had asked Zairn's Head of Security and Logistics to keep an eye on her after Graham refused to take no for an answer. He hadn't shown up yet, but his calls, texts, and emails were enough to give them a scare.

It had to be Trevor. She didn't call for takeout. Groceries had been delivered the day she got home. No one else should be coming to talk to her. She got up and put her wine on the breakfast bar.

Trevor was who she expected to see on the other side of the door.

Boy was she wrong.

"You're wrong," was the first thing he said.

It took a good ten seconds for her to reply. "Knox… what are you doing here?"

"I'm not here," he said, pushing the door away from her hand to stride inside.

This couldn't be good. Hadn't they agreed they wouldn't hear from each other? Showing up was a dozen steps beyond hearing from each other.

She closed the door.

Knox Collier was in her apartment. Right there, standing by the breakfast bar.

"What are you doing here?"

"I have business in Chicago."

"You have business in Chicago," she repeated.

That was an incredible coincidence so soon after they'd parted.

"I'm staying at the Grand," he said. "Unless you want me to stay here."

No prizes for guessing why he'd appeared. "As like a… No, you can't, you shouldn't."

"Shouldn't?" he asked. "Because…?"

A reason. Yes, that was a valid question, answering it would be polite.

"Because… we can't."

"That's not a reason."

No, it wasn't. "We can't… for our friends… it'll get messy."

"No mess," he said. "Have you told anyone what happened between us in LA?" She shook her head. "I haven't either and Zach's forgotten already." Because Knox had such a trail of anonymous women slipping in and out of his bed that the faces blurred? "That's proof we can do this without it getting messy."

Maybe it hadn't gotten messy with their friends and out in the world. In her head was a different story.

"Knox, I'm flattered you'd come over here…" If he had business in the city, it wasn't like he'd flown there specifically for her. Thank goodness! She couldn't imagine the guilt. "But I make horrible decisions when it comes to men. Really terrible. You don't want to get involved with that. Men and me… if there's a chance of something going wrong, it will. It always does."

"Maybe your decision to cut this off is the wrong one."

"I…" Okay, there was logic there. "I don't know."

Warmth rose in his eyes as his lips curled. "You said you didn't do one-night stands, wouldn't want to break your streak, would you?"

"You're teasing me."

She wasn't as good at the flirting and innuendos as Toria and Roxie either. Their confidence, their wit, it got them tangled up with men all the time. Sometimes, like with Zairn, that tangling wasn't such a bad thing.

"Did spending the night with me feel good?"

Color flooded her cheeks. "You know it did," she whispered, her chin dropping.

If she tried to claim otherwise, he'd call her a liar and he would be right.

"Look at me, Blossom," he said. She swallowed as her eyes ascended to his. "Trust yourself. There's nothing wrong with feeling good."

Her friends often said the same. "How long are you in Chicago?"

"Ten days."

Progressing to him, she shook her head. "This can't be… We can't, we…"

"No one has to know," he said. Touching her shoulder, his fingertips floated toward her neck. "You make the rules. You want to fuck and run, I won't sta—"

Leaping up, she grabbed his head, forcing him to crouch to meet her kiss. They weren't supposed to wreck their friends' relationship. But they weren't there. No one was there. It was a secret. They could keep their trysts to themselves. They'd managed it since LA.

Oh, who was she kidding? She was weak. Powerless to resist the pull of his hands on her waist, his body meeting hers. Proximity to this man intoxicated her.

Her hands dropped to his on her waist, holding them there as she walked backward toward the hall and the bedrooms.

"If you're in town anyway… Roxie and Toria aren't home…" She navigated them into her room. "Do you know anyone else in Chicago?"

"No one prettier than you," he said, giving her a boost onto the bed as soon as they were close enough. "You going to give me a real Chicago welcome?"

He crawled onto the bed. Her hands slid onto his shoulders to link at the back of his neck.

Before his mouth found hers, she spoke. "We hook up, you go back to your hotel…"

"Our secret, Blossom."

His confidence inspired hers. "We have this under control. We control it, it doesn't control us."

Though she wasn't entirely sure what "*it*" was.

"No strings. Just fun. Our secret. Totally under control."

"Good," she said on a sigh and tilted her head, pulling him down to touch their foreheads. "I've never done casual."

And she'd be lying if she said Roxie and Toria's ability to split sex from love wasn't something she'd occasionally been jealous of. This was a fling. Ten days. He'd go back to his life and that would be it. Sex. For the sake of sex. She could do that… this once.

FOUR

SAYING GOODBYE AFTER ten days, knowing it was the last time they'd ever be intimate, had been tough.

Submerging herself in the wet heat of the bathtub, the aches of the day waned, and her mind wandered back to her time with him. Too often her daydreams included him; her nighttime dreams weren't exempt either.

The way Knox kissed her, touched her, it provoked all kinds of new sensations and excitement. For a long time, she hadn't understood why no strings was appealing. Now she got it. Now she understood how freeing it was to let loose and give herself to someone without worrying they wouldn't call the next day.

He wouldn't call.

He didn't call.

For one thing, she'd said they shouldn't exchange numbers. The long-distance calling and video thing hadn't worked out for her and colleague, Graham, a.k.a. London Guy. She didn't want to go through that again. Didn't want to go through the excited anticipation of waiting for his call, of being naughty with someone she thought she could trust…

She shuddered.

Thinking back to what she'd done with Graham, her humiliation flamed. Roxie and Toria reminded her all the time that she shouldn't be ashamed of anything. As much as she appreciated her friends and their reassurance, her embarrassment was real.

Counting down the days left with her employer, only three remained. They wanted her to go in on Saturday, which would be fine except she was supposed to be flying to Florida on Sunday to meet Toria. When would she pack? How would she clean the apartment with so little time?

Sunday couldn't come quick enough. Oh, she missed her friends. More than she'd anticipated. Living as a trio for so long, they'd become accustomed to having each other around. This being in three different corners of the country was difficult.

Their lives had been on a collision course with these changes since their LA trip, when they watched Talk at Sunset being filmed. How long ago was that? More than eight months. Geez, time went fast. Roxie and Zairn had known each other eight months and were still going strong. Together and apart, business commitments tugged them around the globe, but the couple always came back together, always returned to each other, their love stronger than ever.

Time… it was a funny thing.

Had it really been a month since Knox left her apartment?

Their affair was over. Finished. She shouldn't still be thinking about him.

Maybe it was easier to think about him than Graham or Brendan, the last two love interests in her life. No, actually, there was no maybe about it. Thinking about Knox made her smile, it turned her on, he'd become her favorite fantasy figure.

And boy was that becoming a routine. Maybe it was being alone in the apartment and the freedom that brought, but in the previous four weeks, she'd pleasured herself almost every day. Way more than usual. No matter how vivid the illusion, it was never as good as the real thing, as his hands touching her, his fingers slipping into her.

With her eyes closed and her head resting on the edge of the tub, her hand crossed her thigh to rest between her legs. The way she massaged her clit wasn't as skilled as his caress. She could only conjure memories of the heat he built low in her belly, how the pressure grew and her breathing deepened as he curled a digit within her, massaging her—

"You're a mind reader."

She shot upright so fast water sloshed left and right. It got in her eyes though she grabbed for her bare breasts, terrified by the intrusion.

Except as she blinked her wet lashes, Knox came into view. Already his shirt was on the floor, he toed off one shoe and then the other.

"Knox," she said, catching her breath. "What are you doing here?"

"You," he said, unfastening his pants.

"How did you get in here?"

"Your door was unlocked."

"My door was unlocked?" she asked, leaning back when he braced his hands on either side of the tub to climb in on top of her.

"We're going to buy you a new tub," he said, kissing her forehead and her temple. "Something built for two."

His arms came around her and he rolled, sloshing the water, switching their positions so he was beneath with her facing him between his legs. His embrace crushed her to him so tight, there was nowhere for her to go.

"The neighbors will complain," she said.

His hands skimmed down her back through the water, yanking her hard against his erection. "Zairn pays the neighbors."

"Not those neighbors," she said. "Downstairs. If the water spills—"

"Blossom," he said, tucking her wet hair back from her face. "Did you miss me?"

Somehow, her imagination had summoned him back to her. "It's been a month."

"You forgot about me?" he asked though his drowsy eyes didn't believe it. He kneaded her ass, using her body to stimulate his. "I missed you."

Her fingers spread on his chest. "You're insanely attractive," she sighed.

"If that means you're powerless to resist, I'll take it."

"Maybe I drowned." While pleasuring herself, but she left that part out. "Maybe I'm dead."

"Is this your heaven, babe?"

Their eyes met. Both her heaven and her hell. "I'm going to Florida on Sunday."

"For the Bahamas trip."

"And I have to work the next three days." Which would take them to Sunday. "Business brought you back here?"

"If that's what you have to think, yeah," he said, losing his fingers in her tangled locks. "Business."

Whatever that meant. They couldn't have sex in the tub even if they wanted to.

"Condoms are in my nightstand," she said.

Had she really been won over so easily? Where were her objections? Shouldn't she be calm and level-headed? Oh, she just lost herself in the way he made her feel. She could object or resist, but she wouldn't mean it.

"How many?" he asked.

"How many?"

Why would he ask that?

"There were ten in the box when I left."

Whether that was true or not, she couldn't say. "I haven't counted them."

He exhaled a laugh, still caressing her. "That's my way of asking how many guys you've been seeing this month."

"Oh."

Yeah, she'd missed that completely.

She kissed his chin, relaxing into being near him again now the panic was over.

"Oh?" he said. "You going to give me an answer?"

"No." She smiled at him. "That's breaking news you don't need."

Didn't the Colliers know everything else? It was just a tease. If he really had counted the condoms before he left, he'd find the same number there when they went through to the bedroom.

"I'd give up the rest to know that."

"Then take me to bed," she said, kissing his chin again.

"You don't want to do it here?" he asked, wearing a grin as he stood them up.

Once again water went everywhere. "I don't want our neighbors to sue." He lifted her out of the tub first. "And I plan to clean this place to within an inch of its life. We need our security deposit back."

"Need it for what?"

As he got out, she pulled the plug. "Do you know how expensive it is to live in New York?"

He probably didn't because he didn't live there.

"I live for free in New York when I visit. A good friend of mine lives there," he said, catching her hand when she tried to pick up her towel. "You don't need that."

He pulled her out of the room.

"You shouldn't leave your clothes on that wet floor. They'll get—"

Sweeping her around in an arc, he rushed her against the wall and crouched to kiss her. Passion, pleasure, desire. The man was a wet dream. Her wet dream and probably that of every other woman in his life.

The pressure of his kiss grew hard, fast, but it disappeared before she was ready to lose it. Her eyes stayed closed, and her fingertips tried to find his jaw, to tempt his mouth back.

"Did you miss me?" he murmured.

Air left her lips with the answer. "Yes."

With the gravity of need inside her, it was unbelievable she hadn't succumbed already.

"Want me to fuck you?" he asked.

A shot of excitement quaked in her pussy. "I… I…" Her mouth dried, she wanted it, wanted him, but her reserve kept her rigid. "I…"

"Don't be nervous, my delicate blossom," he growled in a voice that was anything but reassuring, but it spoke to her arousal. "You want it? You want me inside you?"

"Knox," she whined, her fingertips dropping to his shoulders.

"That what you were thinking about? In the tub… Were you thinking about my cock?" Her head managed to shake, her wet hair probably marking the wall. "No?"

Her mind was blank until need sped her heart. The fantasy came back to life. Fumbling for one of his arms, she took it from its place bracing him against the wall and guided his hand down to the apex of her thighs.

Her eyes fluttered open as feral satisfaction pulled at one corner of his lips.

"I was still at the foreplay," she whispered and gasped when he slid a finger into her.

"Then I got here just in time."

He swirled his finger within her and withdrew to suck it clean. Wow, her heart might have stopped right there, maybe the whole world did.

While she was still off-balance, he crouched to grab her up, squeezing her ass as he carried her into her bedroom.

FIVE

"I'M SORRY I HAD to work late today," she said, loose and sated in her own sheets on their third night together.

Knox shifted, dropping his head back into a pillow. "It's karma," he said. "I've lost count of the number of times I've used that line myself… It's not that late, it's not nine."

"What time is it in LA?"

"Almost seven."

"Dinner time?"

"You want to go out?" he asked. "You hungry?"

Funny joke. How long would their secret stay secret if they went out galivanting together?

"You satisfied my appetite," she said, smiling as she adjusted to look at him.

"I could get used to this kept man thing. You should get cable."

She laughed. "I'm a girl on a budget. Don't you own a cable company?"

"Oh yeah," he said like he'd forgotten his heritage. "Several. In various countries… You want cable?"

"In exchange for sex? No, thanks, I'm moving soon," she said, climbing over on top of him. "You know what I'd kill for?"

"Anything you want is yours, Blossom."

"There's wine in the fridge. Do you want some?"

He picked her hand off his torso and pulled it to his lips. "Stay here, I'll get it," he said and kissed her knuckles. Holding her hips, he guided her onto her back again and got up to put his sweats on. "Back in a second."

"There's a corkscrew in the drawer under the breakfast bar!" she called.

He was already gone but must've heard her. The apartment wasn't that big.

Tomorrow, she had to go back to work for her last day. Official last day anyway, she'd still be on the end of the phone if they needed her.

Knox had been waiting for her when she got home. A man waiting at home after work. A man pleased to see her. He worked during the day. Where? She didn't know. But paperwork had been spread out on Roxie's desk the previous evening. He hadn't talked of a hotel and had been sleeping in her bed both mornings she got up for work. Was he staying with her?

If he was in Chicago for business, shouldn't he have meetings or calls to make? She didn't know much about his business. Or his family. Or his social life. It was sex, they didn't talk about those things.

Maybe he hadn't heard her. And rather than let herself overthink what was going on in her messed-up life, she wrapped herself in the sheet and went to find out if he'd located the corkscrew.

"Babe, what's…?" She tripped on her sheet at the end of the hall, catching her balance on a screeching halt. They weren't alone. "Oh! Uh… Oh!"

"Oh?" Roxie said, whipping around to show her shock. "Jane! Are you kidding me?"

Her roommate had come home, unannounced, and brought someone else. A woman she didn't recognize stood behind Roxie in the doorway.

What could she say to explain this? "This isn't what it looks like."

"I tried that," Knox said.

"You know, I don't even know what is more upsetting about this," Roxie said, sweeping her bangs up for them just to flutter back down. "That both of you lied or that you just ruined my weekend."

Jane tucked the sheet in tight to protect her modesty and distract herself from her own betrayal. What she'd done was unforgiveable.

"We didn't lie," Knox said. "It just sort of… happened."

Roxie was amped. "Believe me, I know these things don't just happen. There's a moment when one or both of you could've turned it around and you chose not to," her friend said, switching to her. "This is like reverse déjà vu."

She and Toria had found out about Roxie and Zairn's relationship in a situation not entirely unlike this one. "I was fine with you and Zairn… I was shocked, but Toria—"

"Does she know about this?"

Guilt shifted her posture. "No."

Roxie took one sure step toward Knox. "Why are you ashamed of being with my friend?"

"What?" he asked, his brows rising. "Who said that?"

"If you're not ashamed, why keep it a secret?"

"You and Z started out secret," Knox retorted.

This was bad.

"That was different. We had no choice with the contest hanging over us. Jane is the nicest, sweetest, kindest human being you'll ever meet. What the hell gives you the right to use her for your own sick pleasure?"

Really bad.

"Sick pleasure?"

"Rox," she said, going toward her friend. "Don't be mad. Please." This was awful. She'd been so selfish. Kidding herself that messing around with Knox would be okay so long as no one knew was despicable. Her weakness could cost her one of her most valuable friendships. Tears gathered on her lashes. "Please, Roxie."

On an exhale, Roxie pointed at Knox. "You don't move." Roxie grabbed the woman behind her and came charging her way. "Girl talk."

In command, Roxie herded her down the hall into her own bedroom. Roxie's bedroom… Given the sex sheets in her room, the choice was welcome.

Roxie let her go to close the door.

The refined stranger offered a hand. "Merci Moore," she introduced herself.

The newcomer seemed overwhelmed. Good. A kindred spirit. "Jane Simmons," she said, shaking her hand.

"What happened?" Roxie asked, grabbing her to rush her back to sit both of them on the bed. "When did you…? In Chicago? He lives in LA!"

This was the conversation she'd dreaded. The one she'd promised herself they'd never need to face. This was Roxie. Difficult or not, she had to tell the truth. "It was in LA," she said. "The night when you were missing… that you spent with Riot Guy."

"Oh my God," Roxie said on a gasp. "I was missing and you were screwing—"

"No! I kissed him." In panic, her hand leaped from her lap. "Just a kiss. One kiss."

"How did that happen?" Roxie asked. "You were all together when I got there. All in the same room."

Confessing was tough. "I was in the restroom, and I guess he didn't know… He came in and I was crying, then I just… kissed him."

Roxie inhaled. The seconds that followed were torturous. Was she mad? Sad? Did her best friend hate her?

Apparently not because Roxie laughed. "Go get what you want, girl. Wow, you're amazing." Diving forward, her roommate gave her a sure hug that she definitely hadn't expected. "You surprised the hell out of me."

"You always go after what you want," Jane said, still a little stunned.

Roxie straightened up. "I'd tell you not to take a page out my book, but it seems to be working for you! Good going. Now you can plan two weddings! Two for the price of one."

"Oh no, shh! Shh! He'll hear you."

"Hear me?" Roxie asked, unimpressed. "Who cares if your boyfriend knows I'm talking about—"

"He's not my boyfriend," she murmured, the heat of familiar embarrassment rushed to her face. "I think he's my… buddy."

"Buddy? Fuck buddy?" Roxie looked at her closer. "Jane, honey, you don't do casual… ever. You do heart on your sleeve, not fuck me 'til I love you."

"I know." Surging to her feet, the weight of truth and insanity burdened her head. Even in both hands it was too much to support. "I know. I know… I think I messed this up."

"Is this him? He thinks because he's some super-hot billionaire, he doesn't have to play by the rules?" Roxie stood up fast. "I'll tell him. He won't get away with using you for sex and casting you aside."

Now was the time to face the truth she'd hidden from herself until that moment. Holding Roxie's arm, she took strength from her. "I think I'm using him for sex."

"You think?"

If Roxie didn't get it, who would? How would she herself understand it? Sex stuff and relationships were so much more her roommates' bag.

"I… I don't know."

"Honey…" Roxie said, seating them back on the bed. "You're gonna have to help me out here."

"I really don't…"

"When did you have sex?" Roxie asked with all the patience in the world. "You said the first time was a kiss."

If Roxie could be calm and accepting, she had to keep her composure. "The night in Crimson, after you and Zairn got together… you left the club and Toria was hooking up with Logan Lowe."

"She told me about that…" Roxie said. "That was the night before I left for New York…" Her head bobbed in a side-to-side nod. "Okay, so you didn't have time to get into it… Though…" She pushed her. "You could've told me about the kiss."

"It was stupid," Jane said, exhaling some of her tension. "I wasn't even listening to what he was saying. I just thought… I wanted to…"

"And that's okay," Roxie said, taking her hand over into her lap. "You went home with him from the club?"

"Toria made him promise to get me back to the hotel safe. We were in the car… I said something about where he lived or… something. Just thinking it would be cool to see a billionaire's house."

"Wow, that is such a corny line."

"I know!" Jane wailed, her head falling onto her friend's shoulder.

Roxie laughed. "So you went back to his place…" The laughter stopped. "Wait, does Z know about this?"

"No. No one knows," she said, her head still on Roxie.

"I thought Kintyre lived there. With Knox."

"I met him," she said, breathing in and sitting upright. "In the morning… I didn't know anyone else lived there and I was trying to get out, to get back before Toria."

And before Knox woke up. Though that was a big fat failure.

"You said no one knows."

"He doesn't know who I am… that I'm your Jane… He didn't say anything. Knox said he wouldn't even know your roommates' names."

"Probably not," Roxie conceded.

"I'm sorry." Somehow, her friend's acceptance compounded her guilt. "I really am! I don't know how this happened."

"Shh," Roxie said, moving in to give her another hug. "He's sort of smug and superior, but he's cute… Wait, what happened to the coffee cart girl?"

"The who?"

"Hmm…" Roxie said, her mind somewhere else.

The woman by the door hadn't said anything. She just stood there, taking in the show. That might've made her self-conscious except Merci appeared anything but comfortable at being included in the private moment. Poor thing needed some reassurance. If Roxie trusted Merci, she would too.

"I…" Merci said, "don't know the coffee cart girl either."

"How did he get here?" Roxie said. "I thought Knox went back to LA with Kintyre."

Maybe saying it aloud would give her better perspective. "A couple of days after the club, when I was home I… He just showed up here." For business. "He did go back to LA before the engagement party and flew to New York with Kintyre."

The engagement party. Yes, Merci's engagement party. She was marrying Matteo Reid, another of Zairn's close friends.

"He flew from Chicago to LA and then to New York?" Roxie asked. "He does know where Chicago is, right?" Now that she mentioned it, that was a little odd. Unless he had business in California along the way. "He came back here after the engagement party?"

"Not right after," Jane said. "He's only been here a few days."

Since Wednesday and they were now on Friday.

Her friend grinned. "Stop looking so scared. This is okay. I'm just confused why you wouldn't tell us. He's solvent and from everything I've heard, his family are okay people… most of them. They'll love you."

She shook her head. "We're not together like that, Rox. We don't talk about the future… We have sex… talk about you and Z, other things going on."

Politics, movies, the weather, just small talk… Though he had met basically everyone in every movie or political arena that came up. He'd even dated a meteorologist. He'd said talking about the weather with her was a whole new level of shooting the breeze.

"I don't mind being part of your sex talk," Roxie said, "but it might freak Z out, so we'll just keep that to ourselves."

She laughed at her friend's teasing. "Rox…"

"It's okay," Roxie said, tucking her hair from her face. "Really, honey. It can be a thing or not a thing, that's your call… But we should tell Toria."

"No!" Another surge of panic and adrenaline. "No, we can't tell anyone… You can't tell Z either."

Roxie leaned back to show her incredulity. "I won't lie to Zairn. Why does it have to be a secret?"

"Zairn isn't my friend, I can't—"

"Right," Roxie said, leaping up on a mission to return to the living room. Her purpose forced Merci out of the way. Despite being eager to follow, the stranger's confusion held her up. In the delay, Roxie's voice carried from the living room. "You want me to lie to Zairn?"

SIX

JANE HURRIED INTO the living room, but Knox and Roxie were already facing off.

"I don't give a damn what you do," Knox said.

She got between them, maybe three feet from each. "Please don't fight," she pleaded.

"You think being with my friend messes up some precious reputation?" Roxie demanded. "You think you're special?"

"I think you need to get back in your box," Knox snapped. "This is none of your goddamn business."

"She's my best friend! He's your best friend!"

"And we didn't tell either of you," Knox said. All she could do was look from one to the other as they argued. "Again, it's not your fucking business."

"Oh, swear at me, Collier, please. You think I won't tell the man I love because you—"

"I wanted to keep it a secret!" Jane shouted over her friend. "It was me. It wasn't him. I didn't want to tell you or Toria… or Zairn." The admission filled the air with surprise. "*I* wanted this to be a secret."

"Oh," Roxie said.

"Yeah, oh," Knox said. "You dial up fast, Kyst."

"We don't keep secrets," Roxie said, ignoring the man in the room.

That was hurt in her voice. She'd hurt her friend. "I'm sorry," she said, her heart breaking.

"Is this because of me and Z?" Roxie asked, more timid than usual. "It wasn't a thing and then it was, I… I never meant to hurt you."

"I didn't mean to hurt you either," she said, fighting to restrain her tears. "I just… this is so different, so… out of character. I thought you would judge me."

"Honey," Roxie said, crossing to link their hands. The warm acceptance in her voice was more than she expected. "I would never judge you, neither of us would."

"You and Toria or you and Zairn?"

Roxie looked at Knox. "Do you know how close he was to coming with me?"

"I talked to him last night."

"He stayed in New York to be in the Gramercy negotiations."

"Yeah, Kinloch's in town," Knox said to Roxie's nod.

He'd spoken to Zairn last night? She hadn't known that. Maybe she'd been asleep. Did he sneak out of her bed to make calls to other people too?

"You want to worry about anyone," Knox said. "We should worry about her."

He was looking at Merci, so she and Roxie did too.

"What?" Merci asked.

"Merci's cool," Roxie said. "She doesn't care about this drama."

"I told Z your whole fake break-up thing was only a good idea if she didn't know about it," Knox said. "In a few weeks, she'll be on her own again. Why do we trust her not to sell everything she knows?"

According to Knox, Merci was only pretending to be engaged to Reid. In the course of that, to distract the media, Roxie and Zairn had fake broken up. It was complicated but working. News of their break-up was devastating… until Roxie called to tell her and Toria it was a ruse to take the pressure from Reid and Merci. As far as she knew, Toria believed Merci and Reid were for real. Though she probably hadn't given much thought to the strangers' relationship.

"You are so paranoid," Roxie said to Knox. "You need to learn to trust people."

"I trust people who have proved themselves."

"And you think Merci hasn't?" Roxie asked. "She went into this knowing it was a lie. Hell, it was her idea."

"I don't think we should talk about this," Merci said, squirming.

Not that the objection slowed Roxie down. "You think the worst of everyone, Knox," she said. "And, by the way, what happened to Coffee Cart Girl?"

"That's nothing," Knox said.

His other woman, maybe. Had he been calling her in the dead of night too?

"I'll be the judge of that," Roxie said. "Are you still seeing her?"

"None of this is any of your business."

"That means yes," Roxie said, resolute. "I won't let you hurt my friend. You won't make a fool out of her."

"This is our relationship," Knox said, gesturing between them. "Our business. You want us to get into yours with Z?"

"If you were protecting him, yes, I would want you to."

"Cool, then I'll call him and tell him what a busybody you are."

Roxie scoffed. "You think he doesn't know that already? When it comes to people I care about, yes, I will get in amongst it."

"Both of you have to realize you're family now," Jane said. Knox's affect flattened further, Roxie just crooked a brow. "Both of you love Zairn. You can't be weird because... You're family."

"Yeah?" Roxie asked. "And you're my family. I'd never let a guy screw around on you, no matter who he is."

Their friendship was still strong. "I know and I love you too," she said, smiling. "I do. I know you're just looking out for me."

Grateful, she went to hug her friend.

Knox exhaled. "Has everyone dialed it back now?"

They broke their hug.

"We can call a truce, with reservations," Roxie said. "If you hurt my friend—"

"And if you hurt mine…" Knox said. Neither had to say more, the meaning was clear. "Jane is right."

"She always is," Roxie said, sighing. "With the exception of men. She makes terrible decisions when it comes to men."

"Yeah, yeah," Knox said. "I hear you."

Was the tension gone? No, but it was under control.

She ventured to retreat a few steps. "Now you two hug and make up. For everyone's sake."

"Can he put a shirt on first?" Roxie asked.

Mm, ripped, tan, gorgeous, she didn't mind being close to his skin. Though Zairn might have a problem with Roxie getting close when all Knox wore was a pair of sweats.

On a shrug, Knox strode off to the hallway.

"Are you okay?" she asked Roxie when he was gone.

"Me? Yes." Roxie's focus darted to her newest friend. "Merci, sorry, this is… Yeah, you didn't know the madness you were walking into."

"Neither did you."

"Can't say life with me is ever boring."

Jane pointed in the direction of her room. "I'm going to…"

"You know the Lurker is outside," Roxie said. "I know why Trevor didn't fill us in, but if the Lurker sees—"

"Thank you," Jane said before going after Knox.

No, he wasn't the type to need coddling, but she wanted to make sure he was okay.

When she got to the bedroom, he was pulling his tee-shirt down over his abs. Oh, such a beautiful body shouldn't be covered up.

Her distraction meant he got in before her to ask, "You okay?"

"Me?" she asked. "Yes, I'm okay." Sneaking around the door, she closed it with her body. "I'm sorry."

"You spend too much of your life apologizing."

"Roxie's told me that too," she said. "You both have a lot in common."

Maybe if they realized that, they wouldn't butt heads so often.

"Zairn's said the same thing."

"You protect the people you care about."

"Doesn't everyone?"

"No," she said, shaking her head. "Not everyone does."

"I do."

Their eyes met. "Roxie does too."

"You don't?"

Before their affair, yes would've been the answer. The fling tested her integrity and she'd failed. "Will you be okay?"

"Will I be okay?"

"Do you need me to call a cab?" she asked. "I'm happy to pay for—"

"Why do I need a cab?"

She blinked a few times as her frown formed. "Have you called your own car? Roxie says there's a reporter out front. Zairn sneaks in the back, there's—"

"I know the way in the back, Blossom," he said, serious. "But anyone who wants to keep working in this industry knows better than to piss off the Colliers."

"Okay." She accepted his confidence because he was the expert. "Do you have a room at the Grand or—"

"What's wrong with right here?" he asked, his eyes flicking toward the bed.

"Roxie's home."

"So? She tell you to kick me out? 'Cause I can go another round." He started across the room. "She still out there?"

Stepping into his path, she caught his waist. "Please don't fight with her. She's my best friend."

The hard edge of his annoyance softened until his shoulders dropped and his fingertips rose to her temple. "You want me to leave? I'll leave. But it's your decision, not hers."

"We have to go our separate ways on Sunday, and I have to work tomorrow anyway."

Moseying in close, he wrapped her in his embrace. "Yeah, that's a whole two nights we can spend together."

That light. His heat. The need for him awoke. Her power to resist weakened when they were making physical contact.

"We've never spent the night together with anyone else in the vicinity."

His smile did so much to reassure her. "And you're worried you'll make too much noise?" he asked, bowing to brush his nose across hers.

A whisper of a laugh escaped her. "You should've heard the noise Roxie made with Zairn."

"I've had the pleasure of being in the next room," he said. "And we can beat that. I know it."

She laughed. "I don't think it's a competition."

"Come on, I'm a guy, and a successful one. That doesn't come with letting the other guy win."

"Zairn is your best friend."

"Yeah, and good luck to him. All's fair in love and—"

Surging up, she grabbed his mouth in a kiss. Roxie knew. The cat was out the bag. Sending him away might assuage her conscience, but it wouldn't change what had been done. They had two nights together. After that, they'd go their separate ways for good.

SEVEN

"FEEL BETTER?"

"You have to pack everything in the right way," Jane said, closing the zipper on Knox's carryall on the end of her bed. "Or your clothes get all crushed and creased."

"Whatever makes you happy, Blossom," Knox said, vaulting off the bed, tucking his phone into his back pocket.

"When you call me that…" she said, turning into his embrace as he gathered her against him.

Familiarity, endearments, they made it so much more difficult to say goodbye.

"It turns you on?" he teased, bending his knees to get his mouth closer to hers.

Why did he always do that? Cradle her in his arms and crouch close that way that made her feel so safe.

Something he was a pro at. It was unfair. Her defenses were useless against him. Somehow, he knew every move to edge her over the line from sane, rational woman, to impulsive, spontaneous harlot.

"One kiss…" she said on a sigh, thinking about the night Roxie went missing. "We were never supposed to see each other again."

Or see so much of each other. Naked. Intimate. As lovers.

"That one kiss…" he said in apparent agreement, tucking her hair back behind her ear, "was followed by incredible sex."

"Not that night!" she objected and squeezed her eyes closed when he smiled. "You're teasing me."

He kissed her forehead and left his lips lingering there. "I am, but I told you we did have sex that night."

"In your head."

"Yeah, in my head," he said. Laughing, his eyes found hers. "At least twice."

"Yet three days went by before you seduced me."

"Took you three days to give me the opportunity," he said. "Thanks for the cliché line."

"It wasn't cliché—I mean, it wasn't a line. I'd never been in an LA billionaire's house before. That's the truth."

"And knowing you like I do now, I believe you meant it. There's not a conniving bone in your body, Blossom."

"You know it was an accident. I didn't mean to sleep with you… I shouldn't have slept with you." Her guilt was one thing, but she also didn't want him to think he'd been manipulated on purpose. "I'd lost my happy ever after, and Roxie lost hers… I wasn't thinking straight."

It felt urgent, like this was her last chance to set the record straight. After the Bahamas trip, she'd move to New York and start a new life. The Knox chapter would close along with the Chicago one.

"Roxie got hers back and I've told you I don't want to hear excuses," he said. "You might not have been on my radar before that kiss, but you sure were after."

Excuses spent a lot of time in her head. With Roxie around, her betrayal was all the starker. She just couldn't get over it. Revisiting, worrying, was her penance. For the rest of time, she'd be the floozy who put a good lover above an amazing friend. She'd had no idea that was her, that she was one of those women. Until Knox.

"I've never done anything like that," she said, nestling her head under his chin, resting it against him. "Been bold like that."

"I'm happy I brought it out in you. Though your new adventurous side did use me for sex and dump me after one night."

Horror pulled her back to gape at him. "I didn't dump you!"

Though, there was no other way to put it.

Why had she kissed Knox that first time? No matter how she obsessed about it, she could never come up with a definitive answer.

His mouth was her kryptonite. The smooth line of his delicious lower lip entranced her, she loved the way they parted for her, how he gave for her every time. It just... was mesmerizing and... Was he talking? She couldn't hear, wasn't sure what he was saying or—

Her mouth leaped to his, stealing whatever he was trying to say, sucking his words onto her tongue as it slipped between his lips. Without delay or hesitation, his responded. How did he do that? Know just what she needed and... Oh, God, if they didn't stop... the span of his hand pressed into her back, holding her to him, sliding south so slow, but it would eventually—

"Stop," she said, shoving back, balling her fists on his chest. She squeezed her eyes closed. "Oh, I'm sorry."

"You know you do that a lot," he said, keeping her tight against him while stroking up and down her spine. "Cut me off to kiss me. I'll get a complex that you only want me for my body."

"This is exactly why we need distance," she said. "I can't control myself around you."

Their best friends were engaged. Why couldn't she get that through her thick skull? There would be a wedding and family events. Their fling had to end so they could move on to being casual acquaintances.

Thus far, every time it was supposed to be over, he'd appear back in her life, and she'd surrender to him all over again. It had to stop. Now. The cycle had to be broken.

Her Bahamas trip couldn't come soon enough. They needed the watershed. Needed the period at the end of their sentence.

"You ever hear me complaining?" he asked.

"No, but you should," she said, flattening her hands to give him a couple of light pushes, enough that he loosened his embrace. "Our friends are sharing a life. There will be birthday parties, anniversaries, kids, events. As long as they're together, we'll keep running into each other."

His smile was slow and sly. "I don't mind running into you. Over and over and—"

"No," she whined, letting her head drop back. "Don't talk dirty to me."

"Why?" he asked, a laugh in his words. In his arms again, she was powerless to resist when he kissed her jaw, her throat, her cheek. "You like it when I talk dirty to you."

"I like everything you do."

"I know," he said, hooking the strap of her dress to draw it down her shoulder.

"No," she said, grabbing the strap and leaping away. "We can't have sex again. You're packed, there's a car outside, you have to go."

"Roxie's home," he said. "There's always a car outside."

"Your car. A car for you."

"I don't want to sound hackneyed, but do you know who I am?"

"Collier Communications royalty," she said. "Media magnate. Billionaire. Playboy—"

"Uh, less of the playboy these days."

"For all your important work commitments, I never see you actually do any work. Don't you have a staff to get back to? Things to be running in LA?"

He shrugged. "Caspian prefers to do it himself."

"You know this is your brother's plan, to be so indispensable you'll lose your status when he takes over."

"He's the oldest, it's his gig anyway."

"He needs you. Even if he doesn't know it, he does."

"Okay, you want to get some food and we'll talk more about this?"

"No," she said, clenching her fists at her sides. "You have to leave. *I* have to leave."

"You want to come to LA with me?"

Though there was hope in his voice, it wasn't optimistic. "No, I'm going to the Bahamas. I won this trip the night we went to watch Talk at Sunset." The late-night talk show. "The same night Roxie won the contest to travel the world with Zairn." He knew all this. She was reminding herself more than educating him. "I'm going to the Bahamas and you're going back to work. Back to your life."

As they were supposed to do after their night in LA. It should never have carried on beyond that. It shouldn't have started in the first place. Was a kiss and a one-night stand an affair? Somehow, it felt like it. Being with him felt naughty. Because of their connected friends? Their coming from opposite ends of the class spectrum? Maybe because she was on the rebound… sort of.

"After this Bahamas thing, you and Toria are moving to New York with Roxie, right?"

"That's the plan," she said.

She, Roxie, and Toria loved their city and hadn't considered leaving it until Roxie fell in love with Zairn. That changed everything. Love like theirs, real, true, fairytale love shouldn't be constrained by zip code. Moving to accommodate that love just seemed right. Roxie shouldn't have to choose between her friends and the man she loved. So instead of one woman moving into his life, Zairn had three.

"It will be harder to keep this a secret when you're living with Zairn."

"There are apartments in the Crimson HQ building," she said, which was where Zairn and Roxie lived. "Roxie said Toria and I can move into one of them."

"So we'll get away with secret sex?"

Charm just oozed from him. And he was too hot. Not cute. He was like pinup hot… or the male equivalent. Calvin Klein ad hot, but older, more mature Calvin Klein.

"That's not what I…" She sighed. "You know I don't think straight when I'm with you."

"You think straight enough to keep telling me we have no future."

"I've never had a secret fling, never had a fling at all," she said, laying a hand on his chest. "I didn't think I even wanted one. We agreed when I left LA that this wasn't going to be a thing."

And he'd shown up in her life twice since then.

"I don't remember agreeing, I remember you saying it."

When he showed up, it wasn't like he only stayed for a one-off booty call either. He'd come and stay until his life forced him away. Their affair was supposed to stay private. Clandestine. Now Roxie knew and Merci too, their secret wasn't so secret anymore. It was getting out of hand. Way far out of hand. They had to put an end to it before anyone else had the chance to find out.

Over. Finished. Done with. Period. No more.

Not only to save Roxie's forever love, but to set her on the path to her own. Her Mr. Right, wherever he was, wouldn't tolerate her coming fresh from one lover to his life. She had to be ready for it. Open to love when it found her. Without thoughts of Knox's hotness residing in her head way more than it should.

Fairytale love didn't start as a secret. It didn't start with an ill-timed kiss and a sleazy one-night stand. And Knox was a Collier. A billionaire from a line of billionaires. Successful. Together. Nothing but potential.

In contrast, she couldn't even form a sentence without pausing halfway through for breath. High-strung, neurotic, anxious, these were words that would describe her.

"We're from different worlds," she said, wishing she could kiss him again. "We always knew this would come to nothing."

"You seem so sure of that."

She smiled. "Thank you for being the most exciting sexual experience of my life."

He laughed and wrapped his arms around her again. "If a guy's got to walk away with a title, that one seems pretty good." He kissed her forehead. "Call me if you need anything."

Tipping her chin up, she showed him a smile. "I'm going to the Bahamas. Paradise on earth. What else could I possibly need?"

EIGHT

BEFORE THE BAHAMAS came Miami.

The Talk at Sunset Bahama trip winners were meeting there. That meant seeing Toria.

As desperate as she was to see her other best friend, her nerves were rattled. Would Toria take one look at her and know she'd been hiding something? Probably. Having such little experience with secret flings, she doubted her poker face would hold up.

Her flight got in late. Thankfully, there was a driver at the airport waiting to pick her up. She went to the hotel and was told her roommate had already checked in and was at the bar.

Fantastic.

No matter what else, she needed a little Toria love. Her friend was full on. Gregarious. Nothing got to Toria, the woman was Teflon. She'd been fired not so long ago, but bounced, taking on the editing responsibility for Roxie and Zairn's documentary instead. Nothing got to Toria. Nothing slowed her down.

The bar was big, bigger than she might have expected, with a huge terrace beyond the open doors. Music played quietly, conversation and laughter lit the air too. It only took a second for the sound of Toria's laugh to capture her attention.

Toria noticed her in the same moment and leaped up from her barstool to rush over. She made short work of the journey too and squealed as Toria pulled her into a hug.

Every ounce of Toria was genuine. What you saw was what you got. She'd believed herself to be the same, but her foray with Knox revealed otherwise. At twenty-six, she shouldn't still be learning such profound things about the fiber of her being.

"Oh, honey!" Toria squealed, pulling back to kiss her cheek. But her friend faltered. "What happened? What's wrong?"

Tears rolled down her face. A yelp of grief preceded her laugh. "I've just missed you so much."

"Do I need to be kicking asses? Is it Graham? Did he touch you?"

"No!" Jane wanted to calm her friend's defensive hackles. "I really am okay."

"Come over here and we'll call Roxie," Toria said, grabbing her arm to drag her to the bar. "We need to call Roxie!"

Only as Toria stepped aside did she see her friend's companion was one of Zairn's assistants. A woman Roxie adopted as a good friend.

"Astrid," Jane said, putting her purse on the bar. "Hi." They hugged. "This must be craziness for you right now."

"Mr. Lomond's put a lot of faith in me," the young assistant said. "I'm honored."

From the corner of her eye, she noticed Toria unlocking her phone.

"We don't need to call Roxie," she said, putting her hand on the phone to push it to the bar. "I just missed you. Am I not allowed to miss you?"

"Yeah, but…" Toria let go of the phone to carefully wipe the tears from her cheeks, along with any makeup she might have smudged. "We talk every day. I didn't know you were so lonely at home." She hmphed. "I feel terrible now."

"Don't feel terrible," Jane said, directing her onto the stool beside Astrid's then going to grab another to sit between them, a little further from the bar. "Roxie was home when I left. Her and Merci are flying back to New York in the morning."

"I don't see why they don't come straight here," Toria said, gesturing around the room. "Think we can talk them into Miami instead of New York?"

She laughed. "Zairn is in some negotiation thing with Reid, Merci's fiancé."

"Zairn's probably afraid of what would happen with the three of us in Miami overnight," Toria said, snatching her hand to put a half-full glass in it. "We're finishing our drinks here, then hitting the clubs."

"Oh," Astrid said, squirming a little. "I didn't say we could definitely—"

"Why can't we?" Toria asked. "You said Jane's flight was the last to arrive tonight. No one else is coming in until tomorrow. You're off-duty."

"Yes, but if Mr. Lomond needs—"

"If Mr. Lomond tries to spout any orders, we'll have Roxie distract him," Toria said. "We have a gal on the inside." She gestured at the bartender for another round, indicating three rather than the two currently there. "Zairn won't need anything else tonight if we loop Roxie in."

"I can't get drunk," Astrid said, looking left, right, behind them and back. "If one of the guests needs something—"

"There's what? Fifty, sixty winners?"

"Fifty-eight, but they're not all here yet," Astrid said. "Every winner has a plus one. And the crew that—"

"You're in charge down here," Toria said. "Delegate and come party with us."

She didn't advocate cajoling anyone into anything, not exactly. Her first instinct was to tell Toria it was too late, or she was too tired. But when was the last time she let loose?

All the worrying of the past few weeks was obviously getting to her if she was randomly bursting into tears.

Though, it wasn't like that was a complete first.

"Call Roxie," Jane said. "If she says it's okay…"

Toria squealed in excitement and was quick to dial their friend, putting the phone on speaker between the three of them as the bartender delivered their drinks.

"Hey, honey!" Roxie answered. "Jane get there okay? I haven't heard from her yet."

"I'm here," she said.

"Hey! Oh, now I'm jealous! You're together. Where are you?"

"The hotel bar," Toria said, her smile focused on the bartender further along. "He's cute."

"Who's cute?" Roxie asked.

"Do you want to flirt with the bartender or recruit Rox to our conspiracy?" she asked, subduing her amusement.

"Oh," Roxie exclaimed, then lowered her volume. "There's a conspiracy? Who are we conspiring against?"

"Your fiancé."

"Well, that's no fun, I do that all the time," Roxie groaned. "I'm pretty sure you're on every Crimson list by now. Did we reinstate the Queens? Astrid should be—"

"I'm here."

"If you're there, why do they need my say so to get into Crimson?"

"We don't need your permission for that," Toria said. "We need you to keep your future hubby busy so we can bring Astrid with us."

"Ah!" Roxie said, catching on. "Have all calls diverted to me, Astrid. I can deal with whatever needs to be dealt with."

"I'm not allowed to do that," Astrid said, her mouth opening in shock.

"Who says?" Roxie asked. "This is easy and—you know what? Please hold."

She smiled at Toria who rolled her eyes as she handed out the glasses. "Holding. Everyone drink."

Astrid needed another gesture of encouragement but did sip eventually.

"Lola Bunny," Zairn's voice startled them all. "We hung up like three minutes ago. What did you break this time?"

"I missed you," Roxie said, her voice deeper before jumping back to normal and speeding up. "I'm going to run things in Miami for a few hours."

A pause. "You're going to run things in Miami," Zairn said. "From Chicago?"

"Mm hmm."

"Why do I feel like Toria's involved in this somehow?"

Toria yelped. "What does that mean?"

"Ah, we're not alone," Zairn said.

"You knew that," Roxie said. "If it's me calling at this time of night, I video because I know how much you miss my face."

"And other parts of you," he muttered. "Anyone else with us."

"I'm here," Jane said.

"Sir," Astrid offered, shrinking in on herself.

She knew the feeling. Toria and Roxie were so confident.

"You want to take Astrid out drinking?"

"We're already drinking," Toria said. "You're a party God, you know how important this is."

"Go party, if you want to," he said, distracted. "But I want everyone on that plane tomorrow."

"Me included?" Roxie asked.

"You have your own plane to catch tomorrow," Zairn said. "Back to me in New York."

Roxie inhaled. "I don't exactly catch it, it waits for me."

"If you want to take Merci down tonight—"

"She's still adamant she's not coming with us on this trip."

"You still think she should?"

"I do," Roxie said. "Would Reid have a tantrum if she did?"

Zairn laughed. "Yeah, 'cause that's something I want to get into with you. Go if you want to go, I'll talk to Reid. Dennis has a charge card for fuel. The plane will take you anywhere in the world."

"The Zee-Jet?" Toria asked. "Yes! Yes, bring it down here."

"There's an actual club on the Triple Seven," Roxie said. "You know that, you've partied there."

And slept off the previous night's party in the same room on a different occasion.

"Can we party on the Crimson Craft tonight? It's sitting doing nothing."

That was the fans name for the Triple Seven on permanent loan from the plane manufacturer to Crimson... or Zairn, she wasn't sure what it said on the paperwork.

"It's at the airport," Roxie said. "There are probably weird rules about that."

Because Toria would invite anyone she came across to join them.

"They were doing tours of it earlier," Toria said. "You know they only go as far as the conference room. No one gets to see what's beyond."

"It's his sex den," Roxie said. "All kindsa stuff going on in there. Whips, chains, gags, masks, plugs, the whole kit and caboodle, quite literally. All black leather and kink—"

"I'm writing this down," Zairn interrupted. "Next time you get on that plane, that's exactly what you'll find." Roxie laughed. "And you're wearing the ring, Lo, it's all on you."

"All of you on all of me should be reserved for a video call," Roxie purred.

"We don't mind listening in," Toria said, leaning closer.

While her friend was playful in her teasing, listening to the couple did something else to her. The flirting was fun, funny to hear. But it was their comfort, their easiness, that she envied. Their love was bigger than most other people ever found. Even hundreds of miles apart, they were strong and sure, enraptured with each other.

"Casanova's got to save something for his reception speech."

"Groom doesn't give a speech at the wedding reception," Zairn said.

"Oh, I meant your welcome to the contestants on Wednesday," Roxie replied. "You're presenting us to the world… again."

Their fake break-up would be officially over when they showed up on the island together and happy.

"You'd look amazing in the black leather, but you wouldn't last a minute in a gag. You'd talk right through the thing."

"Probably."

"No probably, for sure," Zairn said. "We'll have to pick this up later. The hookers just showed up with a couple of keys, I have to go. Astrid, party as much as you want, there are enough people down there. If something comes up, Roxie will be on the end of the phone."

"He won't be on the end of the phone because he has hookers to entertain."

"While the bunny's away… Some of them are just exotic dancers."

"They're not exotic dancers, honey," Roxie said. "Women's clothes just melt away when you walk in the room. Happens to all of us."

"You're powerless to resist."

"Me and every other woman on earth," Roxie said. "Go cash out our wedding fund in dollar bills for those G-strings, Casanova. I'll call you before I cry myself to sleep."

"Make sure you're naked, so I can share pictures with the guys."

"Always. Love you."

"I love you too," he said on a snicker. "Night, ladies."

They chorused goodnight and waited a second for the go from Roxie.

"He's gone," their friend said, "now we can talk about him."

"You two are so amazing together," Jane said, almost swooning. "You set a high bar for the rest of us."

"Hashtag relationship goals," Toria said. "We're not looking for our forever guys tonight. Tonight is about dancing like it's our last day on earth."

Astrid hopped off her stool. "I have to go take care of some things," she said and scurried off.

"Did she just ditch us?"

"I'll call her in a minute," Roxie said. "The rest of the winners arrive tomorrow. The flight isn't until after dinner. You fly to one of the islands and then it's a boat trip to get to Zairn's island."

"It's called the Crimson Isle," Toria said, sipping her drink. "You should be boning up on this stuff."

"I spend enough time boning the boss," Roxie said. "He doesn't care if I get the names wrong, just that I open my legs."

"It's not just about sex," Jane whined, knowing her friend was teasing. "He loves you."

"Nothing wrong with just sex," Toria said. "Though she is right."

"Sometimes just sex becomes something more."

"True," Toria agreed with Roxie. "What time are you getting down here?"

"I don't know. You get Tuesday to hang out and settle in. We arrive Wednesday."

"And because they have their own plane, they can show up whenever they want," Toria said. "Do you have your own boat too?"

"I don't know if we're getting a boat or a chopper," Roxie said. "Astrid's more likely to know than me."

"It doesn't matter. We're just excited to see you."

"I know!" Roxie exclaimed. "The three of us haven't been together in too long."

"I can't wait."

"Me either."

She was excited too. The three of them together should realign her sanity. Being like they were, having each other to rely on, it was the only medicine she needed.

NINE

PARADISE ON EARTH was an understatement.

Endless white beaches gleamed, and palm trees swayed in the refreshing breeze. The fragrant sea air was intoxicating, somehow conveying sheer indulgence and privilege. Chicago was quite a gray city most of the year. Not that it was dull, just that it wasn't as… enlivening.

The top end luxury resort was equipped with anything and everything a vacationer could need. A four-hundred room hotel, thirty private cabana bungalows dotted around the shore, and all kinds of retail and leisure facilities provided a firm foundation. Nothing was left to chance. The resort boasted corporate facilities and a separate block for staff apartments too. Not too bad a prospect. With its very own mountain, there were walking tours, and all sorts of outdoor pursuits suited to all levels of ability.

After the overnight in Florida, they waited all of Monday for the rest of the Talk at Sunset Bahama trip winners to arrive. By the time they got to the Crimson Isle, it was so late that food was delivered to their bungalow and they crashed.

On Tuesday morning, a room service breakfast was delivered, and she got to work unpacking and cleaning their bungalow. Everything was beautiful, it didn't seem unclean, going over everything again was just her way.

Their prize didn't officially begin until Roxie and Zairn arrived the following day. It was nice that winners got some time to get their bearings and acclimatize before the fun began.

"Oh, you are going to love me!"

She hadn't heard Toria arrive back from her jaunt to the main complex, but there she was, rushing across the tiled floor, waving something in her hand.

"What?" Jane asked, turning her back on the ocean view beyond their deck. "What is that?"

Toria pushed the flyer into her hands. "I signed us up."

"Signed us up for what?"

"Love in Paradise!" Toria exclaimed.

That was what the paper said. "Love in Paradise. An opportunity for singles to find the partner of their dreams in this tropical paradise," she read, then handed Toria the flyer back to rush over to the bed. "No. No. No, we can't."

"Of course we can," Toria said, admiring the flyer. "It's like the cherry on the cake. We need this. Need to have some fun."

She went to work remaking the bed she'd already made twice. She liked to think of herself as a supportive friend, but Toria had a habit of forgetting they weren't the same. Roxie and Toria were peas in a pod. All confidence and fire. She envied their dynamic energy all the time.

A dating event? She couldn't do that. Couldn't stand in front of various men and sell herself.

Coming on the trip was supposed to renew them. She hadn't considered dating even a possibility. The vacation was meant to be about friendship. Finding themselves. Learning more about their inner needs and wants. At least, it had been in her head. It was possible she hadn't actually said that aloud to anyone.

"It's not a good idea."

"It's a perfect idea," Toria said. "This is an adventure. What could be more exciting?"

"After Graham... Brendan... I make horrible decisions when it comes to men."

"That's the best part, the island decides for you," Toria said, grabbing her hand the minute she finished with the bed to sit them both on it. "You do not have to find your forever guy. But what if he is here? What if this is where you're supposed to meet him? Can you imagine anything more magical?"

Than a love affair in the sun? Long nights lying together, doors open, ocean breeze caressing their skin, damp from their latest tryst...

Inhaling, she held her breath. How easily she justified being a hussy was worrying. "After Graham, I swore off long distance anything. The people here, the guests and winners, they're from everywhere. We can't fall for someone, build a relationship, when we'll have to break up in less than a month," she said. "I have to be realistic, face facts instead of dreaming."

It was a fantasy. An unhealthy one. Romantic notions got her into so much trouble. This idea of a perfect guy, a grand romance... She couldn't keep chasing it.

Toria frowned. "That doesn't sound like the Jane I know and love."

"That Jane believed in fairytales. She believed in romance and rose petals on the bed. I've spent my whole life thinking I'd have an epic love. That we'd find each other and I'd just know, that everything would fall into place."

"Don't let assholes like Graham and Brendan take that dream away from you. It can happen. Look at Roxie, she found it, didn't she?"

"Roxie goes and gets what she wants. She's strong."

"You're strong," Toria said, tossing the flyer aside to slide closer and join their hands. "Is this why you were upset when you met me in Miami? Tell me what happened to make you feel this way."

"No, I wasn't sad upset. I was happy to see you."

"You don't seem happy now. Something happened. Something you're not telling me about."

"No." Jane shook her head. "The trip to Miami gave me the chance to reflect, I guess. With Brendan, I… I kept thinking I could make it work. That if I changed just a little, if I made this allowance and that, everything would work out."

"Rox and I never liked him."

"I know, but… Graham wasn't an asshole, we just didn't… click, like I thought we would."

"Graham is an asshole," Toria said. "We didn't know it until you said you didn't want to see him anymore. Then he showed his true colors."

She sighed. "Why is it every man I'm with has this other face? This other side. The beginning is great, I think it's real and then…"

Toria pulled her into a hug. "Oh, honey."

"Sometimes I wish I was more like you and Rox. You don't take shit from anyone, but I… I'm not like you. Maybe it's not the men who are the problem. Maybe I am the one who has to change."

"No," Toria said, releasing the hug to cup her face, holding it close to hers, their eyes locked to each other. "You do not have to change. You are so pure and so… You say you wish you were like Rox and me? We wish we were like you all the time." Her blink of surprise wrought a laugh from Toria. "We do. You are the best person either of us has ever known. You're good, inside and out. Every part of you deserves the very best that's out there. You deserve to have every one of your dreams come true."

If only Toria knew the truth. Warmth pooled behind her eyes. "I'm not as pure as you think," she whispered.

The sincerity of her friend's smile twisted the knife of regret.

"Honey, you are pure next to Rox and me. Pure doesn't have to mean virginal or untouched, it means you're the kindest, most honorable and precious—"

"Toria," she gasped, rising away from her friend's compliments. "I'm not precious. I don't deserve your loyalty."

"Why? For years, you and Brendan went back and forth. Every time you broke up Rox and I prayed you'd keep that door locked. You have no idea what he took from you. I didn't even know how much he took, not until right now. How can you think you don't deserve loyalty? You don't deserve love? If *you* don't deserve it, the rest of us are screwed."

Gazing into the ocean, the oblivion beyond felt like possibility. Yet, she couldn't embrace it.

"I have to be more realistic," she said. "Love isn't like you read in books. It's not like the movies. It's not like every story we're fed as children."

"What is going on? Is this opposite day? You've always been the most optimistic of us. Okay, so Graham didn't work out. That's nothing. One more guy down. Who cares? There are still a whole helluva lot more to check out. Someone out there will give you everything you want, and you won't have to change a thing to be with him."

"That's just it," she said, turning her back to the view. "I don't know what I want. What do I want, Toria?"

"You want a man who will treat you right," her friend said, standing up. "You want a man who will adore you the way you deserve to be adored. After Brendan, you put so much hope into Graham… I don't think you knew it until you met him and it was a bust. It feels like another door closed; I get that. But don't let him break your spirit, don't let your loser exes dictate your life. Do you want to go home and regret what might have been?"

No, she didn't.

"You think maybe he's here?" she asked, not convinced.

The glimmer of possibility put another grin on Toria's face. "Better to try and see than give up before it's started."

Her friend was excited about this Love in Paradise program. Toria talked a lot about a lot of things, not all of them panned out. But given they were already there, and Toria was wearing such glee, it sort of seemed like a done deal. Being assertive wasn't her natural state. Standing up for herself against Toria's certainty required a finesse she didn't always possess. But she trusted her friend and didn't want to burst her bubble. If she said no, Toria might pull out too. Could she live with the guilt of potentially tearing down Toria's chance at love?

Maybe it wouldn't be so bad. The island's beauty had to bring out the best in people, didn't it? It was certainly a step up from bustling, gray Chicago.

Love in Paradise could be the clean slate she needed to forget about her streak of bad romantic luck. No one person could be cursed in love forever, could they? Brendan was a bust. Graham too. A new interest should erase Knox from her memory as well. Okay, not completely erase him, but get her over the niggling guilt.

She shook her head. Chase that man out. Don't think of Knox. At all. For any reason.

She paused. That was it. This dating thing might give her some confidence. And it would offer a clean slate. Erase Knox from her body and Graham from her heart… if he'd ever lived there.

"Let me see the flyer again," she said.

Toria came to hand it over.

Under ordinary circumstances, they would never have been able to afford a trip to any island, let alone an exclusive one like Crimson Isle. One of their trio had found their perfect match from being in the Talk at Sunset audience. Maybe they all could. It worked for Roxie, didn't it?

"I was talking to the guy in charge," her friend said. "Nigel Everly. The LIP Endeavour is a pilot scheme they're running to work out the kinks. They want to capitalize on their reputation as a romantic destination. And…" Toria dragged out the word. "As a bonus, if you do find love, you'll be entitled to a free couple's vacation on your one year anniversary. If it's a hit, the resort will expand the program… and make a mint in the process."

"Maybe…"

Her friend dropped to sit on the edge of the bed. "I've had nothing but a trail of random one-night stands for at least a year. You thought London Guy was your happy ever after and he turned out to be a creep. We've got to catch a break sometime, at least one of us does... don't we?"

It was a once in a lifetime opportunity. Anxiety still niggled at her, but it always did. All it took was one. One guy to be special. She didn't even have a bunch of rules or strict criteria, she just wanted someone to love her. Was that too much to ask?

TEN

AFTER SPENDING THE rest of Tuesday in the resort spa, which Toria insisted was necessary, they headed for the LIP induction dinner. Ten men, ten women. It didn't sound like a lot until they were all in the same room and then it was overwhelming.

"Damn," Toria said, looking for their names on the place cards. "There are some hotties in here."

Okay, so Toria wasn't looking for their names, apparently, she was taking in the view instead.

"Let's just sit," she said, catching her friend's hand to draw her toward the next table at the head of the room.

Good. In their seats, they could be calm and wait for the food to be served. Each table held five people, three others came over in a group. One woman and two men. All people they'd met before, Ron, Dale, and Bree.

She'd forgotten Bree's flawless youth. Beautiful. Perfect blonde, delicate features, she'd be a man's wet dream.

"Hey!" Ron said, sitting down while Dale pulled out Bree's chair.

"Hey, we know you!" Toria exclaimed, grabbing her hand.

They weren't exactly bosom buddies, but they'd hung out… among other things.

"Yeah! We were arrested together!"

Her friend wasn't the only one laughing. The guys seemed to think that was a fond memory too.

"You weren't with us in LA, Bree," Jane said. The quicker everyone would forget about her one and only brush with the law, the better. "But you were at the New Year's Eve party in Crimson, New York. That was a great night."

"She's only nineteen," Ron said, resting a hand on the back of Bree's chair. "Not legal."

"I'm twenty now."

"Still not legal…" Dale said, "for bars and clubs."

Creepy. For bars and clubs, but not other things? Had the two been intimate? "Everyone here's supposed to be single," she heard herself saying like a complete killjoy.

Did that even make sense? Everyone else seemed confused.

"We're single," Ron said. "All three of us."

So whatever might have happened between them and Bree was casual. A surge of disapproval was totally hypocritical. Hadn't she just finished her own casual affair? She could feel the blush rise in her cheeks. In an attempt to hide it, she busied herself laying a napkin in her lap.

"Has anyone seen the menu?" she asked, hoping for another subject change.

Thus far the conversation was one false start after another.

Others weren't as willing to move the discussion along.

"How's Zairn?" Dale asked.

"How's Zairn?" Toria repeated, incredulous. "You ask about him before Roxie? Who is our actual best friend?"

"We know Roxie's great. She streams all the time… Man, that woman is so…"

All eyes landed on him.

Toria's head tilted. "That woman is so what?"

"Well, you know, she's… hot."

"Right, mm hmm," Toria said. "That what you were going to say?"

"That's not offensive," Dale said. "Saying she's hot. You're hot, are you offended?"

Jane waited for Toria's retort, except doing a double take, it seemed her friend was dumbfounded. No one ever silenced Toria, never, and she'd been called hot plenty.

"Maybe we should change the subject," Jane said, choosing to be direct about her intention. Subtle hadn't worked so far. "Why did you sign up for Love in Paradise?"

"To get laid," Ron said.

"Ron!" Bree chastised him. "It's supposed to be about love."

"Yeah, but what comes before love?" he asked, leaning in closer. "Sex."

"Yeah, you're a pig."

"I'm kidding," he said and laughed. "Shit, everyone's so uptight around here."

"I think it's amazing that Roxie and Zairn fell in love," Bree said, her smile brightening. "Like a fairytale."

"Me too!" Jane exclaimed, happy to find someone who shared her mindset. "And they're so amazing together."

"I can't wait to see them again."

"Are they really getting married?" Dale asked. "Are they doing it here?"

"I'd do it here," Bree said. "It's so beautiful."

"Yeah, if she's knocked up, they should do it here," Ron said.

"She's not knocked up," Toria sneered. "Why does everyone think she has to be knocked up?"

"You know, it happened fast."

"It happened fast for you, not for them," Toria said. "The world's known about it for less than two months. They've known since the tour last year."

Or Zairn had. Roxie wasn't so quick to pick up on her love. Their friend hadn't sensed her own protection mechanisms clicking into place. She couldn't blame Roxie for trying not to love a man who jetted all over the world. A man constantly hounded by gorgeous, nubile beauties. Zairn owned nightclubs, leisure facilities, entertainment hotspots, the nightlife was his livelihood.

Jet-setting billionaires hadn't been a part of their world before Talk at Sunset. Now Zairn would always be a part of their lives… That meant Knox would too.

Knox's family commanded movie studios, newspapers, TV stations, something of everything media related. They'd been in it since before Hollywood was even a thing. The Colliers were old money, one of the richest families in the world.

Maybe Knox didn't own a bunch of clubs where alcohol was served and music raised heart rates, but he hung out at Zairn's venues plenty. Beyond that, his good looks, the glamour of his family… She didn't doubt a bunch of gorgeous wannabe actresses or anchors tried to tempt him onto the casting couch regularly.

That didn't matter. Shouldn't matter. She shouldn't be thinking about him. They were over. And, technically, they'd never been a thing. Did one kiss, a one-night stand, ten days of casual sex, and a four-night follow-up fling really count as a thing? It wasn't a relationship. No, of course not, they were sex. Just sex. It did make her a little uncomfortable to think of herself like that, to think herself capable. But there was another part thrilled she'd had the experience.

When it came time to settle down, when she found *the* guy, she would go all in. She usually did with her relationships anyway. If she could find a guy willing to give the same, they'd be together forever. He wouldn't be The One otherwise. That was what she was waiting for. Mr. Forever.

Finding him would be the pinnacle of her life. It would be fun to look back on these wild, immature days knowing she never had to live with such uncertainty again.

"Don't answer that," Toria snapped, grabbing her wrist.

Oh, uh, she didn't even know what the table were talking about. "I won't."

"You can't ask about our friends. They're our friends. Human beings."

"It's okay," she said, turning her hand to link her fingers between Toria's. She might not know what the question was, but she understood Toria ramping up to a rage. "We get asked about them a lot."

"It must be intrusive," Bree said.

"Not as much as it is for Roxie and Zairn," Jane said, letting Toria go when a server brought over food.

Another poured wine for everyone at the table.

"When are they arriving?" Bree asked.

"Tomorrow," Jane said because that was no secret, it should be on the itinerary. "In the afternoon."

"Guess they don't have to worry about catching commercial flights," Ron said. "They can show up any time they want."

"Sometimes there are delays," Jane said, glancing at Toria. It wasn't normal for her friend to be quiet. "We'll see them when we see them."

Roxie would be in touch to let them know when they were on their way. Until then, everyone would just have to wait.

ELEVEN

THERE WAS A NEW kind of energy buzzing around their group on the Wednesday. On her and Toria's approach to the main complex in a chauffeur driven golf-cart, groups blocked the usual path.

"What's going on?" she asked, leaning toward Toria who was rubber-necking too.

Roxie and Zairn were due, and it appeared the crowds were eager for their arrival.

Squealing, Toria grabbed her hand. "Oh my God, they're waiting for Roxie! Our friend is famous!"

"And Zairn," she said though it was astounding. "Are they safe?"

"Ballard won't let anyone get hurt."

The golf cart drove away from the path past the upper terraces that were crowded with people too. That wasn't just the Talk at Sunset winners. It seemed like every person on the whole island was waiting for Roxie and Zairn to show up.

Going into shadow, they came to a stop by a side service entrance. She was opening her purse, trying to find her wallet when a hand landed on her shoulder.

"Zairn's taken care of it."

"Ballard!" Toria exclaimed, jumping out of the cart to run around and hug him. He didn't do much, just stood there scowling, but Toria didn't care. "Guess that's proof they got here." She gasped. "Oh my God, they were on that helicopter we saw!"

Wasn't subtle and was maybe what called so many people to the building.

She slipped out of the cart, tossing the strap of her purse over her body. The cart zipped away.

Ballard stalked over to the service entrance and touched a panel to open it. "They'll be here in under a minute," he said, crossing a vast hall with doors leading from it to ascend a set of stairs. The guy was tall and determined. To keep up, they had to jog along behind him. "The car's just pulling up out back."

"The world and their brother must be desperate to see if they're together," Toria said. "If both of them are here… If they're still in love…"

Because news of their break-up was still bouncing around in the media. Speculation was rife about this couple who'd lived so much of their relationship in front of a lens.

"We got them out of New York without any hitches," he said. "Keeping them under wraps is never easy."

"I imagine," she said when Ballard opened a door to lead them into some kind of staging area. The drapes were closed, lights weren't on. "Where are we going?"

Ballard marched to the opposite door to open it for them. "In here."

Light beckoned them. They went into a room with round tables set for a meal—Rox! There at the other side of the space. Their best friend had arrived.

Roxie squealed and rushed toward them as they responded in kind, hurrying to erase the gap between them to grab each other in a group hug.

"Oh my God," Toria said first as they loosened enough to look at each other. "I can't believe you're really here!"

"I missed you so much," Roxie said, kissing each of their cheeks. "Are you okay? Is everyone okay?"

"Everything's better now."

"How was your journey?" she asked. "Did you have trouble?"

"No," Roxie said. "I'd never know anyway, Z takes care of that."

"He tipped our driver."

"He tips everyone," Roxie said, stroking her and Toria's hair at the same time.

"There are so many people out front," she said. "It doesn't seem safe."

"Oh, Jane," Roxie said, grabbing her into a one-armed hug while the other stayed around Toria. "Stop worrying about what hasn't happened yet. Oh, hey, wait…" She stepped back. "There's someone you have to meet." Roxie gestured to a woman twenty yards away, calling out to her at the same time. "Merci! Come meet Toria." Merci got a comforting smile from Zairn before coming to join them. "Toria, this is Merci."

"I've heard a lot about you," Toria said, hugging their new friend.

"We have to go do our thing," Roxie said, hugging each of them. Their engaged friends had business to take care of, speeches and a lot of gladhanding. "Get to know each other in here. We'll come back when we're done."

Roxie walked them toward her fiancé.

"I thought we were having dinner later," Zairn said on their approach.

"We are," Roxie said. "We have a lot of time to make up." The rest of them paused at a respectable distance while Roxie went right up close to him. "Are you complaining about going on a date with four beautiful women?"

"Depends," he said, raising one shoulder in a shrug. "Will I get lucky at the end of it?"

"Not with that attitude," Roxie said, gliding past him.

Zairn's tight smile burst with pride. "Ladies," he said, tipping his invisible cap then about-facing to head for the waiting Roxie by the door.

Their teasing was forgotten or had progressed to something else as they departed.

"So..." Toria said, snatching Merci's hand. "You stomped on Matteo Reid's heart?"

Oh no! Not everyone was accustomed to Toria's directness. Given the engagement was fake, Merci probably wouldn't want to talk about it... or the end of it.

"Give her some space," Jane said, untwining the women's hands from each other to take Merci to a table by the window. "It's amazing here, isn't it?"

"Yeah," Merci said. "Incredible."

"I have to keep reminding myself that half of this is Roxie's," she said, pulling out two chairs for her and Merci.

"I don't think Roxie cares about the money," Merci said.

She smiled. "Oh, she definitely doesn't. That doesn't stop me imagining little Roxies and Zairns running around in the sand, playing in the surf."

Toria took a seat opposite them. "Roxie won't want her kids raised like that. Entitled and spoiled."

She laughed. "Isn't that how Roxie is with Zairn?"

"Yeah, some of it's an act... and she's paid her dues."

"Kissed her toads."

"She ain't the only one," Toria said. "You met all Zairn's friends at your engagement party?"

"Uh, I don't know if it was all of them," Merci said, "but, yes, I met a few."

"Any of them cute?"

"Toria!" she scolded her friend.

"What? She's newly single," Toria said, wriggling deeper into her chair. "Aren't we all ready to mingle...? Zane Dyce is cute, I know that. Zach Kintyre too, but he's on the rebound. Who would want to deal with all that divorce baggage...? Knox is hot, no question, but he's too high maintenance."

She tensed. It wasn't so easy not to think about Knox when others brought him up.

"It depends what you're looking for," Merci said, redirecting the conversation. What a relief. "One-night stand or forever man?"

"Somewhere in the middle," Toria said.

"You can't make it your mission to work through all Zairn's friends," she said.

"Ho, hey, did you just call me a slut?"

"No!" she exclaimed. "I'm worried they'll get jealous of each other and you'll start a brawl."

"You're right." Toria ran her fingers through her hair. "They wouldn't be able to handle me."

"Maybe if you fell in love with one of them…" Jane said.

"Like Merci?" Toria asked. "I was surprised to hear you were through. Roxie said you were really good together. Did he cheat on you?"

"No!"

Her friend just wasn't taking the hint. Toria had no shame. It wasn't malice, she was just that straightforward.

"Takes a lot of balls to walk away from a guy like that," Toria said. "Rich. Handsome. Successful… Sure, the money doesn't matter, but he's a grown up. A catch. Not like the losers we pick up in bars… The losers I pick up in bars."

"You picked up Logan Lowe in a bar," she said, trying again to divert the subject to something else.

"Rock stars don't fall into the category of reliable. He's hot. Wild in bed. But, really, do I want to be with a guy who spends his life around screaming beautiful women?"

"Zairn has a lot of admirers," she said. "It's never been a problem with Roxie."

"Yeah, because Zairn is a grown up. He's mature. Successful. Smart. You know, all the things a woman needs in a life partner."

Not so long ago, Toria said she wasn't the same Jane. Listening to Toria there, it was like she'd done some reflecting of her own.

"Wow," she said. "I've never heard you talk like this."

Toria shrugged. "If Roxie's growing up, we'll have to think about it too. You've wanted to grow up forever, I don't want my kids left behind."

"Who's having kids?"

"Roxie will soon." Toria snorted. "Come on, the amount of sex they have, it's inevitable."

"They're careful."

"That's what they all say," Toria said to Merci. "Did you and Reid plan to have kids?"

This wasn't exactly the best first impression.

"Don't harass her," Jane said. "They just broke up."

"I know," Toria said. "But she dumped him, she had to be sure. It was really brave. I couldn't do it. Date the boss, fall in love, and dump him. What if he makes her life hell?"

"Reid isn't like that. And we don't work on the same floor."

"Yeah, but you must have everyone speculating on what happened, what went wrong. Sometimes there's press on him. Sometimes there's work events. And everyone will want to tell you everything about him. Every time he's dating someone. Probably every time he smiles at someone. People take pleasure in that, tormenting others about their failed relationships."

"Oh my God, you make it sound awful," Jane said. "She'll never want to go back to work."

"I wouldn't," Toria said. "No way. Go back to the same building as my ex? Maybe if he was a grunt like the rest of us, people wouldn't care so much. Even then it can be tough. But to be surrounded by everyone thinking he's so great and so special. To hear about his jetting off with supermodels or spending millions on new assets. Every time there's a company change, it will be her instinct to want to talk to him about it. She'll be left out. Ignored. Shunned. She won't even have the same chances as everyone else."

"Why not?"

"Her boss won't want to piss off the guy on the top floor. Merci dumped him, remember? That means he gets the sympathy and she's the pariah. There'll be no invitations to parties, to meetings, no being on the inside of company secrets. He'll be protected by the people he pays, she'll be lucky to be served in the lunch line."

"You know, we shouldn't talk about our exes," Jane said, noticing how Merci suddenly looked panicked and conflicted. "Tell Merci about Love in Paradise."

"I think they're full," Toria said.

"Yes, but it's a sign of hope for the future, right? Isn't that how you sold it to me?"

Without too much deliberation, Toria went into a speech about LIP. Whether Merci was listening or not didn't matter. The engagement hadn't been real, but Merci didn't look neutral, like it meant nothing to her. Whatever had happened, she sympathized. Men and relationships weren't easy to navigate. It was no wonder every woman lost a piece of themselves each time their dreams were dashed, real or illusionary.

TWELVE

TORIA, AS USUAL, changed about five times before being ready for dinner. She hated being late. Their golf cart cab waited outside for twenty minutes, thank goodness they didn't have to pay a fare.

When they stopped outside Roxie and Zairn's bungalow—the most exclusive, most remote, most protected site on the island—she already had the guy's tip in her hand.

"Zairn takes care of that," Toria said when the guy wouldn't accept her money.

Giving up, she stuffed the bills back into her purse.

The guy drove away while Toria messed around with the chiffon of her dress.

"Come on."

"Who cares if we take our time?" Toria asked when Jane snatched her hand to pull her down the path. "They're not going anywhere."

"It's rude," she said, knocking on the door.

"I don't think we have to knock either." Toria passed her to go straight in. She couldn't even begin to… "We have arrived!"

The beautiful space was open on two sides to the deck beyond. The evening air flowed in freely. Okay, so maybe if half the building was accessible, there was less need to knock.

A bar area stood in front of the kitchen behind. Roxie was back there doing something with bottles. Merci sat in a basket chair just outside, staring out to sea.

"Hello and welcome to paradise!" Roxie said and tossed some fruit in her mouth before continuing to pour.

She and Toria went over. Toria kissed their friend's cheek and took one of the already filled martini glasses.

"What's in this?" Toria asked. "Oh, wait, I don't care." She laughed and gulped it. "It's alcoholic. Passes the bar."

Toria gave Roxie a one-armed hug before going around the other end of the bar to head toward Merci.

"Hey, honey," Roxie said, putting a glass in front of her before pausing to give her a hug, holding her sticky fingers away.

"Where's Zairn?" she asked, moving the glass back.

Roxie poured juice into a pitcher, waving over her shoulder. "On the phone. I think. Somewhere."

"Can I do anything? Do you need me to help prep for dinner?"

Roxie flashed her a smile. "They'll deliver it and set the table," she said. "Billionaire lifestyle, baby."

"I don't mind cooking."

"So, Love in Paradise," Roxie said, her smile growing sly.

"How did you know?"

"I talked to Bree this afternoon. You really think it's a good idea?"

"I really think Toria signed us up without my consent… When she told me…"

"You were scared," Roxie said and shrugged. "Why not have a little fun? Live it up?"

"That's what I thought," Jane said. "After my mini meltdown. Maybe I can meet Mr. Right. I have to be open to it, don't I?" She sighed. "Oh, I don't know, I'm not the most attractive prospect."

Quickly frowning, Roxie stopped what she was doing to turn to her. "You are gorgeous, Jane Simmons. You're smart. Funny. Kind. Wonderful—"

"You're biased."

"Yes, I am," Roxie said, leaning in to rest her head on her shoulder, her hands still sticky. "And Mr. Right will be too."

Her friend went back to the cocktail pitchers.

"I have no job, no apartment, no boyfriend."

"You have the most fabulous best friends," Roxie said. "And Zairn can be boyfriend to all of us. As long as you're following our rules, I'm cool with it. He'll cover all your practical needs. Take us to dinner, buy you flowers, jewelry, whatever you want."

She sighed. "I don't know, love just doesn't seem to be… Maybe it's not meant to be."

"God, if you're talking that way, the rest of us are screwed."

"That's exactly what Toria said."

"Because you believe in love. You've always believed in soulmates, one person meant for another. Don't tell me you've gone and gotten cynical. See, this is what happens when I leave you alone for a minute."

"Graham turned out to be a bust, didn't he?"

"London Guy was a fluke. You'd known him for years. Had your long distance whatever… So you met and there was no chemistry. It happens. You weren't in love with him." Roxie paused to look at her again. "Were you?"

"No," she said on an exhale and put her purse on the bar. "I was in love with the idea of him. How romantic would that have been? Circumstances keep us apart for years. Geography's against us. Then we meet and it's all worth it. The wait heightened the anticipation."

"If you want to marry the guy, marry him," Roxie said, stirring the liquid. "Though he is certifiable. The messages he's sent, the way he's pursued you, that's not love, it's insanity. Is he still harassing you?"

"We've kept our phones off here. The roaming charges are ridiculous."

"We'll cover the bill. It's because of us you're here… But maybe keeping it off is smart, then you don't have to face Graham's infatuation every day. Ballard's already lined up a security team for when you move to New York. Are you coming back to Manhattan after this trip?"

"I only packed for the vacation," she said. "Toria got me a bunch of new clothes in LA." She leaned closer. "She got me two-piece bathing suits."

Roxie laughed. "Shit, babe, I've missed you. Toria just wants you to live a little. We both do."

"Am I really uptight?"

"You know how to let loose, honey. When you let yourself. We love you just the way you are. Mr. Right will love you too."

"Like yours does? You're so lucky."

"Don't tell Z that," Roxie said, offering a piece of fruit to her lips.

As she took it, Toria shouted. "Rox, is there a club on the island? How can this be a Crimson resort without a nightclub?"

"There is a club," Roxie called back. "Though this isn't technically a Crimson location." Even though it had been sold that way. "We're a Rouge subsidiary."

"I'm sorry," Zairn's voice rose at the back of the room, attracting everyone's attention. "Has anyone seen my fiancée?" He came toward them. "She seems to have been replaced by this captivating corporate creature."

He put an arm around her from behind to dip and kiss her shoulder.

"It's you that goes on about it, blah, blah, blah. I have to start carrying earplugs." Roxie turned her head to find his lips. "Everything okay?"

"Yeah, Ballard's coming down."

"More people," she said. "Maybe we should skip dinner and open our own club."

"We don't have enough?" Zairn asked, backing up, turning his focus to her. "Good evening, Jane."

He actually came closer and kissed her cheek before fading further into the room to greet Toria. Her mouth dropped open.

Roxie laughed. "Your face right now."

She grabbed her forearm. "Zairn Lomond just kissed me."

"Yep," Roxie said, popping another piece of fruit between her lips. "He's a sleaze." Except Jane was swooning. "We asked you to plan the wedding. You're friends now. Family." She nodded toward the glass. "Are you going to drink that?"

"I don't want to drink too much before dinner."

"Okay, well I have something to tell you, and the drink might help."

"What?" she asked, struck by alarm.

There was a knock and Zairn went over to answer the door. Staff came in with trays and trolleys, going to the long table on the deck.

"Knox is coming."

The motion of the staff machine setting the table and bringing in food was so mesmerizing, she almost didn't hear her friend.

Almost.

Did she just say…?

When the words sank in, everything else was forgotten. "What?" She sucked in a breath. "Why? When? Why?"

"He called Zairn today," Roxie said. "He's arriving tomorrow."

"Why?" she asked, gasping in the word. "Oh, God, Rox, what if everyone finds out? Did you tell Zairn?"

"No," Roxie said. "You asked me not to. Merci hasn't told Reid either."

Oh, God, Reid, was Merci's ex in the loop? He was friends with Zairn and Knox. If Reid found out, more people might learn the secret.

"This is a disaster. I have to go home."

"No! You can't go home, no way. If I have to tell Zairn to bar him from the island, I will, but I'll have to give him a reason. Him and Knox have been friends since they were kids."

"Won't it be strange Knox just showing up?"

"Trust me, he shows up all over the world, all the time. Guess that's the advantage of being a billionaire. All of them just jet all over to wherever they want as it suits them." Roxie sidestepped to wash her hands. "Z doesn't think it's weird."

"Z doesn't think what's weird?" he asked, startling her from behind.

Roxie didn't miss a beat. "That I have a penchant for oral sex on the beach," her friend said, drying her hands.

"Did Z know you had a penchant for oral sex on the beach?" he asked of himself in the third person.

"Isn't that why we're here?"

His brow came down like he thought his fiancée was nutty. She was a little, but only in the most endearing way. "Is that what you'd prefer for dinner?"

He played it so straight that even she had to laugh.

Roxie had no chance and was laughing when she coiled her arms around him. "Maybe tomorrow night. Might put our guests off if we do it tonight."

"I'm going up to the main complex with Ballard."

"Ogilvie losing his mind?" Roxie asked. Zairn's head moved just a little. "Okay, but if you're going to be late text me, or send a cabana boy."

"What about dinner?" Jane asked when the couple shared a goodnight kiss.

"He eats too much anyway," Roxie said, slapping his stomach.

The rock-hard abs she'd seen in the flesh. Zairn Lomond was not out of shape in the slightest.

"I'll eat with the others," he answered her question, ignoring his fiancée's quip.

"Send Astrid down," Roxie said. "She'll take your place and needs to get to know my girls better."

"I'm beginning to feel like a spare part," Zairn said, though he was smiling, not offended. At least, she hoped that was the case. "Maybe me and mine should take off, leave you and the others to run things."

"Don't be stupid. That's a ridiculous idea," Roxie said, pouring from the pitcher into a martini glass, which she then handed to him. "We need you bankrolling us."

He sipped the bright liquid and handed it back. "Keep practicing."

"You know, I'm the woman who'll bear your children," Roxie said, putting down the glass. "A little compliment, some encouragement, wouldn't go amiss."

When he bowed to murmur something in his fiancée's ear, Jane blushed. From the look on her friend's face, she was witnessing a very private exchange.

Roxie caught his neck as he began to straighten and pulled him down for a long, slow kiss. Turning her back, she didn't want to intrude.

She didn't even know Zairn had moved until the door closed.

Roxie raised an arm and shouted. "He's gone! Let's get the party started!"

THIRTEEN

ALL DAY THURSDAY, it was like waiting for the other shoe to drop. Knox was coming to the island. He could appear any minute. She wasn't exactly expecting him to hunt her down, but she wanted to be ready when their paths crossed.

So what if the guy was coming to hang out with his friend? On this gorgeous Bahamian island… That was normal. Expected. Who wouldn't take advantage of the opportunity? Right? Except… why hadn't he mentioned it before he left her apartment on Sunday?

Because their whatever it was, was over. That would be why. She wasn't privy to his private movements because she was nothing to him. They were nothing to each other. His life wasn't her business.

Throughout the day, Toria had been animated, talking, gesturing, excited for that night's LIP icebreaker. Right then, she was supposed to be picking an outfit. It was just a drinks party. No big deal… Unless Toria found a mate. Usually, they were a threesome. Her, Toria, and Roxie. That meant if one of them found a friend, there was always someone else to keep the other occupied.

Toria appeared in her bedroom with a bottle of champagne and two flutes.

"Do you think we should drink?" Jane asked.

Her friend put the glasses down to work the cork from the bottle. "Damn right we should, this is a party!" she said, pouring champagne then handing her a flute. "We have about three hours until the reception."

Food should arrive any minute. They'd elected to eat an early dinner in their bungalow alone. Or Toria elected for them, to give herself more time to get ready. If it meant arriving on time to the event, she was on board.

"We should get some rest," she said, drinking her champagne faster than was smart before eating.

"Rest?" Toria asked, topping off the glasses. "We have to finish what's left in this bottle and have dinner. We're running out of time to make ourselves gorgeous! You should be excited, honey. We're going to meet our future husbands tonight!"

"Have you seen someone you like?"

Toria made eyes at her, then went into the closet. "Maybe. I don't know." She came out with a bunch of dresses to hang them on the doors and their frames. "Rox said Knox Collier arrived today. He really shouldn't be allowed to show up single when we're supposed to be looking at the guys in the group. Don't you think? He's hot, like beyond hot... you noticed, right?"

Drinking her champagne, she admired the dresses. "I haven't seen him."

Toria laughed. "Not today, but you know what he looks like. We've met before. But I guess that ship will be staying in port."

Toria opened a drawer to fish out some lingerie to show it off.

Smiling, she hid her mouth behind her glass. "He's one of Zairn's best friends. We shouldn't think of his friends that way."

"Yeah, I guess, maybe. I don't know. Zairn doesn't seem like the type to care. So long as no one's moving in on Roxie, he must let his friends have fun with other friends. The guy's a nightlife God. You think he controls everyone in his clubs all the time?"

"Just because we can doesn't mean we should."

That her friend was busy with the silk and lace was a small mercy. Those words hadn't been aimed at anyone but herself. What had she been thinking? Instigating that kiss… that incredible kiss. There was no defense of coercion or influence. Her fling with Knox was all her fault.

"I've heard things about him, you know," Toria said, switching a couple of the dresses around.

"Things about who?"

"Knox Collier. The whole Collier family really. They're too hot for their own good. What chance does any woman have?"

She hid her mouth behind the flute, folding an arm across her body. This was excruciating. "They wouldn't force a woman to do anything."

"Yeah, that would be news, right? Not like they can't control that." Toria leaned back to roll her eyes over her shoulder, then went back to her apparel matching dress to lingerie. "They've all had their share of women. Caspian, he's the oldest, he's had relationships. Knox is just take 'em and leave 'em, totally non-committal. No shock there. He's hot enough to do whatever he wants. He's dated supermodels, actresses, his track record is richer than Zairn's when it comes to hot women and that's saying something."

Phew. It was getting hot in there. Was she sweating? Now it felt ridiculous. What gave her the right to randomly kiss a guy who could literally snap his fingers and have the richest, most elegant women lining up on his doorstep?

"How do you know what they're like?"

Toria shrugged. "I know stuff. When Rox went to him for help getting back with Zairn, I checked him out," she said, pausing to frown. "I'm surprised you didn't, you're usually all about the research."

No, instead of researching Zairn's friends, she'd been busy jumping them. She swallowed. What if Knox told Zairn? He could. She'd have no right to tell him not to. Okay, so, yes, she had already done that, but that was while they were still a thing. No, not a thing.

Toria took a big breath. "The three Collier brothers were destined to take over the world. They have it all. The exotic lifestyle of privilege and wealth. When Camden, the youngest, left it all behind and abandoned his trust fund, the world was stunned."

"I wonder why he did," she murmured.

"Word was he was having some torrid affair with a maid or some member of the household staff."

"Word? Whose word?"

"The media," Toria said like it should be taken as gospel.

Jane wasn't as quick to accept it. "If he was in love with the woman enough to abandon his family, why didn't he marry her?"

"I said 'affair' not 'love,' it was probably just sex. Men like him don't marry maids. They marry models." Apparently not. "But this was forever ago, he was a kid. Like college age. Guys like him don't get married in college." Toria went into the closet and came back with more dresses. "Have you looked through all the clothes I bought for you? I love that Roxie has access to Zairn's accounts."

When unpacking them, she'd assumed her clothes were mixed with Toria's. No way would she have chosen most of them, let alone be seen in public wearing them.

"Yes," she said. "I hope most of them are for you. I'd look ridiculous in clothes like that."

"Are you kidding?" Toria asked, approaching to cup her breasts. "You don't show these babies off enough. You have great boobs. All pert and bouncy. You should take advantage of them while you have them."

"Where are they going?" she asked, pulling her friend's hands from her chest.

"You have a great figure." Toria went to open the top drawer and rummage through her accessories. "I don't get why you think you have to hide it all the time."

She didn't want to embarrass herself. "I don't have to put it on show all the time. That's what Brendan used to tell me. I'd embarrass him if I flaunted myself. Didn't he always say there was nothing to flaunt?"

Brendan was her ex as of a year ago. Why did she find it so difficult to connect with men?

"We're not giving Brendan the airtime. He was an asshole. A complete jerk. You can do way better than a fuckturd like him."

"Just because he was a jerk doesn't mean he was wrong."

Toria stopped to gape. "You're kidding. You don't… you don't think he was right, you can't, no way."

She shrugged, talking about her body was the last thing she wanted to do.

Toria grabbed her hand and put their champagne aside to drag her over to the full-length mirror.

"What are we doing?" she asked when Toria started to undress her.

Her friend didn't answer or wait for permission, she stripped her down to her underwear and forced her to face the mirror.

"Look at that body would you, please?"

Why? Geez, it was torturous.

As she crossed her hands over her belly, she closed her eyes. "Tor—"

"No!" Toria said with actual anger in her voice. "Look at yourself. Now, Jane! Open your eyes! You do it now or I'll ask every guy tonight what he thinks of your figure."

The only thing worse than making her look at herself would be drawing attention to her flaws in a room full of strangers.

She opened her eyes slowly and blinked at the sight of her body. "Why are we doing this?"

"You are gorgeous," Toria said. "Not even like acceptable or passable. Gorgeous."

"Since we found out about this vacation, I've been going to the gym almost every day," she said. "You bought me two-piece swimsuits."

"And you're going to wear them with pride," Toria ordered. "You have boobs women pay thousands of dollars to have and an ass men trip over themselves for." When Toria spanked her ass, she squeaked. "And look at that belly! There are muscles there, you see those? Women hunt their whole lives for those. What is it you think is wrong with your body? I'd trade mine for yours in a second."

It wasn't one thing, it was the package. Every time she was bare, she heard Brendan's sneering voice in her head. "He used to tell me he had to picture other women when we were in bed," she murmured to her shame.

Toria growled. "Yeah, he was an asshole who put you down so he could control you. You're better than that. You booted his ass to the curb, you're free. Say it."

Except they actually only split up for good after she found out Brendan was sleeping with his secretary, who was now pregnant with their second child.

"I'm free," she said.

"Yes, you are," Toria said, wearing a grin. "Now you and I are going to make a pact right now." Turning her around so they faced each other, Toria held her shoulders. "We're not going to say no during this trip, okay? We're going to have an adventure. We're going to be daring, throw caution to the wind and take every chance we can to have the time of our lives. Don't be scared. Don't second guess yourself. If we get the chance to do something fun, or new, or exciting, we're going to do it. We're not going to say no. And whatever happens here, stays here.

"We don't have to find forever love. If we do, great, if not, we say screw it and know we at least had the time of our lives."

"Tor—"

"We're not going to let the Brendans of our pasts into our heads. Here we can be anything we want to be. We can be wild and untamed. We say what we want. Do anything we want. We won't question each other or judge; we'll be a hundred percent supportive. And we won't quiz each other on where we are every minute. If we're out all night or disappear, we're going to let it be until the other is ready to share. That way we won't be panicking, we can relax and have fun. If we have a dilemma, we ask ourselves, what would Roxie do?"

"What would Roxie do?"

"Yeah," Toria said, her head bouncing left and right. "Before Zairn. Like everything in our lives: BZ or AZ." Her friend got back to the point. "Roxie's fearless, right?"

Nothing intimidated Roxie. Nothing.

"Right," she said.

"What would Roxie do?" Toria asked. "Deal?"

"Deal."

Toria gave her a shake. "I mean it, Jane Simmons. I want you to be wild and crazy. I want you thinking crazy all the time. I want you thinking adventure. Take chances. Be confident. Even if you don't feel it, smile and fake it. Please, honey, you deserve this. We both do. Let's have an adventure."

FOURTEEN

HAVE AN ADVENTURE. The words rang in her head during the reception.

Before leaving the bungalow, her choice of a high-neck sleeveless dress provoked debate. Toria let her wear it on the condition she never wore it again. Although it was black, it was short. Okay, so it didn't exactly scream tropical vacation, but blending into the background was her default state.

Some of the LIP men had spoken to her, trying to break the ice, as was the point. The men were polite. Pleasant enough. Why couldn't she engage with them? Because if she started talking, she wouldn't stop. Anxiety made her ramble. Toria was amid a group of three men. The other women were in discussions with their friends and the guys. Everyone was smiling and getting along, having a good time.

She backed away, passed the beaded curtain, and went into the main bar, away from their event.

The bartender came when she put her clutch on the bar. "Can I have a white wine ginger ale spritzer, please?"

"Of course, Miss Simmons," he said and walked away.

Her open mouth closed. She frowned. Wow, the place was impressive if the bartender memorized the name of every guest. Those names had to change on a weekly basis. Maybe more often, the hotel did long weekend specials too.

How many guests would stay every year? She was still trying to figure that out when he came back with her drink. Although she tried to pay, he walked away without taking the money.

Huh. Okay. There were pre-mixed cocktails available in the reception. Those were free. She figured she'd have to pay for her special request. Obviously not. How much would an open bar set them back?

The math distracted her as she sipped. She didn't see anyone approach until a young man was right there next to her.

"Miss Simmons?"

Snapping from her calculations, she turned to him. "Hello," she said. "Can I help you?"

He smiled. "Would you come with me, please, ma'am?"

Uh oh, maybe she was in trouble. That was what happened when Roxie wasn't around to keep her right.

With little other choice, the only option was to nod. "Sure," she said, swinging her hips around the stool between them.

Rather than returning to the reception, the guy led her the opposite way. They went to the vast open doors to a different outdoor patio. Instead of going further outside, they went through a beaded curtain up a set of narrow, shallow stairs.

At the top, she slowed, awed by the panoramic view of the ocean beneath the low awning that kept the private terrace almost concealed.

"Wow," she said, mesmerized by the view beyond the single table.

The single, occupied table.

Knox turned to look at her. "You like?" he asked.

In her peripheral vision, she saw him wave the young guy away.

She admired the stars twinkling above the ocean. "It's… breathtaking."

"Sit down and enjoy it with me," he said.

Like it was that simple.

Tearing her focus from the view, she sighed. "Knox."

"I know, you're pissed," he said, opening his arms to gesture at the hidden space. "No one knows we're here."

"Except the guy who brought me here."

"Marty won't say anything. I pay him to keep bigger secrets than this, believe me." Than secret dates with hidden women? She didn't even want to imagine it. "Come and sit down…" He raised his brows. "You knew I was here, right? RK told you I was coming?" She nodded. "Then this was inevitable, Blossom." No kidding. "Come on, sit with me… please. What's the harm?"

Thoughts like that got her tangled up with him in the first place… and every time after. Still, it would be rude to run away.

Taking her drink to the table, she elected to sit opposite him. Rather than look at him, and his kissable lips, her regard switched to the view. "Why would you live anywhere else when you have access to places like this?" she asked, her eyes wide as she raised her straw to her lips. "It's so beautiful."

"Ah, you get used to it. No big deal."

Being glib wasn't exactly new fare for him. Still, she had to look at him to check if he was being serious. It took him a second to smile.

Returning his amusement, she whispered a laugh, and drank more of her spritzer. "Do you have your own bungalow?"

"Why? Do we need to be more alone?"

"Don't flirt with me," she said, shaking her head. "Is that why you brought me up here? To flirt with me?"

"I wanted to talk to you."

"You should've told me you were coming… on the trip, to this island, Zairn's island. You could've told me in

Chicago. I know it's not my business what you do but… Is that what you wanted to talk about? About making sure I don't say anything? I won't. I haven't."

"No."

"Then what did you want to talk about?"

"Your trip, how's it going so far?"

"Fine," she said.

His head tilted. "So we don't talk? At all? About anything?"

In the past, if they'd been alone for that length of time, they'd be having sex already. The only way to get past that, to build some kind of civil, friendly tolerance for each other, was to be something else. She'd get over her attraction to him if she ignored it long enough… and kept furniture between them, that would be helpful.

"Toria's having fun," she said and drew in a breath. "She's having a great time and signed us up to a 'Love in Paradise' pilot they have going on. It's a matchmaking thing… sort of. I'm still not sure how I feel about it. Not great right now, to be honest, gift baskets were delivered to our bungalow just before we left."

"Gift baskets?"

"Yeah. Full of sex toys! Furry handcuffs, paddle thing, whip, all that fun stuff." Her eyes narrowed as she twisted her glass round and round on the table. "I thought this was a classy resort. Do you know what kind of pressure it puts on women to have sex when you fill their rooms with condoms and lubricant? Are handcuffs and whips what it takes to find love? We should talk to Zairn about it… though, I guess he and Roxie are relaxed about that kind of thing. No one can think women should be cuffed and whipped on the first date."

"The first—"

"That's pressure, right there. And what kind of vetting was done? These guys could be sex maniacs or perverts or something and they're being given all the tools they need to violate trusting women seeking love. Someone should suggest toning it down next time, what happened to good old-fashioned champagne and rose petals, huh? When did chocolates on the pillow become too conservative? Me, I like those ones with the strawberry filling, you know? The dark chocolate ones that are thick and creamy with the pink fondant that coats your tongue, you know those ones?"

Yep, this was definitely a ramble, but she couldn't stop herself, she kept on going. "Anyway, that's not the point… Like we're not freaking out enough already that we have to be switched on and charming at every event, now we have to be worried about our dates pulling out the handcuffs! And spanking, not every woman likes that. I know guys think every woman does, but they don't. I mean… I don't know if I do, I've never done it. But breaking sex boundaries is a stretch when there's no guarantee anyone will even like each other.

"Was there any consideration given to likes and dislikes, hobbies and interests? Is there meant to be a potential match for everyone or are we just the first twenty who signed up? Why do most of the events seem to revolve around drinking and games? I, for one, do not excel in social situations. Unless I'm dancing with my girls. That's the exception. They give me like a buffer, they're my shield, my safe space. Other than that, I would much rather sit in a dark corner with a man and discuss history or politics. Yet for the duration, I'll be stuck in the midst of a group telling sex stories.

"With an equal number of males to females there's pressure on everyone to find a mate. What if eighteen others do? Does that leave me entertaining the man who's left? More's the point, does that leave him obliged to spend time with me? I'll tell you now, that guy out there, whoever he is, deserves a full refund." Blinking, she inhaled. The scent of the sea mingled with that of purebred male. His eyes were closer, twinkling on hers. "I mean, I know no one paid for this vacation, we won our tickets, they were a gift, but…"

His smile this time was more subtle, but somehow more potent. "You're magnificent." Her shoulders dropped as he laid his hands on the table. "Marty!" he shouted, startling her. The young man who'd escorted her reappeared. "Get back every LIP gift basket distributed today."

"The… the—"

"I want two bottles of Cristal in every room and bungalow. Strawberries delivered every morning, rose petals on the beds every night. Get diamond earrings for the women, double stud teardrops, and platinum money clips for the men, get them engraved at each man's convenience. If I see one pair of furry handcuffs on this island again, you'll be looking for a new job, you hear me? We're running a luxury resort not a brothel."

"Ab—absolutely, sir. Understood," Marty said and scurried off.

Her lips parted with the shock of his authority.

He smiled and traced a fingertip down her jaw across the narrow table. "Magnificent," he murmured.

"I thought this was Zairn's island."

"It is," he said. "But we don't care about that shit in our group."

"I don't want to be the party pooper. Maybe everyone else loves it."

"Maybe. But you get points for telling it like it is. You speak up, your wishes are fulfilled."

"I speak too much. You know I speak too much… And I shouldn't be negative. It's a beautiful place. We should be grateful to be here, not complaining about what we're given."

"Blossom," he said. "One thing you should've learned about me so far, I hate sycophants. I've been surrounded my whole life by people spouting what they think I want to hear. Honesty is currency with me."

"I'm not looking to buy you."

"I know," he said and smiled again. "But a conversation costs neither of us anything… We can talk history or politics, whatever makes you happy."

He was trying hard, she had to give him that and always liked how easily he smiled at her. "Politics is controversial for a first date, is it not?"

"A date?" he asked, leaning back in his seat, crossing his ankles. "You're forward." Sheesh, had she just said that?

A date? He'd never once alluded to this being a date. He wanted conversation, that was it. Did he see her panic and sense another rant? Maybe, because one corner of his lips curled. "I like it."

"I don't think straight when you're around. It's not a date because we're not a… We've never been on a date, why should we start dating now?"

"You signed up to the LIP thing, you're here to date."

"I don't have the best track record with men. Especially recently."

"Ouch," he said, almost laughing, but not quite. "Isn't LIP just a month of date after date?"

"There's only two weeks left. It means something to Toria," Jane said, sorry she'd offended him. "She's a good friend. She's been there for me when I needed her. She deserves to find love and needed my support."

"So you're just her wingman? You're not interested in a relationship?"

Squirming, she hoped this wasn't some kind of test that would get her kicked off the program. "I'm not averse to the idea, but… like I said, I haven't had the greatest luck with men, so I guess I'd say, I don't have high hopes."

"I wonder about the men in Chicago if they don't notice you. Do you have a reputation up there or something?"

Although she could hear a thread of teasing, worry infused her. "A reputation? Like I'm a slut or something?"

He laughed. "No, I think if that was what men thought of you, you'd have dates every day of the week."

"I'm not famous," she said. "I'm not wild and experienced in the kinky stuff."

FIFTEEN

HIS BROWS ROSE. "You're not?"

She drank more, keeping her eyes from his. "I'm trying not to reference our previous…" How could they be friends if sex kept coming up? If she kept talking about it? "Look, until our…" They weren't an us, she couldn't say it, wouldn't. "Until our thing, missionary before nine p.m. was adventurous for me." He knew what she was like in bed, he'd been there with her. Plenty. Too much. And now she was on a gorgeous tropical island trying not to remind him of that. "I shouldn't have drunk so much champagne at the bungalow."

"Did you enjoy it?"

"The champagne? Yes, it was very nice." Sitting straighter, she held her straw in her drink. "Toria insisted we finish the bottle, she's a bigger drinker than I am. She says that I have a slow system, I'm not even sure what that means. I'm slow at everything, always have been. Maybe it is my system." She stabbed her straw in and out of her drink. "Men complain I need so much foreplay. Not that it mattered to them. You're the only guy who ever cared about my climax—" She stopped stabbing when her mind caught up with her mouth, her mortified eyes leaped to his. "I'm sorry, I don't know why I just said that."

"You're amazing," he said, grinning. "You just… talk. That honesty, Jane, you don't know how refreshing it is."

Avoiding his unnerving gaze, she snatched for a benign topic. "Did you grow up in LA?" she asked. Brown-nosers must come with the territory. His family owned most of… everything. "It must have been an amazing playground."

"I was sent away to school," he said. "Boarding school and college. I didn't go back to live there full time until my grandfather got sick."

"I'm sorry," she said, reaching over to put her hand on his.

His head tilted as he looked down at the contact. After a minute, it became so awkward that she started to pull away.

Before she could, he flipped his hand and linked their fingers. "He died a year later."

"Was that before your brother's affair?" Shock jolted him. Why did she say that? Where did it come from? Something in her brain was completely broken; being around him made it so much worse. "Geez, I'm sorry." Despite a desire to kick herself, she settled for turning her head away to curse. "God, Jane, shut up. Just shut up. He doesn't want to talk about that."

"You want to talk about my family, we can talk about my family," he said and, to her surprise, didn't toss her hand away. In fact, he seemed to prefer talking to it as he slid his fingers through hers. "Most people don't have the balls to ask."

She shrugged. "Your family is notoriously private." Which was unexpected given how they made their fortune. Maybe it was exactly that experience that made the Colliers wary. "Toria told me about Camden."

"You tell her about us?"

Jane shook her head. "No. For once, she was doing the talking. She said you were hot, if that counts for anything." She blushed as he smiled again. "She reminded me you don't like commitment."

"Did she?"

"Take 'em and leave 'em, is how she put it." She inhaled. "You're hot enough to do whatever you want with women. And men have all the time in the world. You've dated supermodels, why shouldn't you play the field for as long as you want?" Licking her lips, she sipped from her straw. "I don't know how that came around to Camden abandoning his birthright. She said he had a torrid affair with someone who worked for your family when he was young. Maybe I should've read more about the Colliers. I didn't know you'd be here… or that I'd have to do anything oral with you."

Sealing her lips, she wanted to throw herself in the sea. Did she ever know when to shut up?

He laughed and raised her knuckles to his lips. "Jane, baby, don't ever change, okay? Promise me, you'll always stay true to yourself and be exactly like this."

It was amazing he could have such good humor about her being so abrupt. "So he wasn't sleeping with the maid?" Her jaw fell. Had she developed Tourette's or something? "I don't know what's wrong with me," she muttered. "I'm not usually so… I think these things, but if I'm not on a rant, they usually don't come out. It's because you're so attractive. I forget myself when you smile and your eyes light up. I feel like I'm the focus of every star in the sky and I—" Watching the slow, soft kisses he spoiled her hand with, she sighed. Looking into his eyes was a mistake. They weren't smiling now, they were smoldering. "Maybe I should start calling you Mr. Collier to remind myself."

"Of what?" he said. "To my friends, I'm Knox."

"Is that what we are?" she asked. "We're friends?"

Had she embarrassed herself again? It was unfair. He was doing that tractor-beam stare, fixating on her so completely it was impossible to look anywhere else, think straight, or even take a deep breath.

"I want to show you something. Will you come somewhere with me?"

"Somewhere?" she asked, glancing back at the beads that led to the stairs. "Somewhere close by or like Italy?"

"Italy?" He grinned and laughed. "You want to go to Italy with me tonight?"

"No!" she said, looking at the beads again. "I can't leave Toria in there alone with all those strangers."

"I had the men checked out when I heard you'd signed up," he said. "We ran background checks, no sex offenders."

"Oh, well," she said, taken aback that he'd done something so extreme. "I suppose that's good to know."

She righted the short strap of her purse on her shoulder that kept it tight under her arm.

"So, Italy," he said. "Any city in particular? I can have a chopper take us to the airport, the jet pilot can file his flight plan if we let him know in advance where we want to end up. Why Italy?"

"No, I…" This was moving fast. "I didn't mean I… I don't want to go to Italy, I just… in the movies, isn't that where the rich guy always takes the girl to impress her?"

"If I need to impress you, I don't need to take you to Italy to do it," he said and stood up, pulling her onto her feet too. "We'll stay on the island. Marty will keep an eye on Toria and if she's looking for you, he'll text me."

Suspicious, she peered at him. "This isn't a variation on 'let's go to my bedroom so I can show you my etchings,' is it?"

Again, he laughed, but she was actually serious this time. "No, I can't draw for shit… I'll play you a concerto on the piano if you want to go up to the main complex."

"You can play piano?" she asked, taking a long last suck on her straw as he drew her away from the table and her drink on it.

"Yep, and the guitar," he said. "And the saxophone, but that's not as sexy."

"Really?" she asked, following him down a set of external stairs. "I thought jazz was supposed to be the sexiest music."

"Maybe," he said, putting her on the back of a motorbike. He leaned in so his lips were on her ear. "I can't kiss you while I'm playing the sax though."

She was still gaping when he climbed onto the bike and kickstarted it. He seized her wrists and pulled her arms around his torso, then revved the engine to gun away from the bar. They drove for less than ten minutes around the coastal path. He parked and took them off the bike to unlatch a gate labelled private.

One good thing about his friendship with the owner of the island, Knox would have access to all the secret corners no one else knew existed. He took her down a sandy slope flanked by sea oats and around into a white sandy cove surrounded by cliffs on all sides.

"It's beautiful," she said, admiring the stripe of moonlight on the water.

"It is, but this is not why we're here," he said and took her hand to guide her across the width of the beach.

Her laughter rose. In his enthusiasm, he waded into the surf like it was just in the way.

She came up short, tripping on the tide and dropping his hand to back off. "Knox," she called out, her smile hurting her cheeks. "I can't go in the sea!"

"Why not?" he asked, rushing out of the water, frowning at her shoes. He crouched to pick up her feet to slide off her sandals. Still holding them, he stood up, triumphant. "There."

Grabbing her hand again, he pulled her into the cool, refreshing waves. They stayed close to the rocks as he waded out. When the water met the hem of her skirt, she stopped.

Worried, she glanced at the beach behind them. "I can't," she said and took a step back. "It's too deep. It's dark and it's dangerous."

"Hey," he said and came back to her. Stroking his damp fingertips down her jaw, he tipped her chin up. "Nothing bad will happen to you when I'm around. Never. You hear me?"

He was so vehement, she wanted to believe him. Whether it was true or not, he meant it. When she parted her lips, she didn't know what was going to come out, whether she'd agree or refuse.

Then he dipped his head and touched his lips to hers and she forgot that they were standing in the ocean. The water vanished, the rocks, the danger, the fear, the excitement, all of it dwindled into the eye of a vast needle.

It felt like so long since they'd kissed, though it was less than a week. His kiss was better than any other kiss she'd ever had. His insistent mouth was reassuring, but it was her tongue that touched his first. The flip-flop in her belly slid down into her legs and they almost buckled, but as she sagged against him, his solid arm came around her waist to hold her up.

Too soon, his mouth withdrew. She exhaled in a whine when the moment was over. Still hanging in mid-air, she kept her eyes closed and decided it was okay for her to die now. There wouldn't be a better moment than that one.

"You want to go back?" he murmured, his thumb brushing her chin as her head shook in time with it.

His body moved and she whimpered, clutching for his shirt. "Let's stay right here."

Pushing up to her tiptoes, she hoped his mouth would find hers again, but her lips were only warmed by his whispered voice. "Just around that corner is something even better."

"Than that kiss?" she asked, her eyes still hadn't managed to open. "I don't think there is anything better. You feel amazing."

Her honesty was more of a curse than a life choice. Yet he seemed to like it because he groaned and with her sandals hooked around one finger, he slid his hands under her ass.

"Hup," he said, boosting her up into his arms.

This wasn't a casual or gentlemanly lift. He deliberately wrapped her legs around his torso.

Given her legs were covered with ocean water, her eyes opened in a panic. "I'm getting you all wet."

He continued the way he'd been heading before the kiss. "Blossom, I've been dreaming about that all week."

She didn't understand the statement or why her furrowed brow put a smile on his face. "You've been thinking about me getting you wet all week? But I… oh." Really? This amazing, attractive guy had been thinking about her being… wet. When her bashful eyes fell, he pulled her higher on his body. She was so focused on his eyes that she missed them rounding the rocks onto sand. After ten paces skirting a cliff, another beach opened out. Much thinner and shorter than the last, a slope of rocks at the back jutted up into vertical cliffs.

"Wow," she said, admiring the stars reflected on the ocean in the tiny, secluded space.

"It's Plunder Cove," he said. "They said pirates kept their treasures in the cave behind those rocks there… When the tide comes in this is all underwater and it's completely inaccessible."

That brought her away from the beauty for a minute. "How long do we have? I like to swim, but I'm not strong enough to swim against ocean currents," that could be trying to smash her against rocks. "And I'm not dressed for swimming."

"It's okay, the tide is going out."

Pushing on his shoulders didn't grant her freedom. "Okay. Good," she said and relaxed. "You should probably put me down."

"Why?" he asked. "Maybe I like holding you."

Was he teasing her or was her honesty infectious? "I'm not hurting you?"

His smile was as slow as her slithering descent of his body. Not that he let her go completely. No, he just let the circle of her legs sink from his ribs to his hips. He'd been holding her high, presumably to keep her ass out of the water.

"This is about as good as I've felt in a long time, Blossom."

"You have access to the world," she said, touching his temple with a tentative fingertip. "You have a constant parade of ever-changing women pursuing you every minute."

"Jane," he said, becoming serious as he lowered them both down to the sand with enviable control. One of his arms remained around her, while the other moved higher to stroke her bangs from her face. "The only woman I think about is you."

Her wide eyes blinked. How should she take that revelation? "Really?"

"Really," he said and smiled. "I've never had a woman so real and genuine in my life. Never had one kiss me the way you did that first time either."

"Oh, geez," she groaned, averting her gaze. "Don't remind me. My mouth's an embarrassment and a liability."

Clasping her chin, he brought it around to look down into her again. "Your mouth's magnificent."

The intensity in his eyes was ambiguous. He lowered to kiss her again, but she pressed a hand to his chest, holding him away. Anxiety pounded so loud that her ears rang.

"What would Roxie do?" she murmured, fighting to remember her promise to Toria about having an adventure while balancing Knox's expectations.

"Roxie?"

Yeah, he didn't get it, shouldn't get it. Roxie would choose her friends. Every time. Friendship over sex. Without a doubt.

"Sorry, I was talking to me," she said. "I know we've had sex before and everything, but this… I'm supposed to be part of the LIP program. I can't… And Toria doesn't know, Zairn… I'll never find forever if I keep getting caught up in our fling."

"We'll take our time," he murmured and tried to lower again.

Pushing up, she curled her fingers into the solid pectoral under his shirt. "We've never been very good at that."

He wasn't smiling. "We'll be good at it now. You have my word."

"We've done it before. I know I should be a sure thing…" That was probably why he brought her to a private beach. Sex should be inevitable. He wouldn't be used to women saying no. "I'm sorry if you thought I got you on the hook and…" What did he accuse her of in LA? "Shut you down. I didn't mean—"

"Doing it in the past doesn't guarantee anything. You're never obliged to be intimate with me, or any other guy. It's always a default no. Consent is required, each and every time." Again, he tried to kiss and she pushed. "No sex, I hear you," he said. "Can I kiss you?"

"You've been with supermodels… I mean, I'm not… I didn't think about it before because we were… Why would you think about me? I'm a nobody."

"You're somebody to me."

Her teeth caught the inside of her lip for a second. "I turn you on?"

How could that be possible?

Picking one of her hands off his chest, she didn't think about what he was doing with it until he pressed her palm to his fly, to the solid length of him behind. Her mouth opened in a squeak as her eyes bugged out. Was he…? Was he hard? Already? They hadn't even done anything yet.

"That's for you," he said.

"I never understood why… My ex had to think about other women to get hard with me."

"I'm not thinking about anyone else. Why'd you think I had to get out of that bar so fast? Just being near to you does it to me. You do it to me."

Shock kept her still when he slid a hand up her body to angle her head. She didn't argue any more. His soft lips tasted her pulse point, they grazed her skin so lightly that she shivered.

As her eyes drifted shut, he kissed her ear lobe and whispered, "Your ex sounds like an idiot." Toria would agree with him. "I don't want you to think about him when you're with me. I want you to think about me. Any time that asshole comes into your head, you think about me, baby. 'Cause you've got me hard, so fucking hard all I can think about is sinking myself into that sweet body." She tensed, but his soothing hand stroked her ribs beneath her breast. "When you're ready. Not tonight. Not now. I want you to look at me." He took his lips from her ear and tipped her head toward him, but her eyes wouldn't open. "Lay those beauties on me, Blossom." His voice was like velvet stroking her skin. She parted her lips to lift for a kiss, but his caress held her away. "In a minute, I'll kiss those beautiful lips in a minute, I want you to look at me first."

It took considerable effort to leave the dream and open her eyes. Except the fantasy became more intense when she saw her real dream man.

"Knox," she whispered.

"Even the way you say my name is hot," he said, stroking from her ribs to her belly. "You are gorgeous. You've got a killer body, and a beautiful mouth that makes me want to keep you forever… I never feel this way about women, Jane, never. I thought I'd seen it all, then wham, there you were, this beautiful, perfect little siren with a mouth that puts me in my place and a body built to make me dream about sin."

She wanted to believe he meant it. His heavy eyes were definitely preoccupied by something.

"Knox," she said, brushing her palm up his arm. "No one knows we're here."

Picking her hair from her lip, he skimmed the back of his fingers over her cheek. "Are you afraid?"

"Yes," she said, her lips morphing to a smile. "But not of what you might do to me."

"Tell me what you're afraid of, baby."

"Waking up," she said, cupping his face then allowing her fingers to coast into his hair. "Waking up and finding out this was all a dream."

"It's no dream, Blossom," he said. "Close your eyes and let me kiss those lips. I'll prove to you just how real I am."

That was exactly what she wanted to do. Her eyes closed and his lips descended to hers. Three nights on a tropical island and already she'd found paradise. How could it get any better? It could get worse. In so many ways.

But she'd promised Toria not to think like that. This was her adventure and right then, Knox Collier was her guide.

SIXTEEN

DAYS MIGHT HAVE passed. Lying on that beach making out with the sound of the surf and the smell of the sea surrounding them, nothing else existed. His hand had slithered beneath her skirt a while ago, but it stayed on her hip, being very respectful, just as he'd promised.

His lips floated to her neck again and another whimper of pleasure seeped out. She didn't remember ever making so much noise during this part of the process… during any part of the process.

"This is crazy," she murmured as she slid her hand beneath his shirt and felt the ridges of his abs. "Oh, God, your body."

Could she have forgotten how ripped he was? No, but every time she daydreamed about it, she told herself to stop exaggerating. Yet he always lived up to the memory.

"Want me to take it off?" he asked, licking the width of her collarbone with the tip of his tongue.

"No, you'll get cold."

She felt his lips curl into a smile on her skin. "Baby, I don't think there's any chance of that. You're fucking scorching. So fucking hot, my beautiful, delicate blossom…"

"Until you…" she said. When she stalled, he rose to meet her eye. He'd said he liked her honesty. Instead of trying to stop what was in her head, she let it flow. "I didn't know I liked dirty words… but I think I do."

"Is that fucking right?" he asked.

They laughed together.

"I've never had sex on a beach before," she said, scratching her nails against his belly. "Bet you've done it a zillion times."

"There's a technique to it," he said. "But we're not having sex here tonight."

"I know… I guess I'm just… curious."

"There's time for you to be curious," he said, kissing her jaw and her chin then her mouth. "We'll do it on every beach on the island if you want, but not tonight."

"Some of the beaches are very public."

He licked her bottom lip. "Want to see how quickly I can make them very private?" he smoldered. "I can make the whole island private if you want me to."

That was so sweet that her heart may have swooned a little. "Just for me?"

"Just for you," he replied and kissed her again.

That wasn't the first time he'd alluded to going to any lengths for her. She had her own insecurities about men and relationships. Experience taught her lessons. His had to do the same. He hadn't talked about the women from his past, not in anything but generalizations. Maybe other women expected him to prove his worth with shows of wealth.

"Knox," she whispered, pushing his mouth away from hers.

His smile faded in response to her frown. "What, Blossom? What's wrong?"

Easing him further back, she wriggled out from under him and sat up. "I don't know what it is we're doing here or what you want from me," she said, pulling her skirt down to cover her legs.

"Did I do something wrong?" he asked, touching her jaw, trying to bring her gaze around to his.

Instead of the intimate touch, she took his hand to her lap and looked him in the eye because what she was about to say was important. "Despite all the sex, we… We don't know each other well. Can I tell you what I've learned I like about you already?"

"Yes," he said, still concerned.

"I like it when you hold my hand, when you pick me up in your arms, when you kiss me… I like it when you look into my eyes like I'm the only woman in the world. I like that you appreciate my honesty and don't mock me for my rambling. I like that you reassure me when I'm being crazy and insecure." Which she was kind of doing right then. "None of that is about money. I don't want to be bought. Yes, I'm happy that you're successful, that's impressive. You work hard, you're dedicated, great. But as a woman, getting to know a man." She got as serious as she could. "I don't give a damn what you have in your bank account, Knox. I don't. I'm sorry if you think I should or if your other girlfriends do, that's fine for them. But the number of zeros on your checking account won't make me care about you any more or any less. I don't even know if you want me to care about you or if this is a conquest thing. Maybe you don't believe me, I'm sure other women have told you they want or don't want—"

"Jane," he said, touching her lips with his fingertips before ducking to kiss them. "I'm sorry if you thought I was trying to buy you… and I do want you to care about me."

Okay, that was good, and it provoked a spontaneous smile. "You do?"

"I do," he said and glanced at his watch. "It's almost midnight."

What did that mean? Other than they'd been together for almost two hours. "What happens at midnight?"

"You tell me," he said. "You said anything before nine p.m. was adventurous…"

Leaving that thought lingering in the air, it took her a second to remember what she'd said about missionary. "Oh, God, I told you that."

"You did," he said, taking her head from her hands. "I'm happy you did. It's important for a guy to know his girl's rhythms and favorite positions."

Picking up a handful of sand, she prepared to admit more secrets. "They weren't mine, they were Brendan's."

"Your ex?" he asked. She nodded. "So what are your rhythms and favorites?"

Inhaling as she opened her mouth, she sealed it again on an inhale when she came up with nothing. "I... I don't know..."

"You were with Brendan a long time?"

"We were on and off since college," she said. "I think you get used to being what your partner wants you to be, sometimes so much that you forget your own preferences... or I did."

When his brows sloped, she lowered her eyes again. "You lost yourself?"

"I guess. And then Graham distracted me. I used what I had with him as a substitute instead of putting myself out there again... I haven't been with a guy for fun... for just what it was, for a long time."

"That why you wanted to keep us a secret?"

She shrugged, running her fingers through the sand. "I've had boyfriends, but I was always awkward at the sex stuff. I didn't know what to... do with a guy, you know?" Picking up the sand, she scrunched it and let it drift away. "Toria and Roxie talk about it like it's... They're so good at that stuff. And when I get with a guy, my girls ask questions, make suggestions, and I... I know they mean well, but I get overwhelmed sometimes, you know?" He nodded. "Brendan hated that I was so much work. Even to this day when guys ask me out and I go on dates, I always hear his voice in my head telling me I'm not good enough. I just can't let myself... relax. I make excuses and ramble, then I dash off home."

"I'm honored," he said.

She didn't know why he was different, except on this island there was nowhere to run, nowhere to hide. There was no build up to let her anxiety go crazy. But it wasn't just their location. Knox had been different. From the beginning, from the moment she kissed him. Nothing about their relationship, their connection, was like anything she'd experienced with other men.

Lifting her eyes to his, he really did look happy that she had kissed him. She'd kissed plenty of other guys, but that didn't mean she had confidence with them.

"If you want someone more… fun… I'll understand. The island is full of bright, vivacious women. You're not obliged to be polite because we've been intimate before."

"You're the most fun person I've ever met," he said, cupping her face to stroke her cheeks with his thumbs. "And I'm not worried about sex."

Of course he wasn't. "Sure, sorry, I shouldn't have—"

"Get that crazy idea out your head right now," he said, holding her head up when she tried to duck away. "If I didn't think it would send the wrong signal, I'd be jumping you right now."

The playful tease in his eyes relaxed her; he didn't understand the power of that compliment. "Really?" He nodded. "You're just saying that because—"

"I'm saying that because it's true," he said. "You want me to prove it again? I'll put you in missionary right now. It's after nine. I'm game if you are." What a dope, and what a threat. Yet, before her laugh was out, flashes of their past frolics crossed her mind's eye. He tilted closer. "What's in that head of yours, baby? Speak it."

Moving his hand, she swallowed her apprehension and put her hands on his shoulders to push him as hard as she could. He put up no resistance and lay on the sand on his back. Her nervous heart hammered, but Toria had told her to be wild. Wild. Be wild. She had to follow through on her promise. Climbing onto him to straddle his hips, she felt the mass of his erection again. She lifted her hips away but bowed to kiss him.

"I never get to be on top," she said, worried by his grin. There was something mischievous in it and she couldn't read if it was mocking or not. "Is this okay? I can move if I'm hurting you."

But before she could take her leg over him again, he snatched her calf and pushed it back into the sand. His large hands skimmed up, beneath her skirt to squeeze her ass, which didn't help her already frantic heart.

"Satisfy your curiosities, baby," he murmured. "All of them. Take every liberty… Fuck, you turn me on. You don't even know how hot you are."

Taking one hand from her skirt, he cupped the back of her head to pull her down for another kiss.

Something hard and artificial, his phone maybe, dug into her hip as she began to relax enough to let her pelvis sink to his. He made a groan of approval when she snaked a hand down between them, but she wasn't going for the good stuff. As she tried to shift the phone, it buzzed. Blinking at him, it took her a minute to figure out how to form words from her panting, desperate mouth.

"We should get back to the bar, shouldn't we? That's what you meant about the time." Rubbing his chest, she wished she'd asked him to take his shirt off. That was dangerous, her inhibitions were lowering, and she was less drunk now than she had been when they got there. "Are they looking for you? Have I kept you too long?"

But again, when she tried to get up, he took her leg and pulled her down hard. She gasped at the jolt of pleasure that hit her when his solid mass smacked her clit at just the right angle.

"Keep me longer," he mumbled, his eyes closing. "Keep me as long as you want, baby."

When she pushed herself down against the bulge in his shorts, his shoulders lifted and he groaned, louder this time, the sound echoing against the rocks behind them.

"Five more minutes can't hurt, can it?" she asked, reading his expression, rocking her hips on his.

"Five more minutes with your hot fucking body wriggling around on mine," he mumbled, gritting his teeth to grasp her hips as he pushed up. "Might fucking kill me… but it will be fucking worth it… Oh, I'm yours, babe, just keep doing that."

"This," she whispered on his lips as she circled her hips, pressing her clit against him through his shorts. "I've never done this before, like this."

Uncertainty be damned, she was a woman full of confidence, turned on by her effect on this powerful man.

He hissed in a breath between his teeth and cursed. "Fuck, baby, that only makes it hotter."

If he was acting, he was damn good at it. For the first time in her life, she felt sexual, powerful, and wanted to explore what else she could do to this man. He let her be in control, to experiment. If they kept up their affair, she might learn so much more about herself and what it could be like to have a healthy, no-strings sexual relationship.

SEVENTEEN

KNOX CARRIED HER all the way back to his bike. The tide was further out, so she probably could've walked it without getting wet. But it was nice being in his arms and with him taking care of the walking, she could concentrate on stroking and kissing him.

Driving back to the bar was a disappointment. Having to part from him without another kiss was worse. But there was too much chance of someone seeing them together. With a smile, she wandered away from his secluded parking spot and slid back into the reception.

No one had missed her. Toria was still chatting it up, everyone seemed to be closer. Some groups were expanding while others shrank. But nobody was frantically tearing the place apart trying to find her.

Good.

After a half hour at the bar, time was called, and the LIP members were transported back to their rooms. With the excitement of the day, neither she nor Toria were in the mood to chat. They went straight to bed and woke up late meaning they were in a rush to get to breakfast on time.

For other guests, breakfast could be served at individual cabanas or in rooms. Room service was twenty-four seven. But the LIP group were required to eat most meals together, so when they got to the main dining room in the hotel for the buffet breakfast, there were tables reserved with place-cards specifically for them.

Her senses were on overdrive. On the trip to the hotel, the way in, as she sat down, as she went to the buffet, the whole time she was on the lookout for Knox or Marty. She saw neither. As she spooned natural yoghurt into her mouth, she gave herself a mental talking to. Of course he wasn't around. Why would a man like him eat breakfast with the masses?

"Who do you like?" Toria asked, taking a seat opposite her at the small table.

"Who do I like?" Jane scooped some fresh sliced peach from her bowl then pointed her spoon at it as she chewed. "The fruit here is amazing."

"Did you see there were strawberries on our doorstep this morning?" Toria asked and she nodded. Yeah, they would be arriving every morning as per Knox's instruction. "So, yeah, last night, what do you think of the guys?"

She'd be lucky to remember any of their names. "Uh, who do you like?"

Toria leaned over the table. "I know we have that comprehensive orientation thing this morning, Damien says they will lay out all these rules, so I figure we should talk about it, before we can't."

"You think they'll tell us not to talk about who we like?"

Toria nodded and ate some of her food. "I sure do. I mean, if we talk about who we like, the competition will start and we're here for another two weeks. They don't want us scratching each other's eyes out." That was a good point, what other rules would there be? "I think Damien is cute… And Adam is nice too, maybe too nice, I don't know… But Paul, I think he'd be a total animal."

Making herself smile, it wasn't easy to be duplicitous. Had she met any of those guys? She glanced around to see if any faces jogged her memory on names. Nope. Nothing.

"Yeah, uh, Adam seems nice."

Toria nodded, losing her excitement to become more serious. "Okay, I'll leave Adam for you. We don't want there to be any overlap. We'll have to date the same guys but stick to our rules. We can be polite without being forward, can't we?"

That made sense. Hopefully, this Adam wasn't Toria's soulmate; her friend was going to back off in deference to someone who wasn't truly interested in the guy. Too nice wasn't Toria's style. That made Adam the safest bet... didn't it?

"If you really like Adam—"

"He's probably too nice for me anyway, perfect for you."

Good. Her thinking exactly.

Toria sat straighter. It was the guy by the door that did it. The stranger scanned the room, smiled and began to make rounds of the tables.

"Who is that?" she asked.

"Nigel Everly."

She shook her head slightly. "Is that supposed to mean something to me?"

Toria swallowed and tossed a blueberry into her mouth. "Everly is Thena Collier's maiden name. Nigel is her nephew."

Her jaw dropped. Fast. Thena... "Knox's mother?" Suddenly, it got cold. "But that makes Nigel..."

"Knox's cousin. Yeah."

"Did they travel together?" Panic jolted her. "Oh, God, is his mother here?"

Toria laughed. "Knox's or Nigel's? What do you care? I don't think anyone's mom is here. Nigel's the guy I talked to when I signed us up for LIP. Remember, I told you? He's running it."

Yeah, that sounded like her luck. Knox's cousin was the man playing matchmaker. Maybe in his forties, Nigel seemed perfectly fine. Normal. Too normal to be a Collier.

"Oh, God," she whimpered.

"Nigel is a tough guy to read," Toria said. "He was flirting with the women last night. Not like serious flirting, it was cute. Didn't you speak to him?"

She hadn't seen Nigel at the bar at all. Though if he was in charge, it made sense he'd make an appearance at the icebreaker.

"You know I'm not flirt worthy," she said.

Toria exhaled and her spoon fell to her bowl. "What happened to wild and adventurous? We made a deal. No more talking down about yourself. What would Roxie do, remember?"

"Right, Roxie."

Nigel was just a table away and others were beginning to rise. They had to eat fast if they didn't want to be left behind. Glancing around again, she held out one final hope that she'd see Knox, but he wasn't around. Maybe he was thinking about her, or maybe not.

Why did she care?

It was difficult to forget such an intense time with such an overwhelming man. This was a seductive island and the night had been romantic. In the light of day, so much looked different.

EIGHTEEN

ORIENTATION WAS EYE-OPENING. Toria was right, they weren't supposed to favor one partner or discuss who they liked or what took place on dates. The LIP games were designed to be random and force them to spend time with everyone. Even if couples were starting to feel something, they weren't meant to gravitate toward each other. Not yet.

Maybe further down the line they'd be encouraged to single out one mate, but at that stage it was all about promiscuity. Though sex was off the cards. Physical intimacy was prohibited, which suited her just fine.

Perhaps having the rule stated explicitly would give her libido the message.

By the time they'd been briefed, done all their reading, and signed the contracts, everyone was ready for lunch, served buffet style in the hotel again.

Toria was excited about the afternoon activities. 'A Day at the Beach' would give her the chance she wanted to see the men in daylight. Not just daylight, in the full glare of the sun.

Her friend got excited about the white two-piece swimsuit she'd picked out for her. It made her feel naked.

They settled on a sarong compromise, but that didn't cover her midriff or her breasts.

When they arrived at the beach, Nigel was sporting a short-sleeved shirt and pressed shorts. "Everyone looks great," he said, admiring the group as they formed in a semi-circle around him. "Is everyone wearing sunscreen? Nothing else happens until everyone is protected."

Three resort employees came rushing over, bottles and sprays on trays ready for use by all.

The women were like horses at a show, strutting and preening their figures as they slapped sunscreen on each other salaciously. Thank goodness she'd done hers at home. The men enjoyed the show a little too much.

When one of the women sidled up to an interested guy, Nigel waved at them. "Uh, no opposite gender application… for now… please."

Already she was coming to like Nigel.

"What are we doing today, Nigel?" Leanne called out, peeking over her shades at one of the men. She should make more of an effort to work out the men's names so she could identify them when they spoke. Familiarity was made more uncomfortable given her lack of clothing. She didn't want anyone looking too close at her, which should translate from her unwillingness to look at them.

Despite what Toria said, and Knox too, compared to the others on that tropical beach, she was an inferior heifer.

"In the lounge, after dinner tonight, we have speed dating," Nigel announced. "You'll eat and dress in your private cabanas, then be brought to the lounge where drinks and nibbles will be provided." Various variations of approval went around the group. "As you know, we are encouraging variety this week. Bearing that in mind, today's exercise will pair each of you with whoever you'll be joining first this evening." Nigel stepped back to point out to the ocean. In the distance, a series of flags floated on buoys. "Out there are ten flags, the men will swim out, retrieve a flag, and bring it back to shore. The name of the woman you will sit with first is written inside that flag. You will get twenty minutes for your first date and just ten minutes for each subsequent date."

Again, a series of optimistic tones and nods went around the group. Already she could see certain couples making eye contact, smiling, doing that non-verbal flirting thing.

"Each man and woman will meet twice, but only the first date will be twenty minutes long," Nigel said and pointed to a line drawn in the sand near the water's edge. "Men, if you'll line up and women remain behind. On the count of three, the men shall race out to the flags. Women, you may cheer the men along, although there's no way to know whose name is on the flag until you come back to shore and read it."

The men went to the line about twenty feet from the women. Nigel counted to three and the men raced off into the water. Immediately after, the women, including Toria, rushed forward to jump and shout, caught up in the excitement of this show of prowess. Nigel wandered down to join them. It didn't occur to her to move, it was enlivening to watch, but she didn't feel the urge to jump or shout.

"Got your eye on anyone special?"

Her lips curled higher when she heard the purr of his deep voice behind her. Right behind her. Although they weren't touching, she could almost feel the heat of him even under the brilliance of the comparable sun.

"Maybe," she said. "I've been told Adam is nice."

"Which one is he?" Knox asked, remaining behind her.

She kept gazing out to sea so no one would notice them talking.

A grin almost made her laugh. "I have no idea."

"Good," he said. "I'd hate to have him hauled off the island if he's a nice guy." There was a kind of peace that came with just standing with him, even if they couldn't look at each other. "Would you be cheering me on if I was out there?"

That was an easy answer. "Nope."

"No?" he asked, surprised. "Why not?"

"Because I'd be insanely jealous if you got another girl's name. I'd never be able to concentrate on my date if you were in the room."

The hair at her crown moved. Her eyes closed behind her shades as he moved nearer.

"How do you think I feel right now?" he asked in a rumbling murmur. "Jealous doesn't begin to describe it. I hate those guys, literally hate them, and I've never hated anyone in my life."

She softened her voice. "Knox—"

"I know," he murmured. "I know it's why you're here. But that body, geez, babe, I can't believe I'm this close and can't touch you. I want you so bad and these bastards, they're the ones who get to date you. Jealousy isn't a nice emotion, but topped off with resentment… I feel sick."

One of her hands fell, swinging back just enough to touch the edge of his. "No, I…" she whispered. "I don't want these guys. I don't even know their names… I've been thinking about you all day."

"Ditto," he said, his fingertips making brief contact with her hip. "I'll be in the lounge tonight. Somehow, I'll figure—"

"No," she said, shaking her head, fighting the urge to turn. "If you're in the room, I'll be distracted. I already feel bad for the guy forced to spend twenty straight minutes with me."

"The bastard," Knox said. "I'm not supposed to hate guests."

Experiencing an adolescent surge of endorphins said more about her than it did about him. It shouldn't be flattering that he was so angry.

"We shouldn't be talking now, should we?" she asked when Nigel noticed them. His broad smile faltered and although he was wearing shades, it appeared he was frowning. "Oh no."

She stepped forward, away from Knox.

"Don't worry about him," he said and moved in behind her again, so near that his chest brushed her shoulders.

"He's our guide," she said. "In orientation, he told us we had to take part in all activities. What if he thinks I'm not taking part?"

"I'll talk to him."

"No," she said. "You can't use your influence with your cousin to benefit... this."

"Us?" he asked. "I can. Nigel's family. It's not influence, it's blood. He'll understand when I tell him I care about you."

"I have to take part," she said. "If the guys find out I've been physical with someone else on the island, they might be pissed there aren't the right number of women for them."

"If they find out we've been physical, they'll be mad, but it won't be anything to do with numbers. It'll be everything to do with how amazing you are."

She smiled and turned her head a fraction toward him. "We shouldn't be talking, thinking about being physical. We have to forget, we should forget. That's in the past. We're in the past. We're friends. Can be friends. We're going to erase all the memories, forget everything we've done together."

His warm breath fogged her hair. "Want me to remind you what we've done together?"

There on the beach, in front of dozens of guests and the LIP group... and Nigel?

"No. I just... I spent all morning worrying about what might've happened between us last night. We shouldn't be alone together. Never. Not alone."

"Worrying?" he asked. His hand swung forward at her side, his fingers grazing hers as they swung back. "Shit, this is hard, I need to touch you. It's torture having that hot body this close to me... I need to... Blossom, I need you."

Shock would reverberate across the beach if she were to turn and kiss him. So much for not being alone. She couldn't contain her smile but turned it downward hoping no one would see.

"When you touch me, I lose it. I almost collapsed when you kissed me in the water last night. If I feel your hands on my body, I'll..."

"You'll…?" he prompted. "Come on, Blossom, don't tease me."

Was he pissed off? The edge in his voice had thickened.

"I'm not a cock tease," she said, panicked. "I loved being intimate with you… in the past… We can't—"

"Shh, baby," he whispered and brushed his fingertips on her hip again. "Not all teasing is bad; I love it when you tease me."

The nearer the returning men got to shore, the closer the women's screeching came to fever pitch.

"Is it fair someone has to swim out all that way for a date with me?" she asked because whether she liked the LIP males or not, their effort was impressive.

"I'd swim around the whole damn island for one kiss," he whispered.

She shivered. "Knox."

He groaned. "God, when you do that breathy thing to my name… You've got me hard as concrete back here, Blossom."

Her grin was joined by a laugh. "Now you're teasing me."

"I can't tease you 'cause there's nothing I'd deny you."

Maybe this teasing thing was something she should explore.

Letting her arm move, she touched the edge of his hand. "Where do you stay on the island? Do you have a bungalow like Zairn's?"

It took him a second to reply. "An apartment in the central complex."

"You have an apartment…? With a bedroom?"

His snicker was almost a groan. "Yes, baby, with a bedroom you're welcome in every day of the week, every minute of the day, want to see it?"

Nigel walked toward them.

She tensed unable to tease and play while they were being watched. "Maybe another time," she said and tried to go forward.

Knox grabbed her wrist but dropped his hand when she stopped walking. "I need to see you tonight."

"We can't," she whispered, aware of Nigel. "We're having dinner with Roxie—"

"After. After the event."

"I don't know how—"

"I'll send Marty to get you," he said. "Go to him when you see him. Tell me you will."

But she didn't have time to reply.

Nigel reached them. "Jane, is there a problem?" he asked. "Is this schmuck bothering you?"

"No, he was just looking for the gift shop," she said.

The gift shop? She really was an idiot.

Knox laughed. "Ha, yeah, how's it going, Nigel?" he asked. "Everything going swimmingly?"

"I thought it was," Nigel said, looking at her and then his cousin. "Now I'm not so sure, do we have a problem?"

"Just surveying the kingdom."

Nigel wasn't convinced. "Have you ever been to this, the most public beach on the island, before, Knox?"

"No. My visit is overdue."

Should she be listening? Standing between them, she had no choice, but they were family, she shouldn't be eavesdropping.

The LIP men were wading out of the water.

"Jane, you should go and see who has your name," Nigel said. "There's some time to mingle before we go our separate ways for dinner."

"Yes, sir," she said and kept her head down while going to join the other LIP participants.

Toria came rushing over to hug her. "Mikey got my name," she squealed and grinned. "He's gorgeous! Who are you with?"

She had no idea and began to look around for someone who didn't have a partner. "I don't know," she said.

Nigel and Knox were still engaged in discussion. At a distance, while he was busy, she could admire him. How on earth had she managed to capture his interest?

Knox stopped mid-sentence when he glanced her way. He must've lost his train of thought. She did that too. Usually when gorgeous, sexy, attentive, funny guys named Knox were nearby.

He raised his sunglasses from the bridge of his nose and scanned her figure. Did she look different from this angle? Wearing an almost snarl, he took a step toward her, but Nigel moved into his cousin's path and got him talking again.

"Jane?"

Spinning around, a tall, black-haired man was smiling down at her. "Yes?"

"I'm Wayne," he said, offering a hand. "Your date for the evening."

NINETEEN

HER DATE FOR THE EVENING would have to wait. They were due for dinner at Roxie's.

She'd been standing in her closet looking at the dresses hanging inside for half an hour before Toria came in and pulled out a skin-tight, square-neck, purple dress that barely covered her ass. From dinner, they'd be going straight to the speed-dating event.

"It will make a good impression," Toria said.

She tugged at the hem of her dress, feeling it ride up as the cart-cab came to a stop. "What's a good impression?"

Her friend didn't answer, just smiled. They went down the path arm-in-arm and walked into the bungalow without knocking. Roxie was out on the deck with Astrid and Merci.

On her knees facing away, Roxie twisted all the way around as they approached. "Hey!" she exclaimed, climbing off the couch, putting her glass on the central table. "Welcome."

"Thank you," Toria said.

They all hugged and said their hellos. She and Toria sat on the cushioned wicker couch opposite Roxie and Merci. Astrid was alone in the middle of the loveseat at the end.

Roxie was already pouring the night's cocktail from a pitcher into waiting glasses. "Drinks?" When everyone had a glass, Roxie raised hers. "To friends old and new."

Everyone drank, though Toria was quick to tease. "Did you just call us old?"

"Sometimes I can't believe we made it this far," Roxie joked.

"Good point," Toria said and prodded her side. "What do you think of Jane's dress? Stand up, show them." To keep the peace, she did. "Give them a twirl."

"You look great," Roxie said. "New sexy style."

"I've never been speed-dating," Merci said. "Is it fun?"

"You can take my place tonight, if you want to try it," Jane said, anxious about the event.

"Someone may have a problem with that," Roxie said, shifting to her knees again, sitting on her bare feet.

"Someone?"

The way Roxie grinned and raised her glass got Merci sighing. "Reid and I got back together."

"That's great!" Toria exclaimed. "What happened? Did he call you?"

"I didn't say I wouldn't," a male voice came from within the bungalow.

When she turned, Zairn was walking across the room with two others. A stranger and, of course, Knox. Why was she surprised to see him? She shouldn't be. Sitting fast, she snatched up her glass.

"Who didn't say they wouldn't?" Roxie said. "What?"

"We're talking investment portfolios," Zairn said, sitting in the armchair at the head of the table. "We got a tip on a new tech stock. You want in on the action? How much you ponying up?"

"I'm investing myself every minute we're together, Skippy. Investing this beautiful body in the future of your organization. You want an heir or not?"

"Who says I don't already have one?"

"With the amount of sleeping around you've been accused of, I'd be surprised if you didn't have an army of them."

"Toria, Jane," Zairn said. "Have you met Reid?"

"Matteo Reid," Toria proclaimed, crossing her legs. "We were just about to get the skinny on this development."

Zairn explained, "Toria likes to be on the inside of everything."

"Keeps the stars in alignment," Toria retorted.

Reid sat by Merci, which left Knox with one option: the space next to her. The moment his ass hit the seat, she leaped up.

The sudden action got everyone's attention.

As panic rose within her, she fixated on the surest lifeline. "Rox, can we... a minute..."

"Oh," Roxie said, sipping her drink as she got up. "Sure, honey."

She handed her drink off to Zairn and opened a hand to her. Jane grabbed it and tiptoed around Zairn's legs to scurry away as fast as possible.

"You okay?" Toria called as they went inside.

"Fine, we're fine," she said, trying to throw an easy smile back that way.

Whether it came across as easy or not, she couldn't even begin to figure it out.

Roxie led her down the corridor by the kitchen and into a bedroom. "What's going on?"

She fell back against the door. "I don't think I can do this," she said on a gasp like the air was thinning. "I can't do this."

"Speed-dating?" Roxie asked, looking her up and down. "The dress looks great."

Leaping forward, she grabbed Roxie's hand in both of hers. "I almost had sex with Knox. Again."

"Okay," Roxie said with an understanding nod. "And...?"

"And?"

"You've done that before," Roxie said and cringed. "Does he suck at it? If you were faking it at home on the weekend, that's a lot of ego stroking… and you're an amazing actress."

"I can't have sex with him," she hissed. "I shouldn't have sex with him. I keep telling myself over and over that we have to stop, that every time is the last time and then…"

Roxie laughed, stroking her hair. "Jane, honey, you have to give yourself a break. The whole world rests on your shoulders every minute. You don't need to do it to yourself."

"You're my best friend."

"I would hope so."

She swallowed. "Am I one of those women? A woman who chooses sex over their friends?"

"Did he tell you to stop being friends with me?" Roxie frowned. "You know Knox and I have no problem telling each other like it is. If you want me to talk to him—"

"No! He wouldn't, he would never… He's not that type of person."

"So, what's the problem? He's not asking you to choose, I'm not asking you to choose—"

"But Zairn is his—"

"Z definitely isn't asking anyone to choose," she said, the warmth of her smile growing. "Knox isn't my type. He and I have had our differences, but we're both adult enough to say our piece and let it lie."

"You and Zairn, him and I… if it didn't work out—"

"I know, that could be messy… But what if it did?" Roxie asked, the light in her eye sparkling. "What if it did work out?"

She paused. What if it did? "I… I didn't…"

"Zairn has love for Knox, for all his friends, like I love you and my other girls. Knox is a good man. Zairn trusts him in every way imaginable… My guy doesn't love shitty people. Zairn's trust in him is the only endorsement he needs."

Stunned, she tried to shake herself back to reality, but ringing in her ears blanked out her ability to concentrate.

"We're… we're sex," she whispered, still flummoxed. "I'm a wanton hussy who—"

"Oh, Jane," Roxie said, laughing as she pulled her into a hug. "You are not a wanton anything… Not unless you want to be. And if you choose Knox, he'd be lucky to have you."

Some sense was beginning to filter back in.

She retreated from the hug. "We're different and—"

"I am the queen of putting up barriers. The expert at backing away because I won't admit the truth."

"What's the truth?"

"You tell me," Roxie said, linking their hands. "What's the truth, honey? How do you feel about him?"

That wasn't a simple question. She couldn't answer it because she hadn't let herself consider it.

The door opened and Zairn entered, closing it behind him. "Dinner's here," he said. "Everyone okay?"

"Mm hmm," Roxie said, widening her smile. "I love you."

"Okay," he said, his curious brow twitching. "Thank you."

"You know how easy it is to say that to him now?" Roxie asked, squeezing her hand. "And you know I almost fucked the whole thing up."

"We'll wait until you're ready," Zairn said, grabbing the doorhandle again.

"Jane and Knox are sleeping together," Roxie said, bold and unapologetic.

Her mouth fell open. Zairn was right there. "Rox!" she hissed.

"What?" Roxie asked. "If we're all going to be in it, we may as well be in it together." Her eyes stayed on her friend even as she looked to her fiancé. "Anything we should know about him?"

Zairn exhaled and turned back around without opening the door. "Don't ask me, Jane knows him better than I do."

"Oh, God," she groaned, letting go of Roxie to sink into a crouch by the bed, burying her face in the side of the mattress. "This is mortifying."

"Wow," Zairn said. "Did sleeping with me give you this level of self-loathing?"

Someone rubbed her back, Roxie no doubt. "It's okay, honey, just breathe and think of his bank balance." She rolled her forehead to peek sideways at her friend who offered a brief laugh. "I'm sorry. We shouldn't joke. I won't joke… You don't have to worry about anything. We'll support whatever you want to do. Zairn's not going to ask anyone to stop being friends with anyone."

"What?" he asked.

"See," Roxie said, still rubbing. "My Casanova and I are strong enough to weather whatever."

"What am I missing here?" he asked.

Roxie stood up. "She's worried if she and Knox get together and it doesn't work out that we'll have to dump each other in solidarity with our friends."

"Oh," he said. "Knox and I have dated friends before. Dated sisters before… Maybe even dated the same woman at the same time before. We've known each other a long time."

She shot to her feet, spinning to him. "You weren't marrying those women. I'll be uninvited to all of Roxie's celebrations. To everything."

"You know that won't happen," Roxie said. "I love you. I won't dump you for Knox."

"He shouldn't be uninvited to everything either."

"We own nightclubs, honey. We own sports stadiums. Huge cavernous spaces. You wouldn't have to be anywhere near each other if you didn't want to be."

"Why are we planning for the end of the relationship?" Zairn asked. "How long have you been seeing each other?"

"We're not," Jane said, keeping her eyes low.

"You're not seeing each other?"

Roxie leaned against him to stage whisper. "It's just sex."

"Just sex is fine," Zairn said. "Just sex is good… Sometimes just sex leads to not just sex. What does Toria think?"

"She doesn't know."

At this rate, she'd be the only one left in the dark.

"That's an explosion waiting to happen," Zairn said. "Secrets can be dangerous."

"I didn't have to tell her because… Well, because it was over."

"Was?"

Roxie nudged Zairn. "When did he stop seeing Coffee Cart Girl?"

"You know, I don't keep that close an eye on Knox's sex life." Raising her chin, Roxie crooked a brow at her other half. "He ended it your last night in LA, before we came up to the suite."

"The night you gave me my earrings?"

"Yep."

Her friend laid a hand on her arm. "That was before you slept together," she said, still reassuring her. "Has he been with anyone else since?"

Zairn held up both hands. "I'm going to slowly back away from this conversation before someone loses an eye." He dipped to kiss Roxie. "I'll tell the others to start eating. Take your time."

Except she couldn't because they had a LIP thing to get to. That was sort of secondary to the more urgent matter. "Zairn, if you—"

"He won't say anything," Roxie said, coming a little closer as she looked over her shoulder at Zairn.

"This was your secret, wasn't it?" he asked his fiancée.

"Mm hmm."

Zairn just smiled. "I love you too, Lola Bunny." He opened the door to depart. "I love you too."

After he was gone, her friend hugged her again, holding her tight. "You want to come out and have dinner? I can tell Knox to leave."

That would only make things worse. "No," she said. "I'm not afraid to be around him, I just… I need to be stronger."

Because if she wasn't, their just sex fling would go on until both of them were old and gray.

TWENTY

TORIA NOTICED. She didn't say anything, but the way she and Roxie returned to the table was conspicuous. She'd examined every inch of the art on the walls and was running out of excuses not to look anyone in the eye. Given their deal, it was no surprise Toria hadn't asked about her and Roxie's caucus even after they made a swift departure from dinner.

Thank goodness for the excuse to get out of there.

Speed-dating.

Speed-dating was one of those things that always seemed like great fun, from a distance. In practice, it was overwhelming. She only had to talk to ten men… twice. Funny how ten minutes with some men seemed forever and with others it went in a blink.

At the end of the night, their LIP group were mingling, chatting, and she was ready for bed. On seeking out the enthusiastic Toria, it wasn't a surprise to find her with Leanne and Amy. The women had been encouraged to bond that afternoon too. Which worked out because there were other events for single sexes coming up.

"Jane, who do you like?" Leanne asked when she joined their table.

"Oh, shh, shh," Amy said. "We're not supposed to talk about it, right?"

"What are we supposed to talk about?" Toria asked. "I mean, isn't this why we're all here?"

"Right!" Amy said and grabbed a server to order more drinks.

"Not for me," Jane said, touching her belly. "All this talking and drinking, I'm exhausted."

And bloated, she'd spent too long in the second-skin dress.

"Oh no, the night is young!" Toria said. "I heard there was a plan to go to the club later."

Later? It was after midnight already. The event was in the main complex, in one of the hotel lounge bars shut off exclusively for their use. She guessed the idea was to limit contact, so the LIP participants didn't find love outside the group. Oops.

"No clubbing for me tonight," Jane said, seriously considering bed.

Maybe it was all the sun, and emotional turmoil, but she was wiped.

"Okay, sweetie," Toria said, giving her a hug. "Do you want me to come home too?"

The other girls looked sympathetic, but she wouldn't be surprised if they were happy to be down a participant in the competition for LIP male interest.

"No, you stay," Jane said. "Party. Have fun."

Just at that she noticed Marty loitering in the shadow of the doorway.

"I should come in the cab with you, make sure you get back safe."

"Then you'll have to come back alone. No, don't worry. I'll be fine. This is Zairn's island." They weren't in Chicago or some other crime-infested city. "There are always drivers with the carts outside," she said and smiled at the other women as she rose. "Have a good night, and look after Toria for me, won't you?"

They nodded and Toria took her hand. "Lock your bedroom door, I don't want you sleeping down there in the middle of nowhere alone."

Was it habit or were they vulnerable in their isolated location? Most of the other guests got rooms in the hotel. They got a bungalow, probably because they were Roxie's friends.

Bending, she kissed Toria's cheek and said a final goodbye before heading for the door. She didn't say a word to Marty just walked on right past.

He must have followed her out because his voice rose behind her. "Take a left and keep going straight," he said. She walked to the end of the building, and he took her hand to pull her down an alley between two buildings. In the middle of the building to their right was a passage. "Go right to the end into the elevator and up to the top floor."

"But I—"

"That's all I know," he said, smiling, backing away.

Marty disappeared down the alley again, leaving her alone. She didn't know what the place was, she'd guessed it was an administrative building of offices because the alley was signposted private. Maybe she was wrong, or maybe Knox had something else to show her.

Carrying on to the end of the corridor as Marty had said, she found the elevator doors already open and went inside to pick the top floor, hoping to get out of the line of sight before anyone saw her.

What was she doing? Was this a good idea?

She knew what she had to do. There was only one course. Getting it over with might help her sanity. Was she strong enough?

The elevator opened to a curved room with just one door leading from it. No windows. Should she knock? What if this wasn't right? She could be in the wrong place.

The door opened and there was Knox, barefoot and bare-chested. Immediately, she relaxed and started toward him… until his examination of her body got frowny.

"What?" she asked, slowing to a stop. "What's wrong?"

"You were right," he said. Right about what? "I shouldn't be in the room when you're dating other guys, not if you're going to be looking as hot as that."

Oh, she smiled and relaxed again. "I was wearing this at dinner."

"At dinner, you wouldn't look at me."

Going to him, she reached for his face and let her body rest on his. "Zairn knows."

"He told me."

"I'm sorry—"

"How many times? I'm not ashamed of being attracted to you," he said. "And from how I understand it, Roxie told him."

"Does that give you another reason to hate Roxie?"

"I don't hate her," he said, stroking her hair. "I never hated her. And I'll never be sorry to learn she's honest with Zairn."

"Do you resent that I asked you not to tell him?"

His hands skimmed up her back and around to pressure her jaw higher. "What's wrong, Blossom?"

"I'm tired," she murmured.

"Want to go to bed?" he asked, stroking her hair down her back, ending by curling his fingers around her waist.

"I do actually," she said but would delay sleep to do what was necessary. "We need to talk." His single nod was neutral. "Maybe you should've elected to show me your apartment instead of your office."

"Office is the next block over," he said, backing up, guiding her inside.

What? This was his apartment? She'd thought this was his workplace, not his intimate space.

The panorama beyond the curved glass wall on the far side of the room was breathtaking. They were in a kitchen, with a lounge area set up between it and the view.

"This is… it's beautiful."

Closing the door, he turned her away from the vista to show her the open passageway near the front door. "The whole place is circular. The rooms are set up like wedges of a cake, this is the biggest, it takes up almost half. The hallway runs in a ring around the elevator foyer." She got it. The elevator foyer was the proverbial donut hole. "First room on the left is the bedroom you'll be using while you're here, my bedroom. There's a slice of closet and a slice of bathroom leading from it. Next in the corridor is the den, then the family bathroom and another bedroom past that. You'll figure it out."

She pushed her shoulders into his chest. "You think I'll be back here?"

Probably not after they talked.

"I'm betting on it," he said and led her to the couch facing the view.

A deck beyond the glass wall was inviting, but she didn't get a chance to explore. He took her hips to direct her onto the couch.

"You want a drink?" He pointed at her as he went into the kitchen. "White wine and ginger ale, right?"

Toeing off her shoes, she drew her knees up onto the couch to hook her arms over the back so she could watch him in the kitchen. Solid. Reliable. Attentive. Knox Collier was a catch, would be a catch for whoever caught him. She could imagine him taking care of his family, putting the kids to bed, then slipping into the kitchen to pour wine and…

Did men like him think about the future? Dwell on it? Maybe his vision of the future was different. The playboy lifestyle had to be appealing. Would he ever tie himself down?

"Do you want kids?" she asked.

Although he smiled and paused in his job of uncorking the wine bottle, he didn't raise his eyes. Did he know she was watching him? The question sank in. What in the actual…? She dug her teeth into the back of her own forearm. What kind of ridiculous question was that? Who the hell did she think she was asking that question?

"I do," he said. "I'm not in any great hurry for them. I'd have to rethink my lifestyle before they went to school because I wouldn't want to send them away like I was sent away."

Propping her chin on her damp forearm, she had to force herself not to leap off the couch. "I'm sorry, I… I don't know why I asked that. I mean, I had a thought process, but it didn't really come out loud, you know? I guess it seemed like a random question. It was too forward. I'm not trying to be forward. I don't want to scare you. I'm not nuts. I think you're so amazing and maybe, no, I mean, I would totally have your baby, any woman would be lucky to have you—" Rolling her eyes at herself, she growled. "I am not suggesting we have a baby. God, I can't get naked with you and I'm talking about babies. I'm not talking about babies. I don't want to talk about babies. Let's not talk about babies. I'm sorry. Your views on the future, on parenting, they're none of my business. I don't know why I asked. I do. I had a thought process. I should've explained. But no, if I explained, it wouldn't make sense. Well, it would, but it wouldn't, you know? Because it's still none of my business." He came to the couch and handed her a drink as he sank down holding his own. "It was a stupid question, maybe we could just forget I asked and—"

He kissed her and she forgot all about her rant. Even after he eased away, she hung in mid-air, her lips parted and eyes closed, just like last night.

"I think you would make an amazing mother," he said, running his fingers through her hair. "And I won't forget you asked. I don't want to forget a single thing you say. Please, Blossom, stop apologizing for speaking that mind that fascinates me."

"Have there been any murders on this island?"

When he didn't respond, she peeked at him.

"Murders?" he asked. "Uh, yeah, when the pirates—"

"No, recent ones," she said, picking her straw from her drink to circle it around the ice.

"Recent? How recent? Did you see something?" he asked. When his tender hand cupped her face, his concern was overwhelming. Her heart was opening to him more with every second, which was why she needed to finish it. She couldn't kid herself anymore. "I'll get you a panic button… and a rape alarm. If you feel unsafe—"

"No," she said, slipping his hand off her face to link their fingers as she sipped her drink. "Toria told me to lock my door because she was worried about me sleeping alone, isolated in the bungalow. It made me wonder about the crime rate on the island."

He shook his head. "We've never had a murder reported. I think there was a sexual assault about thirty years ago under the previous owner, but security is employed to patrol all night. We encourage good practice of accountability. There have been some fights, nothing serious, but there are so many cart drivers for a reason. No one is allowed out of any of our lounges, restaurants, or bars without an escort. I'm happy your friend cares about you. I'll allocate you your own personal driver and have security posted—"

"No," she said, smiling as she kissed his palm and rubbed it on her face. "I don't want special treatment and I don't feel unsafe here, I was just curious."

"You left Toria in the lounge?" he asked, grazing his thumb across her cheek. Closing her eyes, she sighed. "Marty will keep an eye on her and make sure she gets home."

"I think she'll be partying all night," she said.

"Does that mean you can hang out a while?"

"We have to talk," she said, taking his hand from her face to her lap again.

"You said that. What are we talking about? You want to tell Toria?"

"We have to stop." He didn't react. "I know I've said that before. More than once, but… We have to stop."

"Something Roxie said—"

"No, actually, Roxie endorsed you."

"That's a surprise…" he muttered. "And you're dumping me again anyway?"

"Please don't put it like that," she pleaded. "I don't want to sleep with you anymore. I can't sleep with you."

"Because of Roxie?"

"No."

"Because we're a fling? You like using that word around me."

"Partly, yes. The first part, not the second."

"Because we're a fling and because our friends are engaged?"

Removing her hand from his, she put her drink on the glass coffee table. "This isn't easy for me. Maybe you could make it a little…"

"Make it a little what?" he asked, on the defensive. "A little easier for you?"

"Yes!"

"Why?" he asked. "This is what you want. You've never even asked me what I want."

Bouncing to the edge of the couch, she twisted toward him. "I thought about that."

"About what I want?"

"About asking you."

"But you didn't."

"No," she said, closing her eyes for a few prolonged seconds.

"Why not?"

"Because I don't want to know," she said. When in doubt, go with honesty, that's what Roxie would do. "We can't ever be anything more than a fling. We live on opposite sides of the country and after Graham, I swore I'd never do the long-distance thing again."

"We don't have to be long-distance," he said, resting a hand on her knee. "I'll move to New York."

Her mouth opened, but no words came out for at least thirty seconds. "You'll… You can't do that!"

"Why can't I?"

"Because that puts so much pressure on us. You move your whole life and it doesn't work out—"

"Okay, let me rephrase. I'll stay in New York."

"How is that different?"

"I don't have to quit working for the company. I can do what I do on video calls. Anything I can't, they come to me."

"What about your house?"

"It's paid for, baby," he said, squeezing her knee. "Kintyre's staying there. He won't care about having the place to himself."

"And you'd stay with Zairn?"

"Or Reid. Or I get my own place," he said and smiled. "Don't worry about money, Blossom. I've got us covered."

"You'd do that," she murmured, stunned static while being overwhelmed. "You'd move right across the country for me?"

"To be together, we have to make some allowances. It's only right."

"You've thought about it?" she asked. "Us being together?"

He nodded. "I guess I didn't make that clear last night."

No, he hadn't. He definitely hadn't. "You want us to be together?"

He didn't respond, just looked into her. Asking him what he wanted was always off-limits. She couldn't, wouldn't have asked him to make such drastic changes to his life.

Everything was shifting. Her life. Her perspective. She'd come into that apartment telling herself to be strong, to put a final stop to their fling.

"Does silence mean you don't?"

Did it? "Either way…" she breathed. "Our fling is over."

"It is," he said, his brow stern. "I said no sex last night because this is different. Me coming here, after you, it's different. I don't want to keep doing what we were doing. This is serious. I'm serious. About this… It's up to you what happens next."

Up to her. She couldn't think straight.

Licking her lips, she rested a hand on his shoulder to boost up and kiss his lips.

Forcing herself away, she took a deep breath and whispered, "Can I think about it?"

Though his expression stayed hard, he sank back from the kiss. "Take all the time you need."

TWENTY-ONE

IN HER DEFENSE, she did knock on the front door. When no one answered, she tiptoed inside. They lived together, or had lived together, and she definitely wasn't going to steal anything.

Rather than storm straight in, as Toria would, she knocked on the bedroom door. They weren't having sex, as far as she could tell.

"Is that one of your people?" Roxie's voice carried from inside.

She popped the door just out of its frame. "Roxie?"

"Yours," Zairn mumbled.

"Jane," Roxie said. "Get in here." She peeked around the door. Roxie was sitting up on the far side of the bed. "Come over here." Going in, she closed the door and dropped her purse at the end of the bed. "What's going on? Is it Toria?"

"I need to talk," she whispered, crouching by the bed. "Can we talk?"

"Yeah," Roxie said, scooting back to lift the covers. Slipping onto the bed, she lay on her side, sharing Roxie's pillow. "What happened?"

"I ended things with Knox."

"Oh," Roxie said, stroking her hair. "Are you okay? That's not what we talked about."

"I couldn't do it anymore. It wasn't fair on either of us."

"You want to get drunk? Where's Toria?"

"In the club," Jane said. "She went with some of the LIP girls."

"Do you want me to get changed? We can go up there."

"Take Ballard," Zairn mumbled from the other side of Roxie.

"I'm not waking Ballard up," Roxie said, tipping her head more his way. "It's a nightclub—"

"No, I don't want to—I woke you up, I'm sorry."

"It's okay," Roxie said, laying an arm over her. "We would've been awake if my fiancé could get it up." The bed moved and Roxie laughed. "Ouch, okay, we did it on the beach… and on the deck… We were pretty much at it as soon as the dinner party was over." Her head twisted Zairn's way again. "Your prowess is no longer in question." Roxie's smile faded when their eyes met again. "I'm sorry, honey. How did he take it? Was he mad?"

"I don't know what he was, it was… I'm not used to men like him."

"No, he isn't your regular type. Your regular type is vicious or insane. He won't stalk you… although he would have the means to if he wanted to."

"He wants there to be an us."

"Oh."

"Not a fling, an us."

"And you don't?"

She groaned, fake weeping as she turned her face into the pillow. "I don't know."

"What's the down side? You're obviously attracted to each other. I said already he's a good man and he has his shit together." When she peeked at Roxie, her friend's face was turned away. "You don't repeat anything you hear in our bed, Skippy."

"Never do," Zairn murmured. "I'm sleeping."

"Good, thank you," Roxie said, her fingers combing through her hair. "Tell me why you're not sure, honey. Is it the circus? Because you get used to it. You didn't want to do the long-distance thing again. That's your choice. You don't have to—"

"He said he'd move to New York." Roxie's mouth opened like she meant to talk, but only shock was conveyed in her expression. "What kind of guy does that?"

"I did it. I moved to New York for Z."

"That's not the whole way across the country. It's a two hour flight. You did it because you were in love." Roxie raised knowing brows as her lips thinned. "No, we're not, we can't even… It's ego, is what it is. It's ego, right?"

"If you're asking: does he have an ego? Yes, he definitely has an ego. Do I think he'd be frivolous enough to uproot his life if it were about conquest…?"

"No," Zairn mumbled.

"No," Roxie said without acknowledging her fiancé. Maybe she saw the fear on her face, maybe it was uncertainty, but her friend smiled and stroked her hair again. "You do this with every guy. You always think the worst, like they couldn't just want to be with you."

She wriggled closer. "Why would he want to be with me?" she whispered. "He has… everything."

"He doesn't have you," Roxie said. "Yet anyway. Why is he different from any guy you'd meet in a bar or at work? Because he has money? Screw money. You have access to as much money as you want. You're financially secure so long as I'm financially secure. Which means always."

"Because you and Zairn will never break up."

"Because even if we did, he wouldn't cut me off. And everything's halved in the divorce." She moved like maybe Zairn had made contact again. "Forget about money. Does he make you laugh?"

"Yes," she said in a small voice.

"Is the sex good?"

"Yes," she said even quieter.

"Can you talk to him?"

"About some things. We haven't spent much time going… deeper."

"Maybe that's what you need to do," Roxie said. "Get to know each other better. Talk."

"Yeah, is that before or after he's moved his whole life across the continent?" she asked, shaking her head. "It puts too much pressure on us."

"We can go to LA, if you want that option," Roxie said. "Z can work from anywhere."

"That doesn't take the pressure off. It's commitment before we've even decided if we want to commit."

Roxie frowned. "What's going on? You're usually all in with guys you like. Are you scared you'll hurt him? If you don't want to do this, that's allowed too. If you don't want to be with him…"

She sighed. "It's not very romantic, is it? All this planning. The back and forth."

"So he can't be your forever guy," Roxie said on a sympathetic exhale, resting a hand on her cheek. "Because it's not the fairytale."

"It's childish."

"No," Roxie asserted. "You want what you want. Don't apologize to anyone for that."

"It's ridiculous that I would care."

Roxie smiled. "No, it's what makes you you. I'm so proud of you. You should wait for the real thing. No more Grahams or Brendans, you wait for Prince Charming because you deserve him. You're the kindest, sweetest, most incredible woman. I'm so proud that you see that too."

Waiting for the fairytale was what? A sign of her level of self-esteem. It was certainly higher than it had been with Brendan. If it wasn't, she wouldn't consider saying no to anyone. But she couldn't ask Knox to move when she was unsure. It wouldn't be fair, to either of them. If he moved, she'd never end things, no matter how sure she was they weren't meant to be. And he'd be stuck there, unable to say he was going back to LA, because he wouldn't want to hurt her feelings.

"Should I tell him tonight?"

"Do it tomorrow," Roxie said, unzipping her dress. "Wriggle on out of that. I'll text Toria, tell her you're here."

"Rox," she said, cupping her friend's face. "Thank you."

One thing she'd always be sure of was her love for her girls. No matter what, they were there for each other. With them, there was no such thing as an inconvenient time or place. They supported each other. Up, down, back, forth, they'd always be there for support. For anything.

TWENTY-TWO

"OLD HABITS DIE HARD."

"Hilarious."

The male voices broke through her slumber. Who would…?

Opening her eyes, it wasn't a surprise to see Toria sleeping in front of her. When she tried to roll over, there was someone else at her back. Rox.

"Do you boys need something?" Roxie mumbled, still half-asleep. "Or are you waiting for a show?"

Her friend shifted enough that she could sink onto her back. Zairn was up, buttoning a shirt. Ballard was next to him and… Knox was in the open doorway, a shoulder resting on the frame.

"Damnit, we've missed breakfast," Toria said, tossing the covers aside to jump out of bed… in her underwear.

Without asking, Toria passed Zairn to go into the closet.

Roxie stretched out. "We slept late."

"You did," Zairn said, coming to bend over, propping a fist on the bed to kiss his fiancée. "Astrid's on the deck with breakfast."

"With coffee?"

Zairn smiled. "Yes, with coffee," he murmured on her lips. "Need anything?"

"Not with this many people in the room. We're going to the beach later?"

"Count on it, Lo."

He kissed her again, then turned to leave with Ballard in tow. Knox lingered, their eyes met. What was he thinking? He'd just found her in his best friend's bed. Roxie was there, Toria too, he couldn't think anything untoward went on, could he?

"I'm going to shower," Roxie said, climbing out of bed. "And keep Toria busy."

Knox didn't look at Roxie, all she wore was one of Zairn's shirts, but it didn't seem like he noticed.

"Good morning," Knox said when Roxie had disappeared the way Toria had gone.

"Morning," she whispered. "I came over here last night, I didn't—"

"I know," he said, boosting his shoulder from the frame. "Make any decisions?"

Yes, and that might not be the place, but she couldn't keep him in the dark. Wrapping herself in the sheet, she slunk out of bed.

"Can we talk outside?" she asked, sliding open the patio door.

He followed and she slid it closed behind them again. "This isn't going to go well for me," he said, leaning against the pillar that held up the awning.

"I'm sorry," she said, cringing. "I really am. I think you're amazing—"

"Just not amazing enough."

"It's not that," she said, going closer, reminding herself to be as quiet as possible.

"So it's the distance thing? I said I'd stay in New York."

"I don't want you to stay in New York. I couldn't ask you to—if you moved all the way to New York with me, we would never be sure if it was real or just convenient. We just don't know each other well enough to take a leap like that."

"And I thought you were all about the romance."

Romance… She faltered. Being the romantic, she swooned at the big romantic gestures in movies, in real life, just not in *her* life. Looking at it from that point of view, it was romantic he'd take the risk for her. Hadn't she thought it was romantic that Roxie moved for Zairn?

"I am," she said, giving herself a mental kick. "I am about the romance, but… We didn't have the most romantic start did we?"

"Kissing me in that bathroom, acting because you couldn't resist… seems romantic to me."

And she was busy getting bogged down in all the sex. The kissing. The physical. A soft exhale came with the loosening of her muscles. That mouth. His mouth. The way she couldn't… resist.

Damn, this was getting away from her. "I… uh…"

"Showing up at your apartment 'cause I just couldn't help myself," he murmured, the smolder of his words vibrated through her. "Showing up here. The night we spent on the beach… Am I the only one who noticed?" Apparently. His curled forefinger slid under her chin to raise it. "Don't worry, Blossom. No is not a word I hear when I want something this bad." He stooped to press a short kiss to her lips. "You want romance? You got it."

He left her there outside, hankering after him, wondering what just happened. Did she end their association or fire the starter pistol?

TWENTY-THREE

THEY MISSED BREAKFAST but made it for lunch. Their day by the pool switched to a day at the beach when everyone heard Roxie and Zairn would be making a stop on one of the quieter beaches.

"Do you want to swim?" Toria asked, helping her top off her sunscreen.

Some people were splashing around in the sea. Others stuck by the loungers lined at the head of the beach. Palm trees offered some shade, but not enough she would skimp on the protection.

About fifteen feet behind them, a four-poster beach bed was sitting vacant. No guesses who that was for.

A screech from the waves ignited her panic. When people began running up the beach, she turned but quickly relaxed.

Zairn and Roxie.

She smiled. Their friends were quickly mobbed.

"I'm getting used to this having Zairn around thing," Toria said. "He was cool about last night."

"He was."

"How'd you end up over there?" she asked. "You said you were tired."

"I was… You know me, I get overwhelmed and I… I needed to talk to someone."

"You could've talked to me. Is it LIP? You don't like the dating?"

"I feel like my head is all over the place with men and relationships," she said because it was true. "I second guess every decision I make."

"You have to trust yourself. Like Rox and me trust you."

Should they? Should Toria? The secret was… She'd tell her when they got back to New York. After the vacation and LIP and everything was over with.

"I'm trying."

"The problem is you don't think you deserve anything good. I don't know why, if it's your mom or Brendan still in your head. I wish you could see yourself the way we see you."

"Hey!" Roxie's shout brought their attention around. "Jane, we didn't bring sunscreen."

Maybe they did or maybe they didn't, but the invite was genuine. Roxie gestured them over, so she grabbed her beach bag and went with Toria.

Zairn was on the phone, resting against the inclined head of the bed. In the middle, Roxie was on her knees at his side.

"Where are the cocktails?" Toria asked.

"On their way," Roxie said, unbuttoning Zairn's shirt. "They're bringing food too." Zairn was still talking and only moved to let Roxie maneuver him out of the fabric. "And music as well."

"Are we partying on the beach?" Toria asked, sitting down and scooching over to make space for her.

"Don't see why not," Roxie said, rising on her knees enough to lick Zairn's torso from navel to clavicle.

His hand landed on the back of her head when she got to the top, though his attention was tipped a little away. She kissed the corner of his lips and he switched the angle of the phone to steal her mouth in something much more passionate.

It was brief though and he was quickly back on the phone. "Say again," he said into the device. "I missed that."

"Gotta give the fans something," Roxie said, tossing a leg over to straddle him.

"You give 'em a lot," Toria said and laughed. "We're grateful."

Roxie clapped her hands and gestured for the sunscreen. Leaning over, she gave Roxie the bottle who quickly squirted a whole bunch onto Zairn's chest. He glanced down, but stayed stoic as Roxie opened her hands on his body to massage the lotion in.

Toria groaned. "You know you're living every woman on this beach's hottest fantasy, right?"

"Just wait 'til I take it below the waistband."

Rising on her knees, she turned her flat hand to slide it down his body. Her fingers snuck under the waistband of his shorts to her knuckles.

Zairn caught her wrist and dropped the phone again. "You know how many private beaches we have here?"

Roxie laughed and stole another kiss. "Man's no fun."

"Yeah, she's losing her mind," Zairn said into the phone, looking pointedly at Roxie over his aviators. "Turning our lives into a porno."

"A cheap one too," Roxie said, enjoying rubbing in the lotion, though it was likely the body more than the substance she relished.

Zairn took his phone from his ear to look at the screen. "Look up."

"Hmm?" Roxie asked when he next made eye contact.

"All of you. Look up," he said, taking the phone back to his ear. "I'll call back."

"Look up?" Roxie asked.

Just like her friend, she craned her neck, searching beyond the net canopy of the bed into the azure sky. What were they looking for? There was nothing—

A plane. Three actually. No. Four. One was pulling a banner…

Shading her eyes, she stepped away from the bed to read it.

"You want romance?"

Romance?

Smoke poured from two of the other planes, writing letters in the sky, *"Like this?"*

Oh, God…

She couldn't believe her eyes, the planes, the words, they'd spoken about… Another plane appeared, drawing a big pink smoke heart in the sky. Going another step onto the sand, she was transfixed until the rumble of engines came closer.

What was that?

A plane thundered toward the beach. It was low. Too low? Was something wrong? Were they in danger?

Wait… It wasn't alone.

The echoing sound brought her around, another was coming from the other way. Two planes, headed straight for each other, one a little closer than the other.

A stream of something came from behind the first plane the moment it was over the beach. Pink scattered across the sand and the cheering LIP members. The first plane quickly pulled up and the other coming the other way reached them. Again, a cascade of pink streamed from behind it, falling over her and the bed, spilling in a thick plume until the plane pulled up.

What was the pink payload they'd sprinkled everywhere?

"Wow, was that the resort?" Toria exclaimed, jumping off the bed. "They're really committed to this Love in Paradise thing!"

The others on the beach were as exuberant. It helped that was the moment food and alcohol showed up. Her eyes met Roxie's. Still on top of her fiancé, Roxie had her upper arm on his chest, lying on him with a hand in her hair, holding her head up.

"Someone is," Roxie said.

Toria dipped to scoop up the pink flowers. "What are they?" she asked, handing them off.

The petals touched her palm. "It's cherry blossom."

"Cool," Toria said. "I'll get us a pitcher."

As one friend scampered off, she was drawn toward the other on the bed. "It's cherry blossom."

"Yes, it is," Roxie said. "Which I guess means something to you."

"Thank God it's April," Zairn muttered. "He'll never live this down."

Roxie smacked his chest. "Ignore him, honey. Everyone else thinks it's romantic."

Taking the flower to her nose, she couldn't believe someone, anyone, had done something so bold. For her. It couldn't be real.

"It can't have been… No, we just talked this morning." She'd dumped him. Why would he take the chance? "He wouldn't—"

"You know how many people can get that much cherry blossom together and down here that fast?" Zairn asked. "That wasn't money, that was influence. That was dedication."

The Colliers did have pull. No one could deny that. Most others would have gone for something easier, even rose petals would've done the job, but he'd done it with blossom. Written words in the sky and…

On an exhale, she sank down onto the bed.

Romance. She'd asked the universe for it and, boy, did it deliver.

TWENTY-FOUR

FOOD, DRINK, MUSIC. The hours passed and there was no sign of him. The sun sank down past the horizon and still nothing. How could he do something like that and not show up?

Everything was complicated. Messed up. And she wouldn't be able to make sense of it without at least looking him in the eye.

"He's not coming."

Turning away from the laughter and dancing, it was Zairn who stood behind her, drink in hand.

"He's not coming?" she asked. He shook his head as he drank, watching his fiancée dance in the sand. "Why not?"

"You'd have to ask him." That would probably be the smartest idea. "There's a line of carts waiting on the path." Their eyes met. He smiled and nodded once. "I've got you."

Okay, she needed to go and Zairn would cover. Oh, it sucked to be hiding anything, but she couldn't explain. Not then. Not until she'd seen him.

Leaving Toria again felt wrong, but she had Roxie and a squad of other people. They'd also made a deal to live the adventure. Isn't that what she was doing?

Getting in the cart, asking for a ride back to the main complex, she felt every revolution of the wheels. It seemed forever away, yet time just disappeared.

He might not be in his apartment. He could be in his office. Maybe someone else was with him. The risk was worth it. She had to take the chance.

Her heart raced as she ascended in the elevator. When it freed her, she held her breath and went over to knock. What the hell was she going to say? Her mind was blank. For maybe the first time ever, there were no words.

When the door opened, she released the breath and there he was, shirtless like last time.

"Hi," he said. "I didn't expect—"

Grabbing his face, she almost leaped into his arms as she pulled him down to join their mouths. How could she ignore her attraction to him? She couldn't. This was more now. Nothing easy, but that didn't matter.

He backed up and she heard his foot make contact with the door before it closed. Though he tried to take his mouth from hers, she didn't give him much room to play with.

"Show me your bedroom."

"No," he said, taking her hands off his face, closing them inside his. "No bedroom."

"No bedroom?"

He shook his head and flattened her hands on his torso. "This is not sex. We're not doing that. We're not doing fling again."

"What you did today was—"

"Not for sex," he said. "And I didn't do anything, I just made a few calls, pulled in a few favors."

"You did it for me."

"Yes, I did."

"Because I wanted romance."

"Because I had to show you this is not just sex. Just sex we can get anywhere with anyone. This has to be different."

"Okay," she said, not sure she followed. "So… what do we do?"

On a dazzling smile, he interlinked their fingers to guide her over to the couch before retreating to the kitchen. "Starts with me getting you a drink."

She slipped off her shoes to tuck her feet under her. "No one's ever done anything like that for me before."

"Big grand gestures I can do," he said.

Because they meant something to her. It wasn't about the money, it was his willingness to put himself out there. For her. With no guarantee she'd respond like he wanted. It was the thought. The fact that not only had he put time and effort into coming up with the idea, but he'd actually picked up the phone to make it happen. For her.

Resting a hand on the back of the couch, she laid her chin on her knuckles. "What do you want?"

"What do I want?" he asked, mixing their drinks.

"You said I didn't ask before and you were right."

"You said you didn't want to know."

"I do want to know."

"Now you want to know," he said, showing her another smile as he picked up their glasses.

He brought them over and sat next to her, offering a silent toast before they both drank.

Scooching closer, she rested her head on his shoulder and draped her legs over his lap.

"Did you have a good night?" he asked, combing her hair back from her face. She shook her head. "No? Why not?"

"You weren't with me," she murmured, closing her eyes and sipping more of her drink. "Being around you, it does something weird to me. Is it okay to say that?"

"By now you should know it's okay for you to say anything to me," he said, kissing her hair.

"Then maybe you can tell me why I win the prize? Why would you want more than sex from someone like me?"

"The prize?" he asked. "If anyone has won anything, it's me. You're different, I've known that from the start. Your honesty, your mind, you pulled me in, Blossom. Your kiss, the feel of you, the way you intoxicate me. I didn't think it was possible for anyone to grab me this deep… And here, seeing other guys, you with other guys… You're in bikinis and clothes that… I don't get jealous, I'm not possessive… I wasn't…"

"I never wear bikinis, or dresses like this. Toria went shopping with Roxie's, or Zairn's, credit card. She said I needed a vacation wardrobe and got me a bunch of new clothes, things I'd never normally wear."

"You've looked beautiful in everything you've worn," he said. "Chicago wardrobe and this. You always look beautiful. I bet all the guys down there noticed."

Was that why he hadn't come to the beach party? "Wayne paid me a compliment," she said and held her straw in her teeth for a few seconds before continuing. "I never know with men if they mean it. Isn't it just something you have to say to a woman even if she looks a mess?"

"No woman ever looks a complete mess," he said, "there's always something nice to say, and it's important to make a woman feel good. But I'd never lie and if that means saying nothing at all, then I'd comment on the night or the restaurant or whatever."

"I bet you've been on a million dates. A guy like you must have a lot of notches in his bedpost."

"I won't lie to you, babe. I've dated women through the years, nothing clicked… until I was standing in that bathroom with you. I know it's full-on to say it, maybe you're rubbing off on me, but I knew you were something special within a minute of walking in there."

No pressure then. Something special? One thing was for sure, there was an attraction between them. Another thing was that they came from different worlds. That didn't mean she couldn't try to find something they had in common. If they were going to do this, they had to be able to talk.

"Are you close to your parents?" she asked.

"It's relative. Yes, we see each other and we're in regular contact."

"But…?"

"We talk about business and family, I don't pour my heart out to them."

"Who do you pour your heart out to?"

He kissed her hair and finished his drink, putting his glass on the table behind the couch. "I don't," he said. "Typically. If I need a sounding board or to depressurize, I call one of the guys."

"Your secret posse," she said, remembering the club... the night she'd ended up going home with him.

"Dropped Z in it with that one."

"Which I think you did on purpose," she said, prodding his chest.

"Maybe. They'll bounce. They're through it already. Zairn and Roxie are solid... You know about my family. What about yours?"

"My mom and dad are still together," she said. "I don't see much of them. They live in the city. My mom's super religious. When I was about twelve, she found God... whatever that means. We talk on the phone sometimes, when important things happen. I have my girls for everything else."

"Siblings?"

"Just me."

"Guess your parents knew they hit gold the first time. Why keep digging?" he said with a smile in his voice as he trailed his fingertips down her arm.

She slurped her drink and reached over him to put her glass next to his. The move brought them chest to chest, into alignment for a kiss. But he'd said no. He didn't want to get physical.

What were they talking about? Family?

"My parents are so secure with each other," she said, trying not to blush. "They've been married thirty-five years, but they're still in love, it's... quite sweet really."

"Is that what you're looking for?" he asked, opening his fingers at her temple to spread them wide in her hair. "Thirty-five years of marriage and to still have your guy look at you like he could eat you up?"

Smiling, she bumped her nose on his. "I really don't want to think about my parents and... that."

"Hmm," he said, pushing his lips to one side. "Yeah, might have killed the mood there."

"It's okay, we're not lost yet, but I promise not to seduce you."

"God forbid," he said, admiring her figure. "Dress looks tight."

"It is," she said, wriggling.

"Want to take it off?"

Her smile was instant. "I thought we weren't having sex."

"Doesn't mean you can't be comfortable." His intensity grew. "I want this to be home. I want to be home to you, Blossom."

Oh, God, on a sigh, it was impossible to hide her swoon. Holding herself together took effort. She got off the couch and he grabbed for her like he wanted to pull her back down, so she swerved her body out of reach.

Stretching his arms along the backrest, he drank her in as she loosened the zipper under her arm to slide off the straps of her dress. Slowly, she peeled it down over her breasts, wriggled it past her hips and dropped it to the floor.

After stepping out of the fabric, she returned to the couch, straddling him rather than re-taking her seat. "I liked being on top."

Humming out his approval, he slid his palms from her hips to her waist, to the sides of her breasts and then around to her ass to pull her core to the mass in his jeans.

"I liked you being on top," he said, squeezing her ass. "I like you any way I can get you."

"I can't stay long," she whispered, kissing him once.

"Why not?" he asked, dipping his head back.

"I'm tired," she said and tried to kiss him again.

He avoided her mouth. "You can stay the night if you want," he said, touching the length of her hair against her waist at her spine. "I love your hair."

Always with the compliments.

She coiled her fingers around the back of his neck. "I like this… the way your body feels against mine."

Their skin was flush. The heated sensation was so enticing she wanted to slide out of her bra too, but that might be a step more than she could handle if sex wasn't allowed.

"Can I kiss you?" he asked, stroking her back. She nodded. "Here?" He touched her lips and she nodded, so he did. "What about here?" He touched her neck and she nodded. As his lips explored her throat, she lost herself in their rough but delicate texture against her thrumming flesh. "Here?" Touching her collarbone got him another nod, then he moved to her sternum, and she nodded more slowly. She might be the one on top, but he was directing their union, lifting and moving her to submit to his lips. "I'm not going any further. Kissing is it."

He didn't need to be patient; he didn't need to be calm and understanding. His amazing attitude made her want to pour herself into him.

"I want to go all the way," she whispered, running her fingers from his hair to his shoulders and down his arms.

"I can't help myself around you," he murmured, kissing his way back up. "But I want the long haul, not a quick thrill."

"Kissing is good too. And it does…" She moaned at his mouth's gentle suction on her neck. "Stop me talking."

"Always talk to me. There's nothing you can say that I don't want to hear."

"Let's enjoy this," she whispered, rocking against him. "For a little while."

She was weak. It was pathetic. But he was safe. This was easy. With him, she felt good, and her self-esteem skyrocketed. Addiction to him consumed her. She may never be able to give him up.

TWENTY-FIVE

FOR THE NEXT FEW days, they saw each other at every available opportunity. Toria didn't ask where she snuck off to. Even if she disappeared in the middle of the day. Her friend gave her that slack but had to have suspicions. Most probably that she'd gotten close to one of the LIP men.

Each night she left events early. Everyone was accustomed to her claims of being tired so didn't question her departures.

On the night of the cherry blossom day, she'd gone home after another hour on Knox's couch. But every night after that, Knox sent Marty down to lock her bungalow bedroom door and spent the night holding her in his bed. As per her request, Knox set the alarm for five a.m. each day and drove her back to her bungalow. Well, not all the way back, but to a quiet corner nearby.

They hadn't had sex, not on the island. And, damn, she wanted to go all the way. Being with him, and his mouth, felt too good to resist. If it wasn't for his strength, she'd have given in for sure.

But he stuck to his assertion they wouldn't have sex. He listened when she talked and didn't judge her ramblings.

As she'd lay watching him sleep the previous night, she stroked his hair wondering if what they felt could last.

That morning, she opened her eyes and yawned, stretching her toes to the bottom of the bed. Brilliant sunlight reflected off the ocean; that view never got old. Though it did seem brighter than usual.

Huh. The bed was missing one important feature: Knox.

Sitting up, she gathered the white sheet around her nude body and smiled at the memory of his fingers slipping into her underwear last night. Real sex might be off the table, but that didn't mean he neglected her needs. Knox was always showering her with compliments and when she was around, he seemed to sport a permanent erection… which was a compliment in itself. He was enamored with her, even if she didn't understand why.

"Tomorrow afternoon," she heard Knox say when she stepped out of the bedroom into the hallway. The sheet she held tight at her chest trailed behind her as she moved toward the kitchen. Was he alone? "Do I have time tomorrow afternoon?"

"I checked with Amber, we can make it happen."

She stopped, almost on the cusp of crossing into the kitchen. That was Nigel's voice. What time was it? He shouldn't be there at five a.m. Come to think of it, the sun shouldn't be in the sky either. When Knox usually took her home, the sun hadn't yet peeked over the horizon.

"Okay," Knox said. "Two. I'll be there at two."

"Why are you pushing me out?" Nigel asked. "Don't you think we should discuss what you should say?"

"You want me to talk about how great I am with women, how they respond to success."

"No, I don't," Nigel said. "Because you're not."

"I'm not what?" Knox asked.

The offense in his voice curled her lips.

"Great with women," Nigel said. "You're not great with women at all. They bore you… You have to talk about how you envy what our participants are finding, that the journey they're on is important."

"I would figure they know that," Knox said. "Why else would they sign up for LIP?"

She rested her forehead on the wall. Nigel was talking about her group. The LIP group.

"When you heard about this program, you said you wanted regular updates."

"Yeah."

"Since then, you haven't asked once."

"I've been busy," Knox said. "And you're doing a great job."

And maybe he asked for those updates because he'd learned she was part of the group. Hadn't he said his people checked out all the men? Those updates wouldn't be as important now that they were spending nights together.

"Some of the participants are giving us cause for concern," Nigel said.

"What kind of concern?" Knox snapped.

Was he worried or pissed off?

"We're concerned some of them are not taking the process seriously," Nigel said. "They seem to be more interested in… sex."

Knox's burst of laughter was hilarious. "You've got them parading around in bathing suits and drinking together every night. It's no wonder some of them are horny. Putting a sex embargo on them is a red rag to a bull."

"We are not running a brothel. Isn't that why you wanted the gift baskets removed?"

"Yeah, I'm not saying you shouldn't have rules," Knox said. "If they want to find love, they should be patient. Who wants the guy or gal who's slept with nine members of the opposite sex already? But there will be flirting, maybe some kissing and groping. They'll settle down."

"Some members may not be able to proceed."

Knox inhaled. "You can't have expected they'd all find something real."

"Except not everyone is engaging," Nigel said with judgment.

It took a minute for Knox to respond. "The program isn't suited to everyone," he said, answering like he suspected where Nigel was going. Still, he asked, "Say what you're thinking, Nigel. Who isn't engaging?"

"The woman standing in your hallway right now," Nigel said, unforgiving and unimpressed.

She pulled her lower lip between her teeth.

"What the fuck are you—"

"I saw a burst of sunlight when she opened the bedroom door. I know she's here," Nigel said. "Jane, why don't you come and join us?"

She didn't want to. She'd rather stay there with her eyes closed and pretend it wasn't happening.

"Leave her alone, Nige," Knox said. "You bring your problems to me."

She couldn't hide and let Knox take all the heat, the situation was as much her fault as his. Sidestepping, she slid along the wall until it ran out and she was in the kitchen. Knox stood with his back to her. Nigel was on the opposite side of the counter, his eyes narrowed on her over Knox's shoulder.

Knox glanced back. "Go back to bed, baby. It's okay."

"No, it's not," Nigel said.

Fury darkened Knox's eyes as they cut back to his cousin. "Don't you dare talk to her like that," he growled. Nigel blinked, clearly taken aback. "Jane has done nothing wrong. What we're doing is not shameful."

"What are you doing?" Nigel asked. "This woman is part of a specific program, a romance program, and you've usurped her."

"Yeah, I have," Knox said. "Do you hear me apologizing?"

"He hasn't," she said, rushing forward. She didn't want the men to fight. "I'm sorry, sir. I didn't mean to cause any trouble."

Knox put an arm around her and kissed her head. "Don't apologize to him, Blossom. We've done nothing wrong."

"We have," she said, peeking up at him. "We knew we shouldn't want this. We've been unfair."

"You signed a contract to say you wouldn't have intercourse," Nigel said.

Oh no, was that really in the LIP contract?

Knox squeezed her tighter, landing another glare on his cousin. "Was that a threat? Did you just threaten her? Do you think that's smart? You better watch your step and think very carefully about your next words."

"I'm not threatening her," Nigel said. "I am saying she should not have signed that contract if she intended to renege on it."

"We haven't had sex," she said and lifted a shoulder when Knox looked at her again. "Well, we haven't, why lie to him? Not here on the island while I've been part of Love in Paradise anyway."

"Has that been holding you back? Blossom, tell me you're not thinking of that when we're together."

She shook her head and lowered her voice. "No, I've been more eager than you. If it wasn't for your restraint…"

Knox kissed her head again. "What's the number? How much to buy her out of the contract?"

She gasped. "No!" As she jumped in front of him, the wall clock sent a new shiver of terror through her. "Oh, God, Toria will be awake soon!" Luckily, breakfast wasn't until ten, but it was already eight fifteen. "I have to go."

"I cannot allow you to continue on the program," Nigel said. "You and your friend will have to be removed from—"

"No," she begged, whirling around. "Not Toria, please. If you want to kick me off, that's fine. Just let me talk to her first, please."

"She doesn't know about this?" Nigel asked, examining them. She shook her head. "Why didn't you tell her?"

"What would Roxie do? We made a pact at the start of the vacation that we wouldn't question or judge each other. She probably thinks it's weird that I've disappeared a few times, but she knows I am not great with guys, with flirting and sex—"

"Okay, Blossom, I'll take care of this," Knox said, ducking to kiss her, stemming her rant before it got to full bluster. "Nigel, wasn't another part of this contract that they weren't supposed to discuss their romances? Jane has kept this a secret because she doesn't want to undermine the program. I've told her to skip the dates and excursions, but she goes to support you and the others. She goes to support Toria who believes in LIP.

"Yes, you're right, Jane isn't going to fall in love with any of the participants. She isn't engaged, but she's present, just like you, working to make the program a success." Nigel glanced at her again. "Shit, think about it, Nige, she's dating me. She could've begged off any time. You don't think I wanted to come tell you she was done with the program?"

"Why haven't you?"

"Her. She's the only reason I haven't."

"You've been distracted," Nigel said. "On the beach… I haven't seen you that preoccupied with a woman for a long time. I suspected something was going on."

"It is."

"She hasn't been engaged in the program," Nigel said. "But some of the men… they've come to me requesting to spend more time with her."

"Who?" Knox barked.

Pressing a hand to his bare chest, she soothed him. "Knox," she murmured. "Baby, you know that doesn't matter to me… We talked about this. I miss you when we're not together."

His gaze lowered and she smiled because, for some reason, it had a calming effect on him. She pushed onto her tiptoes.

He read the signal and dipped to kiss her. "If one of them touches you—"

"I carry my panic button everywhere," she whispered. "It pages you directly. With the GPS, you'll always be able to get to me."

"You gave her a GPS enabled panic button?" Nigel asked.

"That's how much she means to me," Knox said. "One good thing that comes from you knowing is it puts you on notice. No one on this island is more important than her. No one."

Zairn and Reid may disagree with that.

"Does Aunt Thena know about this?"

"Not yet."

"Cam's in Florida."

"Yeah, he's going to try to come visit."

Nigel looked at her again. "Cam is Knox's younger brother. He's the easiest introduction to the Collier family."

"Cam's insane."

"He chose love, not money," Nigel said, smiling at her. "We should spend some time getting to know each other, Miss Simmons. Some real quality time."

That might be a good idea. If she was going to be with Knox, connecting with his family was inevitable, but...

"I can't, not this morning," she said, looking at the clock again. "I have to get to Toria before she wakes up and finds me gone, she'll panic."

Nigel looked at his watch.

Knox kissed her head again. "Write a note, tell her you went for a walk and will meet her at breakfast. Marty will deliver it... Or I'll take you down there now."

She rested against him, lowering her volume in hopes Nigel wouldn't hear, "I only have last night's clothes."

"I'll get you something from one of the boutiques downstairs," Knox said.

Toria didn't know every item in her closet, they could get away with it... hopefully.

"Okay," she said. Winning Nigel over, showing him respect, would be vital to her relationship with Knox and Toria too. "My card's in my purse." His mouth opened in an inhale she knew would be an objection. "This is important. I don't want to spend your money."

When Knox gritted his teeth and turned his eyes upward to growl, she smiled. "You infuriate me, woman."

"I know I do," she said and kissed his pec. "But I told you I won't be bought."

"I can buy you a dress," he said. "I'll get the cheapest one in there if that makes you happy."

Hitching up her chin, she let her smile glow proud. "You know what would make me happy?"

"If I took your card to the store and used that instead of mine?"

She nodded. "You read me so well, my love," she whispered and pushed to her tiptoes again.

"You know we don't pay for anything around here," he said, ducking to give a simple kiss. "You never noticed that? We're Zairn's guests, everything's on account."

"Not this. I'll let you pay me in kisses. I'll take as many of those as you'll dish out."

"You could never take everything I want to give you," he said, bowing to kiss her again. "Will you be okay with this bozo for a while, or do you want me to take him with me?"

Nigel was intent on them.

"I'll be fine," she said.

Maybe if she got some time alone with Nigel, she'd get a better idea of his true feelings about her.

Knox rubbed his lips in her hair. "If he upsets you, hit the panic button and I'll come back upstairs."

She wouldn't but nodded anyway and kissed him again before going to her purse. Knox went to put on a tee-shirt as she retrieved her card. She'd never handed her card to a man before, but Knox was unique in her life in a lot of ways.

Once Knox was gone, she scribbled a quick note for Marty who loitered in the elevator foyer.

Coffee was next. She needed coffee… and to distract her from Nigel's scrutiny.

"You know your way around Knox's kitchen," he said, seating himself on a high stool. "You've spent a lot of time here this week?"

"Some," she said, wondering if that was a judgment or an opening observation. "I like to make myself useful and Knox…" Should she be honest? Knox liked that quality in her, she couldn't hide it from Nigel. "He said he put my fingerprint in the system, so I can come up in the elevator and in through his door… We've met here a couple of times."

Nigel's brows rose. "He put your print in the system?"

"I didn't ask him to do it, if that's what you think. He just asked me to put my thumb on his tablet thing. There was kissing and… I'll be honest, I wasn't really paying attention. He didn't tell me what it was about until the next morning."

"You've slept here every night?"

Reading this guy was difficult. Either he was interested, or he was interrogating her. "Since Sunday night, the last three nights. I've told Knox I don't mind sleeping in the bungalow, but he insists he likes having me here and well… I like being with him."

"Just like?" Nigel asked. Exhaling, he spread his hands on the counter. "I'm sorry if I seem harsh, Miss Simmons. But you must understand, there are always women trying to get Knox's attention. Especially here on the island where he's more accessible than usual. Some will go to any lengths for time alone with him. Any lengths… I'm just a little perplexed by you, usually Knox is savvy to women and their ways."

Putting out the coffee cups, she laughed. "Oh, I don't have ways, sir," she said, tucking her sheet in tight. "I do know what you mean, some women are very alluring. I'm awkward and I ramble, I'm not at all knowledgeable about sex… Knox takes care of that. Just last night, he gave me the most intense orgasm of my life. Though I think every one surpasses the last. But this was… incredible." Going to the fridge and drawers, she retrieved what they needed for the coffee, putting it all onto a tray. "You know, I've done it myself, got myself off, but my ex, he didn't care how much I enjoyed sex. I thought it was normal, you know? That sex was supposed to be our own responsibility. I guess with Brendan I could've made more of an effort to participate, you know, to get what I wanted. It wasn't his responsibility to do it. He had no obligation to touch me or make me feel good. I can touch myself, so why should he have done it for me? Knox disagrees.

We talked about it last night and he said it was the partner's responsibility to take care of their opposite. It's different, powerful." She decanted some cream into a small pitcher and then put it away before taking the sweetener from the cabinet. "It's funny, it doesn't even take Knox long to get me there. Last night, he just touched me and boom, I went off. I suppose he'd warmed me up, you know? We'd been kissing a while and he has a really incredible mouth that feels so amazing on my body… especially on my breasts." Righting everything on the tray, she took it to the coffee table and then returned to the coffee pot to check if it was full. "He really is great with women. They don't bore him, he just doesn't click with them. Knox is not a complicated man, he likes to keep things simple, though what he does it's… I'm not even sure there are words for it. And it's not just the sex stuff, he's patient with me, he cares, I'd be falling for him whether he was a fingering pro or not."

She exhaled and looked at Nigel for the first time. There was no time to ask why he was gaping because the door opened, and Knox came back in. He stopped just inside the door, giving it a boost back into its frame with his elbow.

"What?" Knox asked, looking at each of them. "Nige, you look like someone just ran over you with a freight train." Smiling, Knox came forward to hand her a boutique bag as he stooped to kiss her cheek. "Baby, were you maybe just very honest with your new friend? Is it possible you shared a little more than he might have been expecting?"

"No, I—" Her innocence evaporated to shock as she replayed her ramble. "Oh God," she breathed and grabbed his tee-shirt. "I told him that you… that last night you…"

"Made you come?" Knox asked and she nodded, her jaw still loose though her guy was smiling. "That's okay." He put his arm around her and took the coffee pot from the machine. "Don't be so shocked, Nige. My girl had a good time and believe me, she was grateful."

He lowered her to the couch.

Shock kept her in a daze. "I should've been more grateful, shouldn't I?" Knox sat behind her and leaned forward to pour the coffee. Turning, she curled a hand onto his thigh. "I should've returned the favor, shouldn't I? I didn't return the favor." She whined. "Knox, you're supposed to be helping me do the right thing, why didn't you tell me to—"

"Seeing you happy, that was as much gratitude as I needed," he said, kissing her cheek as he poured.

He leaned over her to move Nigel's cup to the opposite end of the table, then sat back to put an arm around her.

"She's a… fascinating creature," Nigel said as he lowered to sit on the other end of the couch, his wide eyes trained on her.

Knox kissed her shoulder; she glanced front and back at each of the men. "Back off, old boy, she's mine."

TWENTY-SIX

TOO SOON SHE had to excuse herself from their coffee conversation to get ready for breakfast with Toria. Her friend didn't question her morning walk. In fact, she didn't miss a beat in talking about the LIP men, even though they weren't supposed to.

After breakfast, they got a briefing about the afternoon hike. Riding the cable cars to the top was something they'd done before. Their planned walk was more challenging than those they'd done in the past. They were provided with long pants, hiking boots, and tee-shirts. During lunch they got another talk on what they needed to carry.

Some of the women complained and it would be a lie to say she wasn't nervous. The safety talks were scary. Don't get separated. Stay hydrated. Who has medical training? How long would they be on the mountain? Maybe she shouldn't have made plans to see Knox later.

Getting up there assuaged some of her concern. Every second got them closer to the base and safety. They'd be fine. They would. The group had been walking a while on the narrowing path; every step was progress.

"Down is better than up," Wayne said, suddenly appearing beside her.

"Oh," she said, smiling. "I suppose it is."

The trail was steep and the drop to the side seemed pretty sheer. It was a daunting warning to be careful of each precarious step.

"The weather doesn't help."

No, it didn't, her tee-shirt stuck to her in a couple of damp spots, and her chest was tight. Was Wayne flirting? Was she supposed to be flirting? She wanted to concentrate not distract herself with—

The scrape of pebbles and dirt came with a masculine wail. Wayne wobbled and grabbed hold of her arm, pulling her with him as he tumbled backwards over the edge. The solid ground disappeared from beneath her feet.

Tumbling and rolling down the gravelly slope they'd been trying to avoid, pain, screams, nothing filtered in. Adrenaline hit hard. Panic. Fear. Rock hit rock, the rush of air passed her ears. Clarity. Scrambling to brace, there had to be something to hold onto. Every time she caught brush or stone, the momentum of her fall kept her going.

Then with a sudden impact, she stopped. Searing pain fired through her shoulder. She screamed, clutching at her lifeless arm. A boulder, right on the edge of a sheer drop had caught her.

Tears burned her eyes, but they were nothing to the agony in her shoulder and raw skin battered and torn by the rough ground.

Wayne.

What happened? Toria! Where was Toria? Someone shouted somewhere, someone. Where were they? Wayne had definitely fallen, and he'd taken her with him. A bush moved. Oh, God, it went off the side.

"Wayne!" she called out and skidded on her knees to the edge of the mountain.

Keeping a little distance from the drop, she peeked over.

"Jane!"

There, about ten feet to her left was Wayne, precariously hanging off the cliff, clinging to the bush hanging over the side.

"Wayne!"

"Jane! I'm going to fall!"

Forgetting the pain in her shoulder, she crawled to him and lay flat on the ground on her chest. "No, you're not," she said, looking around. Up above, some guys were trying their best to negotiate the slope she and Wayne had just careened down. "You're going to be okay."

Those guys might not get to them in time. She couldn't look into this man's terrified eyes and steal his hope or abandon him.

"Jane! I don't want to die! Please! Help me!"

"I'm going to help you," she said. How exactly was she going to do that? Sliding closer to the edge, she put aside her own fear about it giving way and locked her hand around his wrist. "You're going to pull yourself up."

"I… I can't!"

"Yes, you can," she said and smiled into his eyes. "I've seen those abs, you've got this. You've got it. And I'm going to help you." Swallowing her apprehension, she hoped he couldn't read her anxiety. "Keep hold of me." A boulder just beside her supplied an anchor. She kept hold of Wayne and twisted to sit on her ass, planting her feet on the rock. Her other arm was lifeless, but that didn't matter, not yet.

"Jane! Please!"

"Hey," she said, straining, but still smiling as she leaned over to look at him. "With one hand, let go of the bush and grab my arm, I'm going to pull you up, but you have to help me, okay? Just focus on me. Focus on helping me. I need you to help me, can you do that, Wayne? Can you help me?"

"I—I don't know."

"Yes, you can," she said and tried not to groan. "A big, strong guy like you, you can help out a feeble little girl like me. Come on, buddy. Just let go and use me to pull yourself up. Keep your eyes on mine. On three you're going to let go with one hand and grab my arm, crunch those abs and pull yourself up. I know you can do it." Her eyes stayed locked to his, she didn't even blink. "One." She took a deep breath and ensured her footing on the rock was solid. If it gave, they were both going over. There was no safety net. "Two." Knox would never forgive her if she died on this mountain. What was worse, he wouldn't forgive himself. "Three!"

Inhaling, she braced and pulled with all her strength. Wayne switched his hand from the bush to her elbow and cried out as he pulled up with both hands. Gradually, he got higher and higher then his weight was over the top edge.

He fell forward, half on top of her, then scrambled away.

"Hey!"

Tipping her head back, she saw the guys from above finally reaching them. Her eyes closed to the burn in her lungs and the pain in her shoulder. She was alive and more grateful for that than she had been not long ago. Having air in her lungs wasn't something she'd take for granted again.

TWENTY-SEVEN

IN THE MED BAY, she was shuffled in for x-rays and examination by the doctor. Once that was over, he left to get her pain meds. The door opened a second later. The doctor must've forgotten something.

No. Nigel entered, not the doctor.

"Miss Simmons, I—"

The open door flew back on its hinges. Knox stormed in, bowling Nigel aside to get to her.

"Knox," she gasped and rushed into his arms.

"Baby," he said. Grasping her face, he pushed her hair back from her cheeks to plant his mouth over hers. "Oh, baby." He kissed her again and again, she could only inhale the impact of each one. "Why aren't you in the hospital, huh? Why didn't you get on the chopper?"

Wayne was being taken back to the mainland and a comprehensive hospital. She'd elected to stay on the island. There was a full-time doctor and nurse, and the med bay was well-equipped, but that wasn't why she stayed.

"I couldn't leave the island without saying goodbye to you," she said, grabbing his tee-shirt.

"Oh, baby, I'd have come to you," he said, kissing her hard. "Nothing would've kept me away… We'll get you a chopper now, okay? I'll come with you and Toria too—"

"No." She shook her head, still clinging to him, trying to touch every part of him with her only good hand. "The program, we—"

"Fuck the program, babe, I don't give a fuck about that. You are the most important thing." Shoving her hair away again, he crouched until their faces were lined up and although she was a mess, he smiled. "You're the only important thing, Blossom. Just you. I love you. You're it. All there is. When I heard there'd been an accident… Shit, baby, I've never been so terrified in my life."

"I'm sorry," she croaked, but he kissed her again. "I'm sorry I scared you. I'm sorry I fell…"

More people entered. Roxie. Zairn. The former's eyes were bloodshot.

The friends rushed to each other.

"I'm sorry," Roxie cried. "Oh, honey, we were so scared."

"It's okay," Jane said, showing her friend another smile. "I'm fine."

"You could've—I don't even… I can't even think about what might've happened."

"It was an accident," she said. "It could've happened to anyone."

Zairn came up behind Roxie, laying a hand on her shoulder. "Jane, I'm sorry."

"You should be fucking sorry," Knox snapped.

"I've shut the whole thing down and ordered a full safety assessment. This won't happen again, we'll make sure of it. Our former risk assessment firm will be toast."

"Might not be much of you left after the lawsuit either."

Zairn didn't even look surprised. "She can have whatever she wants. We won't fight it."

She couldn't believe these friends were exchanging such words. "Are you kidding?" she asked, amazed by the resentment on Knox's face. "No."

"It's okay," Roxie said, taking her hand. "You deserve everything, all of it. It still won't be enough to show you how sorry we are."

"No. No one is suing anyone. This was an accident. It wasn't anyone's fault." She turned to Knox. "Wayne lost his footing; he was distracted." By her. "Do you really believe your best friend, a man you've known most of your life, would ever have let anyone go up there if he thought it was dangerous? I don't believe it. I won't believe it. Things like this, they're supposed to bring us together. They're supposed to remind us how lucky we are to have each other." She went a little closer. "I was never going to die up there. I wouldn't have let it happen. And now I know that…" Sealing her lips, she retreated to take in the trio. "We have to put a stop to this now. Rox, if they love us enough that they'd turn on each other, it's not right."

The sorrow in Roxie's eyes softened to a kind of clarity. "Honey—"

"It's not right, Rox. Is it going to come between us?"

"No," Roxie said without hesitation.

She shook her head. "I should go back to Chicago."

"Blossom—"

"Will you come with me, Roxie?" she asked, ignoring Knox.

"Yes," Roxie said. "Absolutely. Toria's talking to the doctor. We can leave as soon as you're ready."

"The plane will be waiting for you," Zairn said, the gravity of his voice deep.

"How did I become the bad guy in this?" Knox asked.

She didn't mind landing her own glare on him. "Because you took this traumatic event and chose to face it with anger. You tried to make someone else the bad guy when this was no one's fault. I don't want to be with a person who'd so quickly turn on his friend. Where's your loyalty?"

"My…" Dumbstruck, Knox had never looked so surprised. "Blossom—"

"This was not Zairn's fault. You know him better than this. You should. I know him better than this and I've known him five minutes," she asserted. "You can be sad. You can be scared. But I don't want anyone hating someone else in my name. I was the one there. The one this happened to and I'm fine. I want us to cherish each other, not resent each other."

"She's a smart woman," Nigel said. "She saved that man's life. The idiot caused this. If anyone is to blame, it's him. There's footage of the… Wayne panicked, but Jane kept her cool, and caused herself more pain to save him. What she did for him… she's an impressive woman."

"We'll stay if we know this won't come between you," she said, focusing on Knox. "I know you were scared, but he's your best friend." Already she could see that he'd softened. The accident scared her and news of it couldn't have been easy to get. "Please…"

The men made eye contact. Zairn wasn't easy to read, but Knox's shoulders fell. "Okay, I'm sorry, that was uncalled for."

Roxie stood there not saying a word. In any other scenario, it would be funny, Roxie wasn't made to be passive.

"I feel the same," Zairn said. "Be mad. I'm mad."

"I am mad," Knox said, stepping forward to offer a hand. "But not at you, this wasn't you."

Zairn shook Knox's hand. In the last second, they held, their eyes locked, and a different kind of apology passed between them.

Roxie leaned in. "We still going back to Chicago?"

"No, I want to stay," she said. "Toria's looking for love, we have to see the program through."

"Blossom, no one cares about the program."

She frowned. "I care."

His fingers curled against her cheek. "You know, I am damn proud of you for what you did up there." And that warmed her heart. Until he tensed. "But you ever fucking think about doing something like that again—"

"Okay, we don't swear at the hero," Roxie said, putting an arm around her. She flinched and her friend noticed. "We should get you more pain meds, huh?"

"She gets whatever she wants," Knox said.

"Seconded," Zairn agreed.

"Where are the others?" she asked.

"In a room down the hall," Nigel said. "No one else was involved in the incident… We will have to give them a report of what comes next."

What came next indeed.

"Later," Knox said.

"We need to decide what's happening with the program," Nigel said. "The others will ask if its being continued. We are a man down."

"Like Knox says," Zairn said, "that's not important."

Roxie took her hand. "What do you think, honey?"

"I don't know."

Nigel offered his thoughts. "I think either we end the program early and offer some kind of consolation prize for everyone…"

Like what? Keeping the LIP group there and together was the only way to ensure this didn't turn into a PR disaster. Zairn better have considered that. The island was beautiful. She didn't want one mishap to ruin everyone's experience forever more. He hired people to worry about that stuff, didn't he? They'd be frantic.

And he probably would get sued. Not by her, but by Wayne. Maybe.

"Or what?" Knox asked.

"We find a replacement for Wayne."

"Like who?" Knox asked, stroking her hair while looking at his cousin. "Whoever you get has missed a whole week, which puts him at a disadvantage. He doesn't have a relationship with any of the women and what about Wayne's friend? Is he still here?"

"Dale? Yes, I think they were interested in the same women. Once he learned Wayne wasn't going to die, he was pretty happy to stick around."

No honor among thieves, though it kind of helped them out. Another option was pulling her from the program, but Toria wouldn't stick around if that happened. This was important to her friend, she'd feel guilty for ruining it.

"So how do we find a guy willing to jump into an already established group?" Roxie pondered. "Someone who will know what the group have done until now and be able to identify with their experience on the island? Someone who might have any kind of tiny chance of charming one of the women who already have relationships with the other guys?"

Her friend smiled slowly as Nigel did too.

"What?" Knox asked, sliding a hand into his pocket.

"We have a perfect replacement," Nigel said. "He's all of those things and has a chance of winning one of the women."

"Great," Knox said. "Who?"

Nigel smiled with a smug kind of wry amusement. "You."

"Uh, excuse me?"

"Why not?" Nigel asked. "You can join the group, everyone knows who you are. You don't have to introduce yourself or feel awkward. They've all asked about you frequently, they're curious… And you have Jane."

"Yes," he said, straightening his spine. "And you're telling me I have to date nine other women? You think she'll like that?"

"No more than you like her dating other men," Nigel said. "The timing is perfect. Tomorrow is their watershed day. They were supposed to have that talk with you in the afternoon, if you're joining the group, we'll have to cancel that. In the morning, they're filling out questionnaires about their experiences and eliminating two people from their interests."

"What?"

"Just make sure you tick Jane as one of your prospective mates and you'll be set up to spend more time with her."

"And seven others," Knox said. Nigel shrugged. "No, no way. I don't want to date seven random women."

But it actually made sense. The more she thought about it...

"That's what we've been asking the LIP members to do since they got here, date multiple people. You don't have to be intimate with any of them and most of the activities are group activities. Participants will be given the option to pair off soon. If you and Jane have made friends, you can choose each other and then there will be no more dating. If you're not a part of the group, you'll have to let her pick another man."

"What if we don't?" she asked. "Pair off?"

"Those who don't pair will be set up to date in rotation."

"Could cause waves," Knox said. "Some people's interest might not be requited."

If he was part of the group, chances were every woman would pick him.

Still, the prospect was attractive. And it would mean LIP could continue.

"Wouldn't it be good to spend more time together?" she asked, putting herself in front of Knox.

"And intimacy is allowed this week." Nigel was still trying to persuade him. "Intercourse is still against the rules, but—"

"I'm not signing your damn contract," Knox said. "And if I want to have intercourse"—he mocked Nigel's tone—"with my girl, I will. I don't care about what contract she signed either. No one will sue her for reneging."

"Of course not," Nigel said, surprising her with a smile.

"Maybe my girl's not so bad after all, huh?" Knox said. "Why are you encouraging this? It only means we'll get closer."

"You said you loved her," Nigel said, becoming serious. "I was surprised by her this morning, but I've been watching her resilience all day. She listens, she watches. I saw how she helped... She cares about people."

"Yes, she does."

"And although she's not... conventional... I don't get the impression that she's trying to manipulate you," Nigel said. "I could be wrong. The best women manage it without us seeing it coming. But I don't think I've ever met a woman who's so… genuine."

"Remember that's my friend you're talking about," Roxie said, then looked to her. "I should go find out what's keeping Toria." Jane nodded and accepted her friend's tender hug. When she stepped back, she nudged her fiancé. "Give the woman a hug."

Zairn slipped in next. "I'm sorry this happened. Truly."

"It wasn't your fault," she said, slightly awkward when he put his arms around her.

This was Zairn. Zairn Lomond. Somehow, it still felt surreal. Immediately relief settled and all her emotions rushed out in one heavy sob. And it didn't stop there. So far she'd avoided crying, but now he was holding her, she lost her reserve and the terror poured out.

"That's the medicine she needs," Roxie said. She couldn't move, just kept her face buried against him as the tears fell. "You keep her. I'll get Toria. Knox come with me."

"Come with you? But she's—"

"She'll be fine," Roxie said, rubbing her back. "You okay, honey?"

"Mm hmm," she managed to mumble, still crying.

"We'll come back soon," Roxie's voice retreated. "Love you!"

TWENTY-EIGHT

THE NEXT DAY, the doctor gave her a clean bill of health.

With LIP came breakfast and paperwork. She wasn't particularly hungry and did what was needed. With Knox's speech canceled, they got an afternoon off. Most of their group chose to spend it by the pool, she cleaned and took a nap instead.

Dinner came early. The first LIP dinner that included their new member: Knox. Even though there would be eighteen other people there, it would still be a meal they'd share.

Getting dressed while wearing a sling was difficult. Toria helped her into one of her strapless dresses. When they found it was so much easier to don, every strapless dress belonging to Toria and Roxie became hers. The latter promised to "borrow" Astrid and Merci's strapless collections too.

Their private dining space was an elevated tiki deck they hadn't used before. With a thatched roof and wooden columns, it was perfect, lost in the trees.

A server came rushing over with a tray full of coconut cups, adorned with umbrellas and sparkly straws.

"Miss Simmons," the server said, offering her the tray.

"No, thank you," she said and went to join Toria. "You have my purse?"

"I have your purse," Toria said, gesturing at it under her arm. "I won't lose it."

"I feel naked without it."

Toria leaned in to murmur. "That sure would liven things up."

"Jane! How are you?" Leanne exclaimed, interrupting to rush over and give her a hug.

Every time someone did that, she winced. Hugs were sweet, but she had to brace for the pain they brought.

Amy was right behind Leanne in the hugging line. "I'm so sorry that happened to you. Have you heard from Wayne?"

"Uh, no, I haven't."

Because she didn't carry her cellphone on the island. It wasn't even on. Maybe she should keep in touch with Wayne to check how he was doing. Except they'd never exchanged numbers. If the resort gave out his number on request, she'd be seriously concerned about security and data protection.

Ron showed up with Dale. "Hey," he said. Another hug. "How are you?"

She kept her smile broad but was beginning to feel like a zoo animal on parade. "I'm good."

"That must've been terrifying," Dale said, thankfully forgoing the hug. "Did you think you were a goner?"

"Shut up," Toria jumped in. "Geez, you ever talked to a woman before?"

"Hello, everyone!" Nigel's voice silenced the group and they turned to the stairs. Their host wasn't alone, Marty was just behind him. Knox too. Okay, so Knox was on the phone, but he was there. She'd be less interesting when a Collier was the alternative. "Dinner will be served shortly. In the meantime, drink, mingle, and we'll shout when it's time for the next stage."

As others went over to talk to Knox and Nigel, she lingered with Dale, Wayne's friend.

"How is Wayne doing? Have you spoken to him today?"

"They're discharging him tomorrow… Zairn paid all the bills, pretty cool, right? I guess he's worried about getting sued, but it was still cool he wasn't a dick about it. How long do you have to wear that sling?"

"A few days," she said.

They stood for a score of seconds before he asked, "How long is a few?"

"I don't know," she said on a laugh. "It's not painful, the doc loaded me up with painkillers and muscle relaxants. But he said it could take three or four months to get back to normal."

He winced. "Oh, that's bad. What will your boss say about that?"

Oh, uh, awkward. "I'm… between bosses at the moment."

"Right, you're living off Zairn now."

Something the whole world knew apparently. Her boss didn't need to know because she didn't have one. Her mother on the other hand…

"Would you excuse me a minute?"

"Sure," he said, holding up his drink. "We'll talk more at dinner."

Nodding, she walked backward a few paces, then swung around to weave through others to get to the guy with internet access. She smiled when people noticed her but didn't slow down until she snuck up behind Knox. At least ten LIP members vied for his attention. Nigel and Marty flanked him, acting as filters and security as needed. They gave her the cover she needed to slide a hand into his back pocket to pull out his phone.

His voice got momentarily louder as he peeked over his shoulder, but it was Marty she made brief eye contact with. Knox went back to his conversation without missing a beat.

Retreating to the shadow by the entry stairs, she opened the internet and logged into her email to send her mom a message. It was a relief not to have a boss to notify too. Writing the message took a shocking amount of time. Yes, she had her right hand, but just balancing the phone was tough without her left.

"Everyone, your attention, please!" Nigel called.

She slunk up behind Knox to slip the device back into his pocket. He didn't even flinch. Thank God, he hadn't drawn attention to her entitlement in front of everyone.

A server came hurrying over when she was a few steps away from Knox. "Miss," he said and tried to hand her a coconut.

"Oh, can I have a ginger ale?"

A second server swooped in beside the first to present her with a ginger ale filled coconut. "This is just ginger ale," the server said and murmured something to the first who wandered off.

"Really?" she asked, sipping it to find out he was right.

Glancing over her shoulder, watching the server retreat, her eye found Knox's. What was that look on his face? She didn't know but liked it. He was just hers. Considerate, thoughtful, attentive, admiring her, in love with her. Had he really said that? Had he meant it?

"Miss Simmons!" Nigel exclaimed, dragging her from Knox's ensnaring gaze.

"Huh?"

The women were gathered on one side while the LIP men were on the other.

"Please join your group," Nigel said.

"Right." She hid her embarrassment in her drink. "My group."

"What are we going to do about Wayne's spot?" Dale asked.

"I don't mind dating two of you lovely ladies," Ron said.

Was that a joke? Normally she wouldn't care if a guy were a sleaze, but Toria could end up dating any of these guys. She didn't want her best friend getting mixed up with a prick.

"That won't be necessary," Nigel said, unimpressed.

Good, hopefully that meant Nigel was clued in on who to watch out for.

Marty came up behind her and whispered right in her ear. "Are you cold?"

Turning her head toward him, it was Knox she snagged on, propped against a post on the periphery of the room.

He tugged the edge of his shirt, open over a tee-shirt and mouthed. "Want this?"

She smiled and sipped her drink, keeping her eyes as sultry as she could while whispering to Marty. "Ask him if he means the shirt or the body beneath it because they have opposing answers. If he doesn't know which is which, I'll assume he hasn't been paying attention."

Marty did back away a step but seemed reluctant. The poor guy being the proxy for their flirting, he should probably get a raise. But the young man did his duty. After another stuttering step, he went back to his boss to relay the message. Knox's smile got wider and more salacious.

"Miss Simmons!"

Again, Nigel was shouting at her.

"Yes, sir," she said, trying desperately to remember if she'd heard anything he said.

"It's ladies' choice tonight," Nigel said. "You get to pick your date. We've elected you to pick first, given all you've been through." She might get first choice every night, maybe she could play on this injury thing. "Who would you like to eat with?"

All the men were lined up like she was making a pick in gym class. Pressure. She didn't want to pick someone the other women were interested in. Stepping on toes was pointless.

"Dale," she said, nodding at him as he'd said he wanted to talk more at dinner.

Nigel glanced back at Knox, but she didn't want to look at him. "Excellent choice," their leader said and moved onto the next woman.

When her eyes drifted to Knox's, he was still smiling. Good. Oh, that was good. He wasn't judging her for the choice.

Marty came back to her. "Mr. Collier assumes there was a strategic reason for that decision."

"I can't play favorites, can I?"

And it might be a little too obvious and desperate to slather herself all over Knox. Something she tended to do when they got too close. How long would they stay secret if she was entranced by him? If she kept grabbing and kissing him mid-sentence?

Sensible and reasoned. Yes, that's what she was trying to be. Why was he smiling? He'd have to date one of the other women. Her heart sank as her belly roiled. What if he decided he liked his date more than he liked her?

Marty came closer. "You're eating dinner at the individual tables around the perimeter of the room. After, everyone will move to the central table for dessert and a getting to know you session. Like a group date. Knox ordered soup and penne pasta, both of which can be eaten with one hand. He wants to know if you want fruit salad or cheesecake for dessert."

Did this man never stop being amazing? He wasn't asking everyone else what they wanted or taking a vote, he was giving her the decision. It didn't even matter if he was doing it in response to the accident, it was still sweet.

"Cheesecake with the group," she said. Marty bowed back, but she grabbed his hand to keep him close and rose to her tiptoes to whisper. "But I want fruit later, in his room. No lights. No cutlery. No clothes. And I won't be using my hands to feed him either."

Marty swallowed hard, color brightening his cheeks. "I… I can't say that to him."

On a laugh, she sighed. Yeah, that was probably too far.

Hooking the back of his neck, she pulled Marty down to kiss his cheek. "Oh, you're a sweetheart."

"What's funny?"

She turned around to see Dale coming up beside her. "Nothing," she said. "Sorry, where would you like to sit?"

TWENTY-NINE

DINNER WAS UNREMARKABLE. The deck was circular, with two-person tables arranged around the circumference and one huge table in the middle. Couples occupied those around the edge to eat.

Knox was four tables away seated to face her. She could look right into his eyes. He was too distracting. It helped that he was eating with Toria, who it turned out picked second. She didn't want them falling for each other, but from the frequency of looks they exchanged, that didn't seem likely.

Dale was interesting, not in a sexual way, just generally. Though not as interesting as the hot guy staring at her from across the room. Damn, it wasn't discreet. Did she care? Her hormones didn't.

Nigel and Marty ate dinner together, which was sort of sweet, the older man with the body man. Oh, to be a fly on that wall. What did they talk about?

When the dinner plates were cleared, everyone was invited to the central table where candles were lit around pitchers of alcohol and decadent baked cheesecake.

"This is really good," Ron said, tucking into his dessert.

By the time everyone was served, he was finished eating. The servers moved on to filling drinks as conversation became about how they should get to know each other.

"Who's plugged into the Wi-Fi?" Dale asked. "There's this website that spits out random questions. We should try that."

"Marty," Knox said. His assistant came rushing over, typing into a tablet. The questions were benign enough. Likes, dislikes, favorites, pet peeves, they each answered a question and then someone would hit 'next' to move onto another.

"Miss Simmons?" Nigel asked, keeping a tight rein on proceedings. It was his way to control the fun, prompting and moving on, ensuring everyone got their equal turn to talk. "Your favorite food?"

"Uh…" she said, touching the rim of her glass.

"Oh, don't even pretend," Toria exclaimed, grinning. "Jane is seafood crazy." She had to concede that. "She loves all that lobster, crab, scallop stuff. I've never seen her meet a fish she doesn't like."

She nodded. "That's true I guess."

"You like caviar?" Leanne asked.

She shrugged. "I've never tried it."

"If it comes from the sea, she'll love it."

Knox leaned back and gestured to Marty. Hmm, a sign caviar was going to feature in her not-too-distant future?

The game was interesting, but not exactly riveting.

"I have a question," Amy said.

"Okay, Amy," Nigel said. "What's your question?"

Amy was grinning and bouncing in her seat like an eager toddler. "Knox, do you believe in love at first sight?"

"Wow, that's a big one," Knox said, glancing at her and then to Amy. "I didn't… until recently."

Everyone at the table whooped.

"Toria, you must make a helluvan impression," Dale said. "I haven't been on a date with you yet. Can't wait now!"

Knox looked to her as though to check she was okay. It was nice everyone assumed he was talking about Toria. If the two of them got along, her life would be easier.

"With such beautiful women around," Knox said, her eyes flicked to his, "it will be difficult to make a singular choice."

Measuring her gaze on his, she read the reassurance behind it. He was trying to calm her, using the snare of his eyes to remind her what she meant to him while begging her to relax.

"Tor, you don't seem alike," Ron said. "You and Jane."

"Shit, I could only hope to be like my incredible friend," Toria said. "She's not just pretty. She cares. She's a carer. Smart, funny… fastidious. She's patient, understanding, careful… talented… generous… And her cookies are to die for."

"I always wanted my kids to have a mom who did the cookies thing," Ron said and winked at her.

Yeah, he was a sleaze, but she smiled. "Maybe if there are supplies around, I can make something for the group. I always make too much, at least here there are people to eat it."

"She does these classes at the community college," Toria said, beaming as she spoke to her friend. "She can do loads of stuff, it's amazing what she's learned."

"What kind of classes?" Dale asked.

"Cooking," Toria said. "Cake decoration. Flower arranging. She speaks three languages and has done all these dance classes! Where do you think she got that incredible body?"

It didn't matter that everyone was impressed, Knox was the only person she saw. To her, it was his opinion that mattered most.

"Magnificent," he said, one corner of his mouth tilting.

"She does pottery too and did glass blowing for a while. She really liked that, but the teacher was a jerk who kept grabbing her chest, so she quit."

Discussion moved onto men who were grabby, and the women shared stories. It became white noise, she was still mesmerized by Knox who returned her fascination. They were on almost opposite sides of the table, in perfect position to watch each other.

She sighed.

She could admire him all day and never get bored. His strong fingers turned the base of his glass on the tabletop. Those fingers had done things to her that no other male fingers had. She missed those fingers… sliding into her, tormenting her, arousing her with their deft movement, their speed, their pressure… Her breath caught in her throat. Would she get to experience them any time soon? Her fantasies of them were nothing to the reality.

Now that he was a part of the LIP group, they couldn't sneak off together. If they were the only two who slipped away, the others would talk, and there would be no denying it. Having him in LIP gave them the chance to spend more time in each other's company, but with others around she'd see less of him… as in less of his body. Up close. Under her fingertips, her lips, her—

"Questions!" someone exclaimed.

She blinked away from his smile.

Everyone cheered on the return to the game. Somehow it fell to Amy to ask the questions. They went through first cars and pets. But the next question caused a stir…

"Craziest place you've ever had sex," Amy asked.

People laughed or made 'ooo' sounds.

Bree held up a hand. "Do we really want to talk about that? I mean our exes?"

People became more hesitant. "I don't want to hear about who you guys have screwed," Stacy said.

There was some brief discussion until Amy took control again. "Okay, how about this? We can talk about ourselves, our own preferences or what we want, but we can't talk about anyone we've been with."

More discussion and agreement was reached. Pride glowed on Nigel's face. The guy had rubbed off on them and taught the art of diplomacy.

"Knox, how do you feel about sex?" Amy asked.

Resting a forearm on the table, he shifted his weight. "In general? Providing it's consensual, I'm pro."

Amy laughed. "Do you mind talking about your preferences?"

"I'll reserve judgment for each question," he said and made a point of glancing at her. "No one has to answer any question they're uncomfortable with."

"And we all promise not to sell our stories to the tabloids as soon as we leave," Leanne said.

"He probably owns them all."

The others laughed.

Knox got serious and looked at Nigel. "I hadn't thought about that. Should I consult legal?" Everyone else stopped laughing and looked at each other like they didn't know if he was serious. Knox held for a second and then smiled. "I'm kidding, guys, we're good. I'm not going to admit to anything kinky. Isn't the point of this that my next girlfriend is sitting around this table? She's got a right to know what she's letting herself in for."

"You really think you'll date a woman at this table?" Bree asked. "Like for real?"

Knox's secret smile turned to his drink. "I really think I will."

"Is there like a sex question section?" Ron asked.

Amy checked and nodded. "Yep," she said. "Trust you to ask for that."

The ache in her shoulder distracted her from the first question. When was the last time she took meds? In the bungalow before she got in the shower. She slid her chair out and asked a server for water. He disappeared to retrieve it and she went to crouch between Toria and Knox, touching her friend's knee to get her attention.

"You okay, honey?" Toria asked.

"You have my pills," she whispered, catching Knox's thigh when she wobbled.

Toria twisted the opposite way to rummage in her purse, accidentally bumping her arm in the process.

Cursing under her breath, she buried her face near Knox's hip, hiding the pain so her friend wouldn't feel guilty.

A hand landed on the back of her head. "You okay, Blossom?" Knox murmured.

Although her teeth were digging into her lower lip, combatting the pain, she nodded. "Toria has my pills."

"You need medication?" he asked, concerned. "I can get the doc here to—"

"No," she said and touched his leg again. "Thank you."

He smiled. "I can see right down your dress."

She wanted to pinch him for teasing but grinned instead. "Then be a gentleman and look somewhere else." When his eye narrowed, his intention to do the opposite was unashamed. "Is the server here with my water?"

Knox sought him out and gestured him over.

Amy was still playing games-master. "Knox, you haven't answered the question!"

"And where's Jane?" Dale asked. "She hasn't answered either."

"She's practicing what we're preaching," Ron said on a laugh. "She's on her knees under the boss."

Is that what they believed? That she'd just had the urge to blow Knox and he went with it? Her guy wouldn't like that. He wouldn't like that at all. The only way to calm him, to dial back his rage, was to absorb and deflect with humor.

Instead of focusing on her humiliation, she grabbed Knox's hand under the table and used it to levy herself higher to peek over the tabletop and smile at the group. "I don't think he's that easy, ladies," she said. "You'll have to get him seriously drunk if you don't want him putting up a fight."

Sure enough Knox's face was hard and cold. The glare he pinned on Ron threatened to turn the guy to stone.

"You're going to have real trouble finding a date around here, buddy," Knox said. "I've seen nothing but class from the ladies. Try it sometime or move over and let the real men take care of them."

Ron's laugh faltered. Most others seemed pleased Knox had been abrupt with the man with few boundaries.

The server came from behind to hand over water. With the glass in one hand, she couldn't take the pills Toria was now offering.

"Open," Toria said.

She opened her mouth and tossed her head back when Toria scooped the pills onto her tongue. As she swallowed the water, Knox took the glass.

"Hope you didn't just roofie me," she teased.

Toria laughed and stroked her hair. "Honey, if I was going to roofie you, I'd have done it years ago, don't you think?"

She stood up. "Maybe you did."

Toria got sly, looking left to right. "Maybe I did."

"Please return to your seat," Nigel said from the other side of Knox.

Her man didn't look happy with his cousin. But he was right.

"Yes, sir," she said and left her friends to go back to her seat beside Dale.

"Everything okay?" Dale asked and she nodded.

"So, Jane, what's your answer?" Amy asked. "Oral, do you prefer to give or receive?"

"Oh, give definitely," she said without considering the question. "I hate to receive. It makes me really uncomfortable."

"Isn't it funny how many women say that?" Leanne asked. "No guy ever says receiving makes him uncomfortable."

More conversation ensued, but Nigel brought it back. "I think we have time for one more question."

Though the night was fun, she wouldn't mind getting to bed.

"Okay, last question," Amy said. "I click next and…" She read it with a frown, then smiled and eyed the group before reading aloud. "Name one place you've never had sex but would like to…"

Various answers were given with hers being the beach. They'd never done it there. Plenty of comments followed about where the seductions would be taking place once they'd paired off.

When the answering got around to Knox, it stalled. "Where?" he muttered. "Where? Where…?"

"I bet you've had sex everywhere," Amy said.

"Yeah, a guy like you must get a lot of dates," Dale said.

"No, it's just, if there was somewhere on my to-do list, I did it," Knox said, turning a beer mat onto its end. "I really can't think of anywhere."

"You've done it in all the places mentioned?" Amy asked.

Knox shrugged and pointed at Stacy. "I haven't done it on Johnny Depp's cock, but you know, he has visited the island before, so… maybe…" Everyone laughed. "But there's nowhere else I'm missing."

In all the times they'd talked about what she hadn't done, she'd never considered what he had. She'd never be a first for him. Would never take him some place he'd never been or do something to him no other woman had. She didn't like to think of herself as treading in someone else's shoes. How special could they be if they didn't have any unique memories?

The group rose from the table to say their goodbyes. Breakfast was at ten the next day, as usual. They were supposed to be rafting after, something else she wouldn't be able to take part in.

Dale was a gentleman and offered to escort her home, but she declined. Knox was kept busy with everyone trying to say goodnight.

Toria hurried over to grab her. "If we get downstairs, we can get a cart before they're all gone."

In a quieter part of the resort, there would be fewer carts. Being tired and sore, she was ready for bed. Although she glanced at Knox as she descended the stairs with Toria, he was facing the other way and didn't see her leave.

He wouldn't be mad, would he?

If she'd gone up to him in front of everyone, it would've looked desperate. And awkward. How would it go? She'd say, "*I'm leaving.*" He'd say, "*Okay.*" And that would be it. He couldn't kiss her, and she couldn't touch him. No, she'd made the right decision. It was time to go home to bed.

THIRTY

TORIA WAS QUICK to go to bed. Seemed everyone was tired, the fright of the accident took its toll on all of them. Her friend didn't deserve to be traumatized on a trip that was meant to be a positive experience. But before she'd even finished tidying up, Toria was zonked out in bed.

Her bedroom was at the end of the hall, she went inside and locked the door. It was warm. What should she wear to bed? Stripping off wasn't easy. How would she take a top off over her head? How would she negotiate a sleeve…? Nude was it. She'd only have to take off pajamas to get into the shower tomorrow morning anyway, another experience she wasn't looking forward to.

Just as she was about to lift the netting over her bed, a creak drew her attention to the window that was little more than a screen and thatched shutter. Just as she took a step toward it, a head popped into view scaring the crap out of her, until she identified it.

"Geez, Knox, you scared me," she hissed and went over to slide the screen further back as he opened the shutter and boosted up.

"Sorry, Blossom," he said, heaving himself over the sill and into her bedroom.

He didn't ask permission to close the shutter or the screen but did both. "What are you doing here?"

"You didn't say goodnight," he said, admiring her body as he came to hold her waist. "I want to spend the night."

"Here?" she asked, glancing back at her bed. "You want to spend the night with me… here?"

He smiled and kissed her. "Why not? We've slept at my place no problem. Why can't we spend the night here?"

"Toria for one thing," she said. He was already walking her backward toward the bed. "Did anyone see you come here?"

"I haven't come here yet."

His brow wiggle was enough to make her laugh and surrender.

"Okay, fine, you can stay, but you can't make a sound, okay? Not one peep. Toria sleeps heavy, but if she wakes up and finds a strange man in our room, she'll freak out. I can't do that to her. I'm freaking out and I'm nuts about you."

"I'm not that strange," he said, reaching over to pull the netting aside.

She sat on the bed, a hand on his waist. "Will you take off your shirt, please?"

He didn't hesitate to do more than that and stripped all the way down to his underwear, then tucked his thumbs into the waistband of his boxers.

"Should I keep going?"

Shaking her head, she slid back to sit in the middle of the bed. "I don't think sex is a good idea while I'm busted and broken."

He climbed in beside her and adjusted the netting to ensure it protected them. Kissing her sore shoulder, he kissed each bruise and scrape he could see on her arms. Her legs had been protected by the long pants, but she had a graze on her temple that he kissed too.

"I'm sorry I wasn't there," he murmured. "So sorry, baby."

"It wasn't your fault, it was an accident. Everyone has to stop trying to assign blame." She lay down, but felt weird, so sat up again. "You're on the wrong side of the bed."

For her injury and from the side he was usually on.

He didn't question her, just climbed over and lay down on his usual side. "I want to hold you, but I don't want to hurt you."

It took them a while to find a position that worked, but when they did, she relaxed. "I haven't set an alarm."

"There's no one looking for me at the hotel," he said. "Marty and Nigel know what's going on, they'll cover if they have to… As long as Toria stays out of your room in the morning, we'll be fine."

Toria sometimes came in to talk to her over coffee or to help her pick out clothes. If that happened, they could always hide Knox in the shower room. It was nice not to have a clock hanging over them. For a minute, she felt like they were just a regular couple… Until her clarity from earlier returned.

"I'm never going to be special to you," she said.

"Whoa, what? You're the most special person in the world to me," he said, offended. "Why the fuck would you think—"

"Not romantically, sexually," she said. "You've done everything. We'll never have anything… unique."

"You are unique and that makes everything special," he said. "And there are plenty of places I haven't had sex that I'd love to try out with you. I just didn't want everyone at the table to know it."

How he knew what had caused her insecurity was a mystery. The guy really paid attention.

"Like where?" she asked, bumping her chin on the forearm he'd wrapped around her shoulders.

"Like right here in this bungalow," he said. "I've never had sex in this bed… I've never had sex in your new Manhattan apartment, I might like to do that one day."

"You'll really visit me in New York?"

He paused. It would be amazing if he just surprised her one day. It wasn't like she'd been intimate in the Crimson HQ building either.

"Would you want me to visit?"

"I'd love that," she said, grinning. Being completely out in the open would be amazing. "Unless…"

"Unless what?"

She pressed her palm against him. "We're living in a bubble here, aren't we?" she whispered. "The accident, us, it will all be a bigger deal when we're off the island. Zairn can control who comes here, he can keep the media at bay, but…"

"You think I can't keep the media at bay?"

"I'm sure you can, I… It will be different, that's all I mean… I don't want us to hide from the real stuff. We'll have to deal with it. If you want us to be together, you'll have to tell your family."

"I'm not ashamed of this, Blossom. I'll tell them the second you're ready. I'd have told them ten times by now if you didn't insist on keeping this secret."

"You don't want to wait? To be sure this is what you want. On the island, it's like a dream, it's not always going to be this way."

"No, because once everybody knows, there won't be your place and my place anymore. No one will be *visiting* anyone."

She moved to peek up at him. "You want to live together?" He didn't respond. She sat up. "I can't. We can't."

"We can't?"

She shook her head. "I can't do that to Toria. We're losing Roxie to Zairn. I can't leave her too."

"You're not losing Roxie, you'll still be living in the same building. Z is strict about security up there. If you want to go sneak into Roxie's bed, or Toria's, in the middle of the night, no one will bat an eyelash. If Z hasn't approved your credentials already, he will when you live there." Though the point was valid, she hesitated. "When I'm in New York, I stay in the Crimson building more often than not. If I'm sleeping in a bed under the same roof as you, doesn't it make sense that bed be yours?"

In an ideal world. They'd just have to wait and see how Toria reacted when she found out about the relationship.

"I'm trying to be fair."

"I know and I'm trying to help. Isn't it better to know where my head's at?"

Than wonder? Yes, it definitely was.

She sighed. "I know nothing about the minds of men," she said and grinned. "I think you'd have figured that out by now." She yawned and settled back down on him. "Will you help me in the shower in the morning?"

"Course I will," he murmured, his voice distant as he kissed the top of her head. "Get some sleep, Blossom. Thank you for letting me stay. I wouldn't have slept for worrying about you if you hadn't let me in."

Her eyes closed and she turned her mouth against him. "Sleeping in your arms makes me happier than I've ever been," she whispered. "Thank you for being you, Knox."

"Ditto."

THIRTY-ONE

BEYOND HIS INNUENDO and need to touch her all the time, Knox was a real help in the shower. His patience shone through again as he soaped her up and rinsed her off. He went as far as to wash her hair with complete concentration despite being hard the entire time.

At one point, without thinking, she'd touched him with a curious fingertip, but he'd bowed his hips back and told her his control was already slipping. Contact would end him. That's what he said. She didn't know exactly what that meant but appreciated it with a zing of excitement.

In the closet, she picked out clothes then sat. "This feels backwards," she said, resting a hand on his shoulder as he crouched to help her into her panties.

He'd towel-dried her skin but hadn't done anything for himself. "Dressing you?" he asked. "You're hurt, we're together, helping is in the job description."

"It shouldn't be a job. We can have sex, if you want to——"

"I want you to feel better," he said. "I'm a guy who likes to get things done." He landed his hands on the bench either side of her. "Being powerless isn't something I like... I'm not accustomed to it."

"I imagine," she said and stood as he drew her dress up her body to tie it at the back of her neck. "But you shouldn't have to… you don't have to do this."

He came around to kiss her. "I want to do this."

"Will you be at breakfast?"

"Yes," he said with a shrug. "I'm part of the group now, right? Dale won't have anyone to sit with. I need to find out if he thinks he's in with a chance after your date with him last night."

She nudged him and smiled. "I think he's sweet, but there's no spark."

"Babe, if you're comparing him to me that's unfair. There's a full-blown fucking nuclear something going on between us. You might think there's no sizzle, but I don't believe there's a man alive who doesn't want you."

Leaning in, she pouted in hope of a kiss. "You're biased."

"Why? Because I'm in love with you?" he asked. There it was again. Hadn't Roxie said Mr. Right would be biased too? "I'm okay with that." He kissed her and went into the room and the window he'd snuck in. "Keep Toria in the kitchen and I'll slip out around the back, okay?"

She nodded and unlocked the door while he slid open the screen and untied the shutter. "You'll need to close this when I'm out," he said, pushing the shutter open on its pole.

Right, she'd forgotten about that and crossed to join him.

He slid both hands to her cheeks. "You're amazing, Blossom. If you don't reserve the first and last dances for me tonight, I'll clear the whole damn island before sunrise."

Compared to him, she was nothing. When he stooped to kiss her, she sank into the union like it was their first all over again.

Only being able to put one arm around him was irritating, but his dedication hadn't waned even in spite of her injured arm. His mouth was amazing, warm, inviting, trying to entice her to more. His splayed hand slid down her back, forcing their bodies tighter together. Oh, it was tempting… too tempting. How could she resist—

Someone screamed. She and Knox broke their kiss, but it took a second to register Toria in the doorway, shock written all over her face.

All of them stood completely still and quiet for a score of seconds. What was she supposed to do? She couldn't lie, she'd been kissing Knox, right there in her bedroom, first thing in the day. Could she say he'd come around early? No, because why would he and how did that explain the kissing?

"What the hell kind of pervert are you?" Toria shrieked and stormed over like thunder enroute to crash on Knox's head.

She put herself in front of him. "Don't," she said, opening her good arm out to the side. "Please, Toria, you have to listen."

"Listen?" Toria asked, anger as strong as ever though she didn't try to muscle her aside, another allowance for her injuries. "This is because of the accident, isn't it? You came here to have sex with a vulnerable woman!"

"Jesus," Knox exhaled. "Sex? Now I know where you get it from, Blossom." His focus was quick to return to Toria. "You complimented me for caring enough to sit by her bed at night in the med bay. Why do you think I did that? You think I do that for every injured person in the vicinity?"

Toria looked to her, then back at Knox. "Why did you do that?"

"Because I'm in love with her."

"Knox," she whispered over her shoulder. That might be a little full-on for Toria's introduction to their relationship. She picked up her friend's hand. "We've been seeing each other since… well basically since LA."

Toria's mouth fell open.

Her guy curled his fingers around her good shoulder and pulled her back to lean on him. "This didn't start after the accident, it started the night Roxie disappeared."

"When I went to the restroom," she said. "I ran into Knox and… I kissed him."

Toria's eyes bounced to his. "She kissed you?"

A smile bled into Knox's voice. "Like hitting me with a two by four. She got me on the hook right there."

That would soften her friend. "I'm sorry I didn't tell you," she said. "We finished it before I came to the island. It was over. You told me to be wild and… then Knox showed up and kind of helped me with that. You said we wouldn't talk about what we got up to. What would Roxie do? But it wasn't just that… I didn't want to jeopardize your place in the LIP program by involving you in my screw up."

"It's not a screw up," Knox said into her crown, giving her a reason to smile.

He was always correcting her when she downplayed what they were.

"We weren't supposed to fall for each other, babe," she said, turning her mouth to her shoulder. On instinct, his hand slid over to meet that kiss. "You know I was supposed to hook up with one of the LIP guys."

Toria gasped. "Oh my God, that's why Knox agreed to join the program? To keep it going."

"And to spend more time with Jane, yeah," he said. "I wouldn't let her out of my sight after the accident. I can't make sure she's safe if I'm not there."

Examining them, Toria deflated in an exhale. "I don't know whether to hug you both or cry."

"Why cry?"

"Because…" Toria said, linking their fingers. "In like a week, we'll be in New York, and he'll be in LA. Long distance relationships are really tough."

"We've talked about that," she said. "We're still figuring it out."

They hadn't made any decisions; there would need to be more talking.

"It's a subject that freaks her out, Toria," Knox said. "I'm trying to ease her in."

"Ease her in?" Toria asked, folding her arms.

But he wasn't intimidated. "I'm learning her rhythms and how to keep her cool."

Toria faltered. "Oh my God, that's what you were doing at the table last night with that weird staring thing. I wondered what the hell that was about." She gasped. "And, Jane, you held his hand, under the table when Ron said that stupid thing. I thought you were just being nice, saying thank you, but it was a thing, wasn't it?"

"I knew he'd be upset," she said. "He gets kind of defensive when people are negative about me or say anything derogatory."

"I'll ruin the fucker. Have the guy arrested for something," Knox grumbled, obviously still pissed. "Maybe we can find drugs in his cabin. Any dick who disrespects you gets the full Collier treatment."

"Oh, don't," Toria whined. "At least let me ride his friend first."

"You want that schmuck?" he asked with disgust. "There could be something wrong with you."

Luckily, Toria accepted the tease without getting defensive and played him right back. "Not all of us like our guys to be white knights. Some of us prefer them a little rougher round the edges."

"Well, have at it, Tor," he said. "I'm for anything that keeps guys away from Jane."

That got him another gasp. "Yeah, how have you been coping with that? Some of the guys really like you, honey."

"I talk to Knox about it actually," she said, hoping to explain there was more than just a physical attraction between them. "He's been really supportive and knows I have to take part to keep up with the program. The next few days will be tough. When people pair off? As Knox put it, there will be some unrequited attractions. If I hadn't got with him and liked a LIP guy, maybe that guy wouldn't have liked me. It would be difficult, depressing."

Toria's brows got angry.

"Uh, I didn't say that," he said.

"You told her that no other guy would like her?" Toria exclaimed. That wasn't what she'd meant to imply. "If you even think of doing anything like her stupid, slimy bastard of an ex—"

"I am nothing like Brendan," Knox barked, firing some fury of his own. "And I'd happily put my fist through the guy's face if he walked in here right now. My people are already building a strategy to ruin the fuck."

Their mutual hatred for Brendan gave them something in common, but she didn't want them exchanging too many insults.

"Knox is nothing like him."

Her friend might not have heard her, it appeared she was in shock again. "You told him about Brendan? About how he treated you?"

She nodded. "Yes, why? Shouldn't I have done that?"

Toria smiled. "Yes, you should have, I'm just surprised. You're usually so self-conscious about sharing that stuff."

"I had to tell Knox he shouldn't expect much, you know…"

He kissed her head again, brushing his lips back and forth against her. "And I have since told her it's bullshit. She has an amazing body and is fucking dynamite. I wouldn't change a goddamn thing."

Impressed, Toria's brow rose.

Her grin crept up as she shared. "And Knox makes me come."

Toria's smile got wider. "Wow, he must be doing something right."

"Lots of somethings."

That had to be enough for her friend because she leaned in to kiss her cheek, then rested a hand over Knox's on her shoulder.

"So you're together?" Toria asked, looking only at her as she nodded. "You're going to pick each other when it comes to the pair off?"

She peeked around at Knox. "I don't know. We haven't spoken about it. Are we?"

If they picked each other, the secret would be out. The world would learn about their relationship.

"Once you do, everyone will know you're together," Toria said like it was a forgone conclusion. "There would be no other reason to pick each other, unless… unless you came to some deal that would get you both out of entertaining others, but…" Her friend walked away, her fingers curling around her chin as she pondered. "There are still group tasks…" Whirling around, she pinned Knox under her gaze. "Do you know what they are?"

"If there's something specific you want to do, I can make sure things are reorganized to fit it in."

Toria grinned at her. "Go you bagging the big guns, Janey, girl," she said. "This could be fun."

"Uh, no," she said, shaking a finger at her friend as she approached. "We do not use Knox's connections and we don't let him use his connections for us. We don't do it. We don't use him for his money, for his knowledge for—"

"You've been dealing with this since day one, haven't you?" Toria leaned sideways to look past her. Knox must have nodded because her friend did too, then took her hand. "Listen, honey, it's okay to let your boyfriend do stuff for you. He won't think you're being ungrateful or grabby. Just because he does something for you doesn't mean you owe him anything. You can still tell him to go to hell if he tries to stick it in your ass or something. If he was a regular guy back in Chicago, you'd let him buy dinner or pay for a movie, right?" She shrugged. "This is the same. We use Zairn's connections, don't we? Roxie doesn't get weird when he puts his hand in his pocket. Get used to letting your guy treat you sometimes."

"Treat me or you?"

"Both," Toria said, enjoying the tease. "Oh my God…" She got serious. "How are you going to tell Roxie? Is Zairn going to be okay with this?"

"They know," Knox said, which took the burden from her.

Toria faltered. "They know?"

"Roxie walked in on us in Chicago… before we came down here."

"And Zairn?"

"Roxie told him."

Toria nodded but looked to Knox again. "Is he okay with it?"

"Of everyone in our circle, I'm one of the surest bets. We've dated friends before."

"Dated sisters before," she said.

Knox narrowed his eyes on her. "Uh, yeah."

"Maybe even dated the same woman at the same time before?"

His curiosity excited her. It was fun being on the inside.

"Well, that won't happen here," Toria said. "Zairn won't leave Roxie for anything, and Roxie is a million percent not your type, Knox."

"How do you know that?" she asked.

Toria shimmered with glee. "Because you're his type, honey. You have to be if he loves you."

"Are you pairing off, Toria?" Knox asked, coming up behind her again.

"Me?" Toria asked then shrugged. "I don't know. There are a couple of the guys I like. Unless one of them really blows me away soon, I don't think I'll be picking one guy. That's allowed, right? Finding love would be great, but if all I get is fun, I'm okay with that. Jane was the one I was worried about. If you're really a stand-up guy, I won't have to be so worried about that anymore... will I?"

"I'll take care of Jane," Knox said. "But she worries about you, which means I worry about you."

Toria glared. "That's sweet. But don't think I'll be returning the favor until I work out if you're for real. Jane has been through more than her share of shit with men. I won't let another guy tear her down. I don't care who you are or how much money you have, you are not going to hurt her and get away with it."

When Knox didn't say anything, she turned around expecting to find him angry, instead he was smiling. "Toria, you and I are going to get along just fine, don't you worry."

THIRTY-TWO

SHE WAS THE WORRIER.

Knox stayed for coffee and left with them through the front door, though he departed before their cart arrived. Accepting his goodbye kiss in front of Toria was strange but being out in the open came with a comforting relief.

Toria had a thousand questions at breakfast. Sharing with her friend was fun. The honesty was freeing and gave her the chance to ask a few questions of her own about how she should be dealing with the relationship.

Knox had breakfast with Dale and sat with his back almost to her, giving her the opportunity to spy on him without worrying he'd see her drooling.

Usually, Nigel came in to guide them, and he wasn't around yet, so no one was rushing.

With her sling's restrictions, would she be able to do any of the day's activities?

"Did you take your meds this morning?" Toria asked, picking up her coffee cup for a refill as the server passed.

"Yes," she replied. "I have to see the doctor tomorrow, I might see if he has something stronger."

"You're in a lot of pain?" Toria asked, watching the server fill both coffee cups.

"Not a lot, but if he loads me up, I might be able to get this stupid sling off."

"You hate it?" Toria asked, sipping her coffee after the server left their table. "I don't blame you. It must make Knox's job a nightmare in the sack."

All morning, she'd been teased about sex. She was still paranoid enough to keep her voice low when talking about it. "We're not having sex, how many times do I have to tell you?"

Her friend shrugged. "You're sleeping together, and you have had sex…" She frowned. "Why did you stop doing it?"

"I don't know," she said, her focus drifting to her coffee. "I think it's because we started casual. I used to say we were just sex and that upset him, so…"

"This is him proving he's real."

"Yeah, ever since the plane thing on the beach—"

"Wait! That was for you? That was him?" She shrugged at her friend who gradually grew elated. "Oh my God, he's your prince."

Warmth of hope and excitement bubbled within her. "He is romantic. Not always in the way I think of it, but… He's giving me so much more than I expected a guy could give."

"Still, he's in love with you for God sake, you have to throw him something."

She laughed. "When I'm out of the sling, I'll think about it."

"Though…" Toria said, scanning the room, maybe for listening ears. "He said he loves you… I didn't hear you say you loved him." She kept using her cup as a distraction. "Oh my God, you don't love him? But you're not having sex to prove it's not just a physical thing, or… Okay, I'm confused… Do you love him?"

Tracing a finger around the rim of her cup, she exhaled, struggling to put her thoughts in order. "He said he loved me after the accident," she said. "It was an intense moment. He was scared and I was… I was frantic. We were both emotional."

"So you think he didn't mean it," Toria said, her voice soft.

"I wonder if it matters," she said, hating herself as she looked at her perplexed friend. "He can love me, and I can love him, but our lives are so different. You said it yourself this morning, how would it ever work? He's a physical guy and I like being physical with him, but I can't fulfill all his needs long-term, we both know that."

"Sex? You think you can't satisfy him in bed?" Toria asked and growled, banging the side of her fist on the table. Most everyone else in the room turned, including Knox. Her friend didn't care, she leaned over the table, lowering her voice. "That's Brendan talking. Get him out of your head. I guarantee your new guy doesn't want your ex in bed with you."

"It's not just that. His work is… He's a powerful man. Here on the island isn't a reflection of how our lives would be. He can't walk away from who he is. His birthright."

"And you shouldn't ask him to," Toria said. "But you can work it out. Until you're ready to get married, you can do it long-distance if you want to. You have to decide where you're going to work first. If New York isn't where you want to be…"

Though the offer was in those words, they were fearful too. "I don't want to be away from you and Roxie."

"We can talk to her. Maybe she and Zairn can—"

"Rox already put that option on the table."

"There you go," Toria said, inspired. "We'll live in LA."

"I can't ask Zairn to do that. I can't have everyone move their lives across the country for a relationship that might not be forever."

"It's forever. You're a forever person, Jane. And if Knox loves you, he's thinking long term… And let's face it, your mom is going to love him."

Her mom. How would her mom react to Knox? He wasn't religious. Her mom would want her married in a church… she didn't want her daughter living in sin.

"This is crazy talk," she said, shaking her head. "He's never going to meet my mom."

Toria reached over to take her hand. "It's only crazy if you don't want it. But if you love him, you have to tell him. It doesn't matter if it's tough. You can make it work. You are capable of anything, honey. Anything at all. If you open your heart to Knox, you'll do whatever it takes to keep him, I know you. Are you telling me that he's not worth it?"

Admiring his profile again, she wouldn't ever find another man on earth who would be more worth it.

Nigel came in and clapped his hands to get the attention of everyone in the private LIP breakfast room.

"Due to the unfortunate accident…" Nigel declared, "it has been ruled too dangerous to raft today."

Some sounds of disappointment went around the room.

Oh, she squirmed. Would the others blame her for them missing out?

"Will we go another day?" Dale asked.

"Yes, it's been moved to next week," Nigel said. That was a relief. "We're going to have another beach day." Cheers went around the room, and she smiled at Toria. "Everyone return to your rooms and grab your gear. We'll meet on the shore in an hour. Carts will be waiting at each of your locations to transport you. There will be games, and a picnic lunch will be provided. Please remember, you must stay hydrated."

Nigel went to Knox and the men talked as everyone else stood up and began to leave.

"Does he have a bungalow?" Toria asked as they headed for the door, staying a distance from the back of the group.

Marty joined Knox and Nigel at the breakfast table.

"Who?" she asked, arguing with the strap of her purse.

She'd elected to wear a long-strap purse because she could hang it over her body on her good shoulder, but she had to keep it light and away from her injured arm.

Toria leaned in to whisper. "Knox. He has to stay somewhere… other than your room at night."

They reached the outer porch at the front of the hotel, and she nodded to the building at the end of the complex.

"He has an apartment down there."

"Show me," Toria said, taking her hand and pulling her two steps toward it.

Jane laughed. "No, we know he's not in."

"We don't have to go in…" Her friend was in a wild mood. "But maybe he leaves the door unlocked."

"He doesn't, it's security protected," she said, wiggling her thumb.

"With a fingerprint?" Toria asked, linking their arms. "You should get him to authorize yours. If he loves you, he can't object to you having a key to his place."

"He has authorized it."

Toria stopped leading her toward the stairs. "Then let's go!"

"No," she said, laughing at Toria's exuberance. "Why would you want to snoop in his apartment? It's so rude."

"You can tell so much about a guy from his place," Toria said. "I'm curious."

"It's perfectly normal," she said. "He does have a great coffee machine though."

"Fantastic," Toria said, grinning. "I need coffee."

She glanced backward. "We just had breakfast and there are like five coffee bars to choose from if you want coffee."

"What about his office?" Toria asked. "Have you seen where he works? Roxie says Zairn has an office. His buddy must have one too."

"No, I haven't been in his office. Why would I be in his office? His apartment is private, and the office is swarming with people." They got to the end of the porch. She paused when she saw the ice-cream cart. "You think it's too early for ice-cream?"

Toria tightened their link. "Nope."

"Do we have time for ice-cream?"

"There's time," Toria said, guiding her to the vendor. "Let's have ice-cream."

THIRTY-THREE

THEY WERE SITTING on a wall in front of the hotel, eating their ice-cream cones, when Knox started descending the porch stairs with Nigel and Marty. The men didn't notice them.

"Sometimes it's surreal to look at him," she murmured, losing herself in the wonder of him.

"'Cause he's so gorgeous and he's all yours?" Toria asked, swinging her legs.

"Yeah," she said, grinning. "That's exactly why."

Toria put an arm around her. "And what do you feel when you look at him? Are you thinking about anything except sex?"

Yes, she was thinking about how much she wanted to see him smile. How much she wanted him to hold her. How much she loved hearing his voice.

Her smile grew and she glanced at her friend. "I'm thinking I'm pissed I haven't seen his office."

Toria laughed first and she followed, flicking her tongue over the tip of her ice-cream. "Do those guys know about your relationship?"

"Nigel and Marty? Yeah," she said. "Why?"

Her friend didn't answer just inhaled and opened her mouth to call out. "Who do I see about filing a complaint?"

What was she doing? The shout attracted the attention of the three men. As soon as Knox saw her, he smiled. Did he even notice Toria was there? The foliage behind them offered shade. The solitude of their corner was the reason they picked it. Maybe they were too in shadow for him to see them both.

"So this is where the prettiest thing on the island is hiding," Knox said as he approached with Marty. Nigel loitered in the background on a cellphone. "How was your breakfast, Blossom?"

"Good, but I felt like ice-cream," she said, tipping her head back to gaze up at him. "It tastes amazing." Lifting the cone, she offered it to his lips, his smile got saucy as he licked. "What do you think?"

"I know at least one thing that tastes better," he said.

"What?"

Curling his fingers around hers, he moved the cone aside and stooped to kiss her. "You."

Flattering as it was to receive the compliment, she ducked her chin and hid herself against him. "Knox, we're outside."

"You could've eaten upstairs," he said, looking up. "There's ice-cream in the freezer... You could've called the store, they'd have sent up full buckets of whatever you're eating."

Trying to remind him of her aversion to taking advantage, she tilted her head. "The hotel employees don't know you're seeing anyone," she said like that was enough.

Knox pointed at Marty. "Call this guy, he'll get you anything you need."

"Not anything," she said, smiling at Marty. "Did you tell him about the fruit yet?"

Marty's blush was so cute. He dug his hands in his pockets while trying not to look at his boss.

"Fruit?" Knox asked. "What fruit? She wanted fruit and you said no? What am I missing? He values his job more than that."

"It's not important, don't threaten to fire him," she said. "I wasn't intending to go upstairs anyway."

Toria laughed. "I tried to get her to take me to your place, she said no."

"Why?" Knox asked, looking at her, not Toria. "My place is your place, you know that."

Another grin from Toria who was enjoying her ice-cream too much. "You'll regret saying that, boss man."

"Why?"

Toria cupped a hand around her ear to whisper. "Because after you two pair off, I'll expect you to make yourself scarce. I'll be using our place as a fuck pad to audition the guys I like."

Screwing up her face, she winced before she laughed. "Really?"

Toria's brows rose as she opened her mouth to lap up more ice-cream. "Oh, yeah."

She blinked at her ice-cream. "I think I lost my appetite," she said. Her impressive friend left her awe-struck. "I envy the confidence you have with guys. You just… do it."

"The best way," Toria said and nodded at Knox. "And you can just do it with him."

She gave her ice-cream to Knox, then clutched his upper arm to hop down from the wall. "We have to get ready for the beach and all the carts are gone… We better start walking."

"Walking," Knox said. "Ha, my injured girl, walking." He nudged Marty. "You hear that joke?"

Toria laughed, Marty too.

"I can walk," she said. "My legs are fine."

"They are fine, baby. I can vouch for that, I've seen 'em up close. They're real fine," he said and lowered, but she backed away before he could kiss her. "Right, no kissing, sorry."

"As soon as you pair off, he'll be all over you like a rash," Toria said, sliding down off the wall. "Once you're public, you won't have to worry about boundaries."

Would that be liberating or terrifying? What would happen? Would the world learn about them? Would there be reporters? She'd seen Roxie deal with that. By proxy, it was fun. The idea of experiencing it firsthand was more than a little daunting.

"Did I leave my purple sarong at yours?" she asked Knox, trying not to focus on what would be for fear it would freak her into a ramble. "I think I did, I had it the night I grabbed my kaftan thing… maybe I should wear the kaftan today? The sun is going to be at its peak while we're on the beach… I tan, but I don't want to get too tanned, you know, and it's dangerous, the statistics of—"

"We're going into meltdown mode over here," Toria said, putting an arm around her. "Please excuse my friend."

"Your friend is magnificent," Knox said.

She looked at Toria and then at him. "I didn't mean to do that."

"It's okay, I implied something sexual," Toria said. "It was my fault."

Sex made her uncomf—no, it wasn't that. It wasn't the sex talk that made her uncomfortable, it was asking Knox to restrain himself when in fact, that was the last thing she wanted him to do.

Her gaze landed on him, focusing hard until he smiled. "Why are you looking at me like that, Blossom?"

"I want to have sex with you," she murmured. Everyone else seemed to pause. "I mean, I actually want us to be… I don't want you to restrain yourself… I'm not afraid."

Knox took the compliment to mean he could hold her.

Toria cleared her throat. "I think that's a cue for the rest of us," she said and gave Marty a poke.

She hadn't meant that minute and wriggled from her guy's embrace to link her arm with Toria's. "We have a date at the beach," she said, unable to take her eyes from Knox's. "We'll see you there?"

"Bet your beautiful ass you will, babe," he said and again tried to kiss her.

Laughing, she dodged the kiss and pulled Toria away.

Marty went with them and held up a set of keys. "I'll drive you guys," he said like it was a completely spontaneous suggestion.

Yeah, right, it was Knox's doing. No doubt about it.

THIRTY-FOUR

MARTY WAS STILL OUTSIDE waiting for them when they came out of their bungalow in swimwear with their beach bags. Toria had talked her into wearing a short sarong. Something had happened to her modesty on the island, it was slowly dwindling.

Everyone else was already gathered when they arrived at a new, smaller, beach. Flags flapped out on the water again, much further out than last time. Her neck prickled.

The groups were mingling, male to female. As she and Toria approached, Nigel waved his hands.

"Thank you everyone for being punctual," he called out.

Leaning in, she whispered to Toria. "Are we late?"

"Right on time."

Nigel was training the group, even if he didn't realize it. He stood on a rock with Knox just below him. Marty left them to go join his boss.

Nigel cleared his throat. "We have some sports activities planned today. We'll have sand races, some volleyball, and a water relay. We also have Frisbee and kites and will have a sandcastle contest after lunch." The suggestions went down well. She wouldn't be able to take part in most of them, but they would be fun to watch. "I'm sure you've noticed there are flags on the water again. Since our swimming race worked so well the last time, we are going to do it again. This time our men will swim for the privilege of joining our ladies for dinner and dancing tonight in a private banquet hall." The men seemed into the idea like they'd suggested it to show off their prowess. Worry crept in. "As usual, before I will allow any games to begin, I will remind you all to stay hydrated and insist everyone wear sunscreen and top it off throughout the day. Please, apply it liberally."

He was about to step down from the rock when someone called out. "Can we touch the ladies now?"

On their first beach day, Nigel had insisted on same-sex contact only.

On that day, he nodded. "With their permission, of course."

"Watch this, I'm off to find Mikey," Toria said then paused. "Oh, but you're—"

"Go have fun," she said.

Toria kissed her cheek and scampered away.

Taking sunscreen from her bag, she ignored the squall of women around Knox and went straight to Nigel. "Will you help me?" she asked, approaching his profile.

He turned, clearly surprised she was there. "You… you want me to help you?"

She nodded and followed his gaze to Knox surrounded by women asking for help and offering to slather him up.

"I need someone gentle who won't make it about sex," she said, holding up the bottle. "Please."

They moved away from the group and around the edge of the rocks, concealing them from view of the others. She didn't want to be on show. While he squirted some cream onto his hand, she scooped her ponytail out of the way.

Her shoulder should be fine, right? Sometimes she didn't feel a thing, then contact would be made and agony would burst through her. Nigel really took his time applying sunscreen to her shoulder, her arm and her neck in all the places it was visible around the sling. Where he could, he put it underneath.

"I have to say Miss Simmons," Nigel said, giving her back the bottle as he rubbed sunscreen on her uninjured shoulder and arm. "I have been very impressed with the way you have conducted yourself."

"Thank you," she said. "Conducted myself in what?"

"In your relationship," he said, holding out a hand for more cream before moving to her lower back. "I have seen Knox with a lot of women through the years and most of them don't have your… reserve. Today, for example, you saw how the other women responded to him, but didn't cause a scene or make him uncomfortable. You carry yourself with grace and, as far as I know, you never blame him for how others treat him."

"If I'm honest," she said, pleased they were talking about her relationship and not the accident. "I don't like it when he touches other women, when they cozy up to him, but… I'm aware he's an attractive man. He's rich and successful, eligible. Women are always going to desire him, and, to an extent, he has to be polite. He represents his brand. Business depends on him not alienating people."

Nigel moved in front of her, his hands creamy, and blinked at her décolletage. "I believe you can reach…"

She smiled. "Yes," she said. "Can you help with my legs? Bending is tough on my arm."

"Of course," he said and took more cream before squirting some into her hand and putting the bottle in the sand. "You are level-headed, practical, I like that. You are a reasonable woman, and Knox hasn't always attracted those."

"I take that as a compliment, sir," she said, applying the cream to her breasts and neck as well as her face. "I always thought you didn't like me. In Knox's apartment, when you found out about us…"

"I was rude," he said. "But, as I tried to explain, it's important for me to look out for Knox, family is important."

"I know that," she said. "And I appreciate it. Loyalty is important."

Still crouched in front of her, Nigel looked up, and said nothing.

She had cream left in her hand and intended to ask what she should do with it.

Before she could, a new male voice joined them. "I'm not going to tell you how seeing this creeps me out."

Knox approached around the end of the rock.

She smiled. "You work fast."

"Me?" Knox asked, waving a finger at Nigel. "I turn my back for two seconds and you make your move on my girl? I think he's the fast worker here, baby."

"Knox," Nigel said, rising, rubbing his hands together. "She requested my help."

Knox's teasing menace turned on her. "You like your men mature, Blossom?"

"I needed help," she said. "And you were busy."

"Not too busy for you."

When he got to her side, she smeared the rest of her cream on his chest and sighed, envying the women who'd creamed him up. "How did you do all those women so fast?"

"Do?" he asked with an impish grin. "I set them up in a human chain."

So he hadn't done them, he'd made them do each other. Instead of rubbing in the cream she'd smeared on him, he took her hand, spread it on his torso and made her do it for him.

"Stop it," she said and tried to pull away.

"You're nervous 'cause it feels so good."

"Stop playing with the girl and help her," Nigel said, taking the sunscreen from the sand and slapping the bottle on his chest. "I didn't finish with her legs."

Nigel stalked off and she kind of wished he hadn't. Now she and Knox were alone, but only ten feet from the others. Lowering to sit on a rock, she stretched out her legs and he dropped onto the sand beside her.

He squirted out way more cream than he needed and started at her ankle, moved higher, over her shin, around her calf, then massaged over her knee.

The heat of his hands and the ease of their movement was making her weak. The sensation of those fingers sliding and caressing was difficult to tolerate at the best of times. Now all she wanted to do was moan and let her head fall back. She had to divert, to find some other focus before she threw herself at him.

As his hands slithered up her thigh and beneath her sarong, she caught his wrists. "I don't want you to swim," she said.

The idea of him going out on the water and never coming back filled her with a terror she couldn't ignore.

"Swim? Why not?" he asked. "You don't have to worry about me dating other women, Blossom."

"It's not that. It's dangerous," she said, clasping his shoulder as he crawled over to slather cream on her other leg. "What if something happens to you out there?"

He stopped with the cream to show his concern. "Is this about the accident? You're worried that because one thing went wrong that other things will too? I know it hasn't been your experience, but the island's safety record is—"

"It's about me not wanting to lose the man I love," she said, pulling herself closer as comprehension slipped onto his features. "Knox, I feel like I've waited my whole life to spend this vacation with you. I'm absolutely terrified something horrendous will happen to blast this dream apart."

Something about the way his smile crept higher made her think he hadn't really been listening, to the last part at least. "You love me."

"That's all you heard?" she asked, trying to be stern and failing. "I'll love you a lot less if you swim out into the ocean and get eaten by a shark."

"Don't worry, I plan to be in the middle of the pack," he said. "Swimming is kind of my thing and I've been doing it in waters like these since before I could walk." His grin burst again. "And now that I know I've got your heart, I don't plan to abandon it."

"No one plans on getting hurt," she said, digging her nails into him. "Please, baby, stay on the sand with me."

But he didn't look like he was going to acquiesce. "How would we explain that?"

"I don't know, say the insurers won't cover you or something."

"That will go over real well with the guys."

"And is it their admiration you want or my trust?" she asked. "You're going to swim out all that way for a date with another woman, I mean, what if you die with Stacy's name in your hand?"

He frowned. "Which one's Stacy?"

"The blonde with the silicone implants," she said.

That didn't help. "There are a lot of women out there with implants."

Her head tilted. "And just how do you know that? Nobody asked me about my breasts when I checked in."

He smiled and slid his hands higher under her sarong. "I would've if you'd let me."

"I don't want those hands on me," she said, trying to push them away with her one good hand. "Not if they've been all over every set of LIP implants."

"Yeah, that's where they've been," he said, sitting back on the sand. "You can tell by eye. Dale was telling me at breakfast how many of the girls had been confirmed as implants." Then he shrugged. "It's something guys talk about."

Fake or real, lovely, but it did beg the question. "Did you talk about me?"

"Did I talk about your breasts?" he asked, his brows almost shooting off his head. "Why the hell would I talk about your boobs with some guy I don't know?"

"So you'd have talked about them if you did know him?"

He peered at her. "Are you trying to start a fight with me?"

"Why would I do that?"

"I don't know," he said. "But you're pissy. I wouldn't talk about your tits with any guy… or girl for that matter. I don't talk about our intimacy with anyone but you. You talk about it a lot more than I do, you seem happy to talk to anyone about what we do in private."

Her mouth opened, was he really throwing that back in her face? "You know why I do that! I don't mean to talk about it, sometimes things just spill out of me. I don't have good impulse control. You've known that since the day we met."

"You talked about it with Toria," he said, rising onto his feet, brushing the sand from his legs and hands. "And RK… Haven't you?"

"That's different, girls talk about that stuff," she said, struggling to get up, but refusing his offer of help. "And I've never said anything negative. I'm proud of how far I've come with you, and it hasn't been an easy journey. Toria knows that I've struggled with men. You should be happy for me. I could've shut this down on night one, but I let you in and now you're telling me that you're talking about my breasts with strangers."

Stepping in close, his voice became an aggravated hiss. "I didn't say that. I said he was talking about it. In fact, he mentioned you and said no guy could confirm or deny because they hadn't gotten close enough to touch you… I was proud of you for that."

"And then you told him you had?"

Knox growled. "No, why the fuck would I—"

"The race is about to begin." Nigel stood a few feet away, scowling at them. "Knox, you have to join the men."

"I'm talking to Jane," he said, his attention snapping back to her.

But she wasn't going to fight with him, not there, not like that.

She marched past to head for Nigel. "Actually, we're done. Thank you, Nigel. Knox would love to take part in the race so he can grab himself a pair of fake breasts, since those are his preference."

Shock took Nigel aback. "You asked her to get breast enhancement surgery?"

"What?" Knox squawked, still behind her, probably where she'd left him. "No! What the fuck? No!"

But she didn't wait to finish the fight, she went around the rocks and was pleased to see the group had moved further down the beach. While the men lined up, the women stood behind them, stroking and cooing.

Most of the women moved between men, sharing the love, but there were pairs forming. Bianca stayed with George, Jodi with Victor, and Wes held Susan's hand. How would things change when people were allowed to pair off officially and show affection? If they got three couples out of this program, it would be a success, in her view.

The eager men chomped at the bit. Nigel and Knox came around the rocks to join them. She was staying back, behind the others. Toria had noticed her snit but was stroking Mikey. That was fine, she didn't want to talk about pig-headed Knox anyway. When he stormed over to the men, his glare was so fierce even the women thought twice about approaching him.

"Women step back," Nigel declared, angry too. "Now, please!"

He could go out there and get himself killed. Her heart was pounding. She wanted to reach out, but Nigel counted to three and the men raced into the water.

THIRTY-FIVE

MUCH LIKE BEFORE, the women ran into the shallow tide to call to their men. Frozen on the spot, she watched Knox's head rise and fall in time with his strokes. He took a clear and early lead, maybe he'd been right about his skill level.

Nigel came up beside her, but she couldn't take her eyes from Knox. "If you care about him, you have to trust him."

"I love him," she said, keeping her gaze focused as her fingers curled around her throat. "Oh, God, I love him so much…" He cut through the water with nothing but finesse. That ability reassured her heart enough that she smiled. "He's amazing… I wish my emotions didn't drive me to be so crazy around him, but they do. I was so scared I would lose him."

"And now?" Nigel asked with curiosity.

She took one step. "Now look at him go," she said, flinging her good arm around Nigel. "I don't even care if he comes back with another woman's name, that's my guy out there. My guy."

Pride was exhilarating. A ball of adrenaline formed in her throat, sending a web of need through her torso to twang against her core. Knox was out there, capable, strong, fast. He was already lunging up to grab a flag while the other men were trailing behind him.

Nigel said something she didn't hear as she rushed forward to slide in beside Toria.

Her friend glanced at her and smiled. "Looks like someone already got his girl."

Knox was on his way back. Most of the other men were still trying to get to the buoys. He slowed and stopped to watch the other guys grab their flags. Maybe he was worried about outshining them and chose to stay with the group. She hoped it was that and not that he was tired. He'd want to make sure no one got into difficulty, which may be why he stayed behind until the very last man grabbed his flag. Only then did he start back to shore.

Taking care of the guests wasn't exactly his job, but he cared about his friend, about Zairn's success. After her accident, it was possible he wanted to avert another. Maybe he kept an eye on the pack just because he was a good man. It didn't matter who was first anyway, he'd grabbed a flag. No one was recording finishing positions.

The other men tramped onto shore, claimed their women, and registered their names with Nigel before collapsing on the sand to lap up some TLC.

She was the last woman standing on the edge of the water when Knox strode from the waves like an Adonis, his flag secure in his hand. They'd been fighting, he'd be within his rights to completely ignore her. But in spite of his glare, he came to meet her when she rushed into the surf and put her arm around him.

"I'm sorry," she whispered on him and was pleased when he squeezed her. "I get crazy when I'm scared."

His lips found their way onto the top of her head, and he crouched to pick her up to carry her back onto shore with one arm. "There is no other woman," he said, slipping his flag into her cleavage. "And there never will be."

"I didn't even care whose name you got," she said, wishing she could do more than let him carry her to her beach bag.

A towel had been laid out beside it. Knox's? Marty must've set it up, but it didn't matter.

Knox crouched to seat her on it, then leaned back to look in her eyes. "I don't leave your safety or happiness to chance," he said and nodded at his flag between her breasts. "You want a drink? Marty!"

As they waited for his body man to approach and take the drinks order, she took the flag from her cleavage and opened it. She already expected it to say her name as she had been the only woman left on shore, but tears came to her eyes when she read it.

"You knew which flag to grab," she whispered more to herself than to him, "that's why you raced out there so fast."

"Don't give me grief for cheating, Blossom, Nigel made a good point about—"

"Thank you," she said, finding his gaze, smiling slowly. "Cheating is wrong, and I don't normally support it, but I need to be with you tonight, Knox. I just… need you."

He lay on his side on the towel, propping himself on an elbow. Their position had been set up further away from the group, nearer the rocks. Everyone else had split into couples or small groups and didn't notice anything weird about them, maybe. She was too mesmerized by her guy's eyes to care right that minute.

"Toria asked if we were going to claim each other," Knox said. "In the pair off."

"Is this us talking about whether or not we're going to write each other's names?"

"I'm going to write your name, I've known that since before I agreed to do this," he said, tracing a circle on her knee with his fingertip. "I'm bringing it up because Nigel made a good point to me before the race. If we're going to be exclusive, it can't be a shock to the rest of the group. I've been… frustrated, that I can't be around you, that I can't be tactile. We can't be full-on together in front of the others, but it's not a crime to prioritize you."

"I don't understand."

"I was in a mood and didn't realize it. When all those women came to me about the sunscreen thing, I got pissed off. It was tough not to show it. I knew you'd need help, I wanted to be the one to help you, and you're the only woman I want putting her hands on me… I thought I had to take it, but I don't. The LIP group is getting closer, Nigel says he's noticed couples forming. Even though they're not supposed to be explicit that's a natural part of the process. The point is, Blossom, you are my priority and it's okay if the group notices. Maybe I can't kiss you, but I can ask you to dance, pick you for dates, and I can do my damndest to impress you… It's what guys do. If I had just come into this competition and decided you were the girl I wanted, I wouldn't be anywhere near another woman. I'd be making it clear you're the only one I want, not only to you, but to the other guys."

Marty came over with drinks and she was pleased to sip the refreshing iced ginger-ale.

"Do you want wine in it?" Marty asked her.

She shook her head. "No, I might have one tonight, but only if the boss is around, okay? Don't let anyone else take me home, I don't know how alcohol will mix with my meds."

"He's been on strict orders not to let any other guy near your bungalow since you got here," Knox said.

She gave his shoulder a shove when he leaned in. "Are there strawberries on the lunch menu?"

"There are now," Knox said, turning his eyes up to Marty who nodded and scuttled off.

She shook her head. "You shouldn't do that," she said, but was getting used to his generosity. "I was making conversation." Twisting her glass into the sand, she wriggled down onto her back and closed her eyes. "I love the way the sunshine feels on my body."

"I love your body," Knox said.

She smiled when he dipped his fingertip into her belly button. "Are there any nude beaches on the island?"

His finger stopped circling her navel. "You can go naked at Plunder Cove… if I'm around."

He was a dork, in the most wonderful way. "Toria asked me, and I said I didn't know. Really?" She twisted her head toward him, though her eyes didn't open to much beyond slits behind her shades. "You thought I wanted to take all my clothes off outside?"

With his weight braced on an elbow, he dipped toward her. "I thought I was maybe living a fantasy."

She caught his shoulder before his mouth got too close. "You're just through saying you can't kiss me."

Maybe he'd forgotten, but he stalled. "Uh, yeah, I wasn't going to kiss you… I was just exercising."

He pushed forward and back in a side push-up five times.

She laughed. "If we had another towel, we wouldn't have to lie so close to each other."

"Why do you think we brought just one?"

"In a resort of this size, located on an island surrounded by water, I'd think there would be more than one towel?"

"You would think, wouldn't you?" he asked. "I should probably talk to someone about that."

Interest tempted her closer. "Did Nigel say who he thought would pair up?"

"He might have mentioned some names."

Lying on her back was uncomfortable on her arm and it was beginning to ache. "Is your tee-shirt around?" she asked, though she hadn't seen him in one, maybe he hadn't brought one with him.

"Yeah, hang on." Rolling to his back, he stretched away from her and then came back a second later to hand over his tee-shirt. "You need help putting it on?"

She shook her head and began to fold it on her body using one hand. "No, I just need something to support my elbow.

He scooted onto his back. "Use me, like last night."

"I can't do that," she said, it was sweet of him to offer. "And we were more spooned last night, I was kind of half lying on top of you."

"I don't mind," he said. Although he was smiling, he meant it. "You need to do what will make you most comfortable. Your health is the most important thing."

"Yeah, I'm sure the rest of the group will buy that," she said, trying to tuck his tee-shirt under her arm. Knox rolled it tighter and helped to slide it in. "Once word gets out that I need to lie on men, I might get other offers."

"Good point. Let's not do that," Knox said. "But another towel will be more comfortable."

"I thought there were no more towels."

"No more towels to lie on. As supports for your arm, we have a bunch of those."

Lying on him would be her ideal. She wished he could kiss her, and they could just be themselves out there.

Unfortunately, she'd have to bide her time until that was possible. "Who did Nigel say would pair up?"

"I can't tell you that."

"Wes and Susan are obvious," she said, ignoring his teasing refusal. "George and Bianca too."

"If you know the answers, why did you ask?" he asked, locking his fingers behind his head.

She couldn't lie on her side but did turn her head toward him. "You know, I can't play volleyball or Frisbee... I've never flown a kite though, that might be fun. What's a water relay?"

"Exactly what it sounds like," he said. "We put a basin of water at one end of the beach and an empty basin at the other. Then everyone has to find something to transport the water in. You scoop up the water from one end and carry it to the empty basin. The first team to fill their basin, wins."

"We should play that one first," she said.

"Why?"

"Because when guys get drunk, they get stupid. Someone will end up peeing in their basin or something."

Knox laughed. "Yeah, I've seen that before... I can't believe you've never flown a kite. There are some amazing stunt kites at the hotel. We do kite surfing sometimes, that's fun... I wouldn't let you do it with one arm though."

"There are a bunch of activities at the hotel I haven't tried yet. And I'd love to go back to the spa. Nigel should factor a spa day into our itinerary."

"I'll make sure he does," he said. "I can give you a full-body massage any time you want. No charge."

She grinned and tipped her face to the sky. "You're so generous, Mr. Collier."

"Hey, what did Toria whisper to you outside the hotel earlier when you were eating ice-cream? That was kind of rude," he said. "By the way, I don't mind you talking about our sex life with a friend like Toria. You trust her, she's been there for you."

"What about Roxie?"

"From experience, I know she's not shy about discussing her sex life. If you trust your friends, I trust them."

"Zairn trusts her too. And he trusts you."

"That's a lot of talking about sex. Hope you're proud of how far we've come together."

"We haven't come together in a while," she said and raised her shades to make eye contact with his devouring gaze. "In too long."

"We will, Blossom, don't worry your pretty head about that... What did Toria say?"

"That after we pair off, she wants me out of the bungalow," she said and touched her fingertips to his hand resting on her belly before he could get mad. "Not in a bad way. It was a joke about me making myself scarce so she could use the bungalow as a fuck pad."

"Ah," he said and turned onto his side, supporting his head on a curled arm. "She wants you to move in with me, that's why she said it in context of my place being your place."

She nodded. "Something like that, I guess."

"We've been sleeping together at night anyway. Now our friends know about us, we don't have to hide."

"The LIP group doesn't know about us, and you have a guys' night tomorrow."

"I do?"

"Yes," she said. "Because I have a girls' night. The following night we're supposed to have a cookout on the beach and sleep under the stars."

"Wait, we what?"

"Everyone on the beach," she said. "It's like camping, that's what Nigel said."

"I have to sleep with you and eighteen other people?"

"Nineteen I guess if Nigel is staying with us," she said. "Or twenty if Marty is with us too."

"Hmm… I don't like that."

"After that we have a free day. We're only supposed to see our roommate, you know, the person we came with. No other LIP contact. I guess that's because they want us to have a chance to relax, think, and talk to our real-life friend before the big decision the next day."

"What big decision?" he asked. "And how the fuck do you have all this memorized?"

It was embarrassing, but she had to be honest about the reason. "I don't remember the day itineraries. I remember the night stuff because I tried to plan how we might see each other. I think we should sleep at the bungalow as much as we can before decision day. I don't want Toria to be alone down there."

"Decision day?" he asked again.

"When we pick who we want to pair with," she said. "It's a big decision. Some people might be struggling with it. We're not just deciding who we want to be with here, we're deciding if there's anyone we might want to keep seeing. Anyone we want to start a real relationship with."

"We?" he asked. "Is that what the rest of the group are deciding or what we're deciding?"

Was he worried?

If only she could roll onto her side to see him better. "I'm not picking anyone else," she said. "I haven't bonded with any of the guys in LIP. You should know that. You're the only guy I want to be with."

"But is it real?" he asked. "Toria was quick to say we'd never work out. That pissed me off."

They couldn't have that conversation on the beach with everyone else so close by and a list of activities on the cards.

"I don't think either of us can know how this will work out when our time here is up."

"You want to move to the island, we'll move here…" Another flight of fancy. It would be so easy to get swept up in him. In them. "Have you thought about it? About what you want from me… long-term?"

That was a big conversation, she took a deep breath. "I'd be lying if I said I hadn't," she admitted. "But I also have to say, I've tried not to think about it too."

"Why? Why don't you want to think about it?"

"I'm only here for a limited time," she said. "I only have nine days left… Sometimes it feels like our relationship is on this clock. Every minute I love spending with you is a minute closer to the one I'll have to leave you."

His serious eyes searched her. "You're right."

"About what? You think this will never work out?"

"No, that we shouldn't think about it now. Why the fuck do you keep saying it will never work out?"

He was offended again. Pissed, just like he was about Toria's assumption. "I think… I'm scared to let myself believe it, to give myself to what I feel because… I've never had luck with men and—"

"It only has to happen once," he said and sat up, a sure sign he was angry.

When he was angry, he got tense and he couldn't lie down when he was tense.

"Then tell me what you're thinking," she said. "Tell me how you see this working out. Help me believe… please?"

When he turned to look down at her, he didn't come out with a detailed plan. He opened his mouth, then closed it again. It was easy to get mad, easy to be offended by other's assumptions, but it was harder to sit quietly and face the truth.

Love wouldn't be enough to get them through, they would have to decide to be together and come up with a plan. Without one, they would drift apart and that would be harder to face than a harsh clean break.

THIRTY-SIX

"I'M LOOKING FORWARD to this," Toria said as they hopped out of the cart at Roxie's. "A girls' night is overdue."

"Roxie will know where the guys are, won't she?"

"Yeah," Toria said, taking her arm to start them down the path. "Not that you should be thinking about your lover boy tonight."

"I'm not thinking about Knox." The blush in her cheeks probably said otherwise. "The two groups might run into each other if we don't know."

But, yeah, that was only part of the reason. They'd seen each other that afternoon and been forced to go their separate ways for dinner. He might have offered to come to the bungalow to eat, but Toria had her process for getting ready, so she had to decline. Going through their routine was fun. Having Roxie around would've made it better.

Toria opened the door and in they went. Music played quietly; the lights were low. And there was Roxie on the deck, wrapped in Zairn's embrace, moving to the music.

They stopped. As her feels flourished, she bet even Toria swooned.

They stood there, saying nothing so as not to break the mood. That there was love. Security. Forever. That was what it looked like.

Until the door behind them opened and someone came striding in.

He stopped short. "Blossom?"

She turned to him as Toria walked toward the deck.

"Is Zairn joining your group tonight?"

"Yeah, we were meant to meet at mine, but I got a call—"

"Thanks for coming down," Zairn's words brought her attention back around.

"What's going on?" Knox asked, sliding a hand onto her good shoulder.

Zairn and Roxie were coming back from outside. Toria stood in the central sunken seating area.

"Everyone should sit down," Zairn said, guiding Roxie's hips to keep their bodies together as he sat.

Toria sank into the loveseat. "Oh my God," she said, gushing excitement. "This is it, isn't it?"

"I'm not pregnant," Roxie said, bursting everyone's bubbles. "Don't hold your breath for babies. I still have a lot of the world to see. Zairn has promises to keep."

It was as Roxie turned a smile to her fiancé that his serious expression provoked hers. Usually, they teased and played, but it was like seeing Zairn's solemnity reminded Roxie to be severe.

"No one's breaking anyone's confidence here," Zairn said, looking at them. "You two are in, right?"

"With each other?" Knox asked, directing her down to sit on the long couch perpendicular to Roxie and Zairn's. "Yeah. What's this about?"

Zairn's attention moved to her. "You trust everyone in this room?"

"You're scaring her," Roxie murmured, coiling her arms around the one Zairn had across her lap. "I told you I should do it."

"Go ahead," Zairn said, relaxing.

Roxie took over. "Graham's in Nassau." The air rushed from her lungs. "You don't have to be scared. You're safe here. He'll never set foot on this island."

"Oh my God," Toria gasped. "London Guy is a psychopathic homicidal stalker!"

"She's safe."

"Here," Toria screeched. "What's she supposed to do? Live here forever? As soon as she leaves the island, she's vulnerable—"

"Ballard and Tibbs are on their way," Zairn said. "Stone and his people arrive tomorrow."

"They're amazing, honey," Roxie said. "The best of the best."

Graham. "Are you sure it's him?"

"We're sure," Roxie said. "Z's had people on him since he landed in New York."

"You think he was looking for her there?" Toria asked. "Oh my God. Oh my God!"

Her friend freaking out didn't help. Graham was waiting for her. Like an ominous cloud hanging on the horizon ready to consume her.

Her hand found Knox's and he locked their fingers together.

"Maybe he's… maybe he's on vacation… maybe it's a coincidence."

"Z's people know what they're doing," Roxie said. "They checked that out. He's been scouting for a way onto the island."

"Crimson Isle?" Toria asked, Roxie nodded. "The guy is deranged. We can't let him get to her. God knows what he wants… What's going to happen when he finds out she's seeing someone? What if he's jealous? What if he gets angry?"

"You're not helping, Tor," Roxie said. "We'll look after her. We're going to do this together."

"Okay," she said, trying to quiet her anxiety. "Okay… This is fine." She stood up. "Are you ready, Rox?"

"Ready?" Roxie asked and looked at Toria then back to her. "You want to go out?"

"I'm safe on the island," she said. "I'm safe here… and we don't know Graham means any harm. If I talk to him—"

"You won't talk to him," Knox said, rising at her side. "He'll never hear your voice again."

"Don't bully her," Toria said. "We make decisions together. Support each other. We don't dictate and command—"

"You want her to talk to him?"

"No!" Toria said, flying to her feet. "Did you hear me say that?"

"I hear you bitching at me when we should be fighting the threat!"

"We are," Roxie said, leaping up before Toria could reply. "All we care about is keeping her safe!"

The three of them yelled more at each other. Disoriented, in some state of shock, she couldn't hear the words. Zairn watched her. Calm. Unmoving. Assessing the scene, or rather her in it.

What did all this mean? Would there be an incident if she left the island? Would someone get hurt?

Taking Zairn's side nod as direction, when he got up to leave the room, she followed. They went down the hall and into his and Roxie's bedroom.

"Need a drink?" he asked when she closed the door.

He took the stopper from the crystal decanter on the corner of the dresser.

He glanced back over his shoulder to see her nod.

Normally, she didn't drink Scotch, but the liquid enticed her closer.

He poured three fingers into two glasses and handed her one before going to open the sliding door to the side deck.

"I love Roxanna more than she realizes," he said, gazing down the beach to the water beyond. "I love her more than I realize most of the time."

"You're lucky to have each other."

"We are," he said, swigging some Scotch while extending an index finger to the patio chairs with a table between. They both sat. "Knox is loyal. Loyalty means everything to him."

"I know his heart is in the right place. Toria and Roxie are used to jumping in for me, protecting me. They're scared. Everyone will calm down when the shock clears."

"Are you shocked?"

"Graham's messages were full on… My cellphone has been off since we got here. I don't know what he's sent recently."

"That may be why he got on a plane."

"Maybe he was worried about me?"

"Or didn't want to lose you. I can't tell you whether this guy is deranged and wants to hurt you. Until we know for sure, we have to assume the worst. Better to prepare for that and be wrong…"

"Than think the best and be surprised."

"Ballard is thorough. Stone's people have protected Roxie, I wouldn't risk your safety, Jane. We're family now… and always will be."

Oh God, and now she might cry. Rather than look him in the eye, she gulped the Scotch.

Too much. Pain. It burned her throat and she coughed.

"I promised myself I wouldn't drink tonight," she wheezed, her eyes watering. "On painkillers, without Knox around—"

"You're safe here… and you're entitled to a drink given what's going on."

They'd never really talked, just the two of them. "You must know him well. Knox?"

"I do. He likes to fix things, like a lot of us do. And Colliers are heard. They're not diplomats, they're dictators. In the nicest meaning of the word. Don't judge him on his reaction tonight. He's scared, just like I would be if Rox was in this position."

Licking her lips, she looked down into her glass. "Roxie says it doesn't mean anything. That the money doesn't mean anything." Their eyes met. "Would you give it up for her?"

"Every cent."

He hadn't even paused for breath. Why when Zairn said it about Roxie was it romantic? But for that devotion to be turned on her…

"He's an incredible man. The best lover I ever had. Smart. Kind. Funny… But when he mentions staying in New York with me…" her gaze dropped again. "Sorry, I shouldn't be—"

"It's a different mindset. Rox says it takes time to adjust. Still sometimes she forgets… Nothing is undoable. Knox could move to New York, you fight and break up a week later, and he can hop a jet back to LA. It's not commitment if you don't want it to be."

"It's overwhelming."

"Don't forget, I'll follow my Lola wherever she goes. Take her to LA, she has access to all my accounts. Buy a house, settle in, I won't be far behind."

She smiled. "I love how much you love her. And she's… secure with you."

"You're not secure with Knox?"

"It's difficult for me to picture our life. You and Roxie lived together as you traveled, you learned each other. Being here with Knox… it's hardly real life. I don't know anything about his work, his family. I know they keep in touch, but does he see them? What would they expect of me? What kind of life would we have? Working nine to five, paying the bills, that's what I'm used to. His life isn't that."

"Have you talked to him about this?"

She shook her head. "It's… He talks about us being together in New York. But would he be happy? He's chosen not to live there—"

"Knox did live in New York. Still does on and off. It won't be a culture shock for him." Though it might be for her. Yet, she was used to city living. How much different could it be? "If you're not in this, you have to tell him now. Break it off before he gets in deeper… if that's possible."

"I don't want to hurt him," she said. "I want it to be real and…" A feeble smile curled her lips. "Usually, I'm the dreamer in my relationships… It feels like he's throwing himself into this, into me, and I don't know if I can live up to his dream of me."

"The thing about guys like him, guys like us," he said, his smile becoming something more profound, yet amused. "We're all looking for a woman like you." Surprise impacted her. "I know it's… People see the glitz and the glamor. They think about the jets and the models, the money, the lifestyle, but we're just as human as you, as anyone."

"What do you mean?"

"Some people get sucked into it. To an extent, we all do at some point. In the early days, the novelty is difficult to resist. There's excess. We make mistakes. Sometimes people get hurt." That stole his smile. Was he thinking of Dayah? His focus drifted up to the water. "And then a woman walks in wearing Lola Bunny pajamas and slaps you down hard, treats you like any regular Joe." He looked at her. "We want something real. Something genuine." He smiled. "I'm not sure there's anyone alive more genuine than you, Jane. Be real. That's all he needs. You are the dream he has of you."

Sound from the bedroom heralded the interruption a second before it happened.

"What have I told you about bringing other women to our bedroom?" Roxie asked, smiling as she appeared on the deck with them. "That's what the guest rooms are for, Casanova." Zairn's eyes stayed on hers, waiting for her to respond perhaps. "How you doing, honey?"

"Better," she said, keeping her smile on Zairn for a second before raising her attention to her friend. "I feel better."

"Yeah, he's weird like that," Roxie said, taking Zairn's glass as she slid a hand onto his shoulder to descend into his lap. "Knox is on the phone."

"With?" Zairn asked as Roxie sipped.

"His brother."

"Figured," Zairn said, holding Roxie in place as his hips rose and he retrieved his cell from his pocket. "He'll need a chopper."

"Why is he on the phone to his brother?" she asked. "Did something happen with his family?"

"Yes," Roxie said as Zairn typed. "You're his family, honey."

Toria tripped out the door, startling them. "I called the front desk, they'll let the others know we won't make it."

"Oh, I don't want to ruin everyone's night."

Knox came out, phone still at his ear. "Z, is—"

"The chopper'll be on the roof in ten," Zairn said. "Car and security waiting at the other end. Room reserved in Nassau, but the chopper is his, he can come straight here after if he wants. Dalton with him?"

"No, he'll stay at their worksite," Knox said then raised the microphone. "You get all that, Cam… Yeah." He hung up and looked at her. "You doing okay, Blossom?"

"Am I doing okay? I don't know what's happening. You were yelling at each other five minutes ago."

"I know, I'm sorry," Knox said. "That's not what you need."

"Why were you talking to your brother?"

"Because I trust him," Knox said. "He'll put eyes on this guy, say what needs to be said."

She appealed to Roxie and Toria. "I don't know what that means."

Toria came over to crouch in front of her. "You can't be a prisoner on this island the rest of your life. You'll have to leave sometime."

"And when you do, no one wants a crazy person waiting for you," Roxie said. "This has to be taken care of."

"He hasn't done anything illegal, yet," Zairn said. "If he does, our people will make sure he's punished for it. But until he does…"

"He's free to roam around," Roxie said. "We won't let this go until there's an ocean between you."

"And my brother will help him understand screwing with us is not a viable option."

"Your brother… is he like a bodyguard or something?"

"He's an architect."

That didn't exactly enlighten her. "Oh. Okay."

"And a Collier," Knox said. "He doesn't leverage it much these days, but he has access to all the strings."

She wasn't much wiser.

"Do you want to stay here?" Toria asked. "They have three guest rooms. If you'd feel safer with all of us under one roof—"

"Yes," she said, nodding. When times were strained, or they needed comfort, the three friends under one roof were a valuable support. "If that's okay with everyone."

Roxie tapped a finger on the back of Zairn's arm around her. "That means Hatfield's out."

"Yeah," Zairn said, typing on his phone again. "Ogilvie's going to love this."

The woman in his lap curled against him, burying her face in the side of his neck. Marty appeared with a tray of drinks and Toria jumped up to scamper over to the young man bearing alcohol.

"You understand why I'm not doing this myself," Knox said, stealing her attention when he approached. "They don't follow Cam anymore; they gave up on that long ago. If I go there, if Zairn goes, it's a story."

"I understand," she said. "I don't expect anyone to… I appreciate it, but… I don't think Graham means to hurt anyone."

"Maybe not, and I can't say I wouldn't do the same if I was in his position. He's lovesick."

She raised her hand, tangling their fingers. "Do you mind… me staying here—"

"Whatever you need, you get," he said. "If sleeping here, close to your girls, is what you need, I'm in favor."

"Will you stay with me?" Something crossed his expression. He hadn't expected that request? Maybe it hadn't occurred to him to be anywhere else. "We don't have to share a bedroom, or a bed if you—"

"By your side is the only place I want to be," he said, bowing to kiss her. "I won't leave you."

THIRTY-SEVEN

EXCEPT HE DID because she woke up alone. Showering wasn't easy, but she was becoming accustomed to working around the sling. Not that it would be a part of her life much longer. Hopefully. The doctor was meant to assess her again that day. Fingers crossed he'd let her ditch it.

Without Knox around, she had no way to know exactly what the day held. They should be allowed to go about their lives as normal, shouldn't they? If Graham wasn't on the island, there was no threat.

She couldn't wrap her head around it. A threat? How could Graham be a threat? How could anyone be so obsessed with her that they'd travel around the globe trailing after her?

Tying her hair up was impossible with just one hand. Looping her hair tie around her wrist, she left the bedroom seeking out one of her girls. Someone would be around, she could hear voices, she just couldn't figure out who—

In the mouth of the hallway, she stopped. The kitchen, the living room, the place was teeming with people. All stopped when they noticed her and there wasn't a friend among them.

Someone came rushing in from the outer deck. Roxie. Thank God.

"Okay, sorry," Roxie said, weaving in and out of people. "I know this is a little…" She screwed up her face, waving a hand. "But it's not that difficult." Her friend put an arm around her waist. "Toria's on the beach with Merci and Astrid." The only people in the entourage she actually knew. Roxie began pointing at people. "That over there is Ryder Stone." He raised a flat hand. "All those scary guys over there are his men. They don't say much. Down on the couch is Ogilvie, we only like him sometimes. Next to him is Warren Dunlap, lawyer. Opposite is Terry Elson, our Head of Public Relations, and Mr. Salad, our press guy, you've probably seen him around." Some of the faces were familiar from Roxie's night MIA. "Over the—"

"Where's Zairn?" she asked.

None of the new names would stick in her befuddled mind.

"He's on a conference call outside. With Knox, Ballard, Reid, and Knox's brother." She squeezed her waist. "Who is super yummy, by the way."

When she blinked at her friend, Roxie laughed and let go to slide the hair tie from her wrist.

"Toria's words?" she asked as her friend went around back to tie up her hair.

"It's like we have a hive mind," Roxie said, running her fingers through her ponytail. "You want to come outside?"

If Knox was there… "Yes," she said. Roxie linked their arms to lead her across the room past all the people. "Is Toria interested?"

"In Cam? Probably." Her friend's smile grew wicked. "That I'd like to see."

"Toria knows how to seduce a man."

"Not this one," Roxie said as they went onto the deck. "He's an anomaly."

What did that mean?

The men stood around a high, glass patio table in the far corner.

Zairn noticed them first and raised his chin. "Okay, Lo?"

The question flagged their presence to the others. Her shoulders loosened when Knox's gaze landed on her. Everyone else faded away, and she went straight to him.

"We came to see what you boys are whispering about," Roxie said, going to her guy.

She tried to put an arm around Knox, but he crouched to kiss her, holding her head in both hands. "You okay, Blossom?"

"There are a lot of people here," she murmured. "Too many."

"There's no such thing when it comes to your safety," he said, straightening up, putting an arm around her to hold her half in front of him. "The rest you know, but that one there…"

He pointed across the table at the guy opposite him.

"He's a Collier," she said, recognizing the look immediately.

This one was rougher, in khaki shorts and an off-white tee-shirt, the pressed and presentable gene had skipped him. He had scruff on his face and his hair was just long enough to be tucked behind his ears while remaining wild on top.

"The baby one," Knox said.

"Camden Collier," he said, mischief lighting his eyes as he examined her. "You know there's an irony here that I'm struggling to articulate."

"Keep struggling," Knox said, kissing the top of her head.

"You want kids?" Cam asked, putting her on the spot.

"Do I want kids? I… Yes, someday."

"You care about the billion-dollar lifestyle? The yachts and diamonds and all that shit?" She shook her head. "You want to be famous? In the papers? On every screen?"

"No!" she asserted, taken aback. "Absolutely not."

Cam grinned over her at his brother. "She's perfect."

"Find your own," Knox said, coiling his arm around her to hold her tight against his body.

"Mimi will have kittens about this," Cam said. "You know she'll drop down and have a litter right there." He looked to Roxie and Zairn. "She coming to the wedding?"

"Mimi?" Zairn asked. "I don't know, Jane's planning it."

"The wedding?" Cam asked, enjoying that tidbit. "Two for the price of one?"

"Who had money on him falling before Casp?" a voice came through the phone on the table.

"No one," Cam said. "Casp's too in love with himself. No one had money on Zairn being the first to go either."

"I wasn't the first," Zairn said, his arm draped across Roxie.

"Kintyre doesn't count," the voice said. "He got divorced."

"And we were all devastated about that," Knox said without an ounce of sincerity.

"I want to meet her."

"Jules?" Zairn asked his fiancée. "No, you don't want to meet Jules."

"Why not?"

"Kesley dotes on her, hangs on her every word."

"I like Kesley," Roxie said.

"Which screws with everyone's head."

Her friend rolled her eyes and she laughed. "Roxie gets along with everyone."

"That's what makes her perfect for Zairn," Cam said. "You guys just tripped and fell into it, didn't you?"

"Toria is single," Roxie said. "If you want to take your pick from my friendship pool like your brother."

"Cam isn't wild enough for Toria."

"Astrid."

"Too young. Ballard would feed him his balls."

"Bree is up at the hotel. She's younger than Astrid, but has no scary cousin trained in killing people… that we know of."

"What's wrong with young?" came the voice through the phone. "Young doesn't complain. Young likes jewelry."

"So you don't have to treat them well?" Roxie asked. "You're not making a good impression, Rourke."

"Most every other time I've spoken to you, Kyst," Rourke said, "you've been naked in a guy's bed."

"The same guy," she said, squinting at the phone. "I've been naked in the same guy's bed."

"And I commend you. I like a woman who knows her place."

"You know who won't be invited to the wedding with that attitude?" Roxie asked. "Xavien Rourke."

"I've got 'em lined up, baby, better book the date early or you won't be blessed with my presence at all."

Opening her mouth, Roxie inhaled, but Zairn clamped his hand over it. "Don't go down this path with him, Lola. It turns him on."

"You spoil all my fun," Rourke said with a laugh in his words.

"Yeah, but you've met your match in Roxie, she won't back down. Ever."

"She's no match, she's amateur hour."

"Says the guy who owns the multibillion-dollar global platform designed around people disagreeing."

"Debate," Rourke said. "Huddle is about debate. Exchanging ideas. The free flow of information."

"Which is why you're on the line," Ballard said, his first contribution. Reid was quiet too. "We want the opposite. Stem the information and find out what he knows."

"And what dirt we can use," Knox said.

"Illegal hacking is what you're talking about."

"Can you do it?"

"Can I do it?" Rourke scoffed. "I did it last night. It's already done. Someone owes me big."

"I do," Knox said. "And you can cash in any time."

Roxie talked about Zairn's friends in much the way she thought of her girls. Knox spoke the same way. It was doubtful any of them would request payment or say no if one of their posse was in a jam.

Turning in Knox's embrace, she sought his attention. "Can we talk…? When you have a minute."

"I have a minute," he said, easing away from the group. "Keep me updated."

His arm stayed around her as they went back inside, past all the bustle, and down the hall into the bedroom they'd shared the previous night.

"Okay," she said to herself, exhaling. "I have an appointment with the doctor today."

He closed the bedroom door. "He can come here. Are you worried about your arm? Are you in pain?"

"No," she said, smiling and unclicking her sling to ease it off. "He said I'd only need it for a few days. It's been four days so…"

"You're done with it? Blossom, what's wrong?"

His concern was touching. "Nothing. I was just… thinking."

His eyes narrowed as she approached him. "About what?"

"Us."

"Okay," he said, dubious. "What about us?"

"I've been waiting around for you to come up with a plan." The fingertips of her injured arm walked onto his hips and up under his tee-shirt to his abs. The others wandered around the back of his neck. "I stressed myself out waiting, wondering…"

"You never have to stress yourself out. You want a plan—"

She yanked him down hard, forcing her mouth to his. All the stress and fear went away as he sank into their kiss. Yes. Whatever became of them, however their relationship worked out, there would never be a happier place than right there in his arms.

His hands splayed on her back, pulling her body to his that bowed over her, deepening their kiss before retreating.

"Don't tell me no bedroom," she panted as his mouth descended to her throat. "I love you."

His smile was fierce when he landed it on her. "You love me?"

"I love you," she said, a laugh of joy bursting out of her.

Bending his knees, he scooped her up, coiling her legs around him. "I don't want to hurt you."

"Promise me you'll never leave," she said, losing herself in the sensation of his lips on her neck. "Promise we're forever."

He took his time about laying her down in the bed and rose to meet her eye, brushing her hair from her face as he did. "I love you, Blossom."

"Zairn said he'd follow Roxie anywhere and I realized… I don't care where we are so long as we don't have to say goodbye."

"Where'd you have this revelation?"

"Alone in the shower," she said. "I didn't know where you were and… I want to know where you are."

"We'll know where each other are, Blossom. Always." His smile came with an exhale that was almost relief. "Roxie says that's no way to measure love."

"And she's right," she said, her hand rising to his cheek. "Because it should be immeasurable."

"It's immeasurable," he said, kissing her quick. "Off the fucking charts immeasurable."

She laughed. "Good, now take your shirt off."

Didn't take him long to rid them both of their clothes. She tried helping, but he was much more decisive in his actions.

"I missed you," she said, stroking his body as he came down on top of her. "No more games. No more deception."

He kissed her lips. "No more fling."

"Forever?"

"Forever," he said, lowering to kiss her mouth again.

Wrapping her legs around him, she gave him space to keep kissing her, to redirect his mouth to her neck, her breasts. All of her was his. She'd fought it. The fear was easier to embrace. In the shower, it had been… Usually, she was the dreamer, that's what she'd told Zairn. Why was Knox different?

Obsessing about that kept her from sleep the previous night, which may be why she'd slept through him getting up that morning.

Why didn't she dream with Knox?

Why didn't she lose herself in the possibilities?

Because, for the first time, she was with a man who'd make all her dreams come true. Not the money or the material, he cared so much that he prioritized her over everything else. No obstacle was too big. No barrier insurmountable. Every time she tried to put a wall in front of him, he broke it down.

When he kissed her clit, she tensed. Yet, just as quickly, her body relaxed. This man didn't want her to be self-conscious. Didn't want her thinking of what came before him. This man loved her. With him, it was more than words and no kind of manipulation.

"Knox," she whispered, her fingers twining in his hair. Sealing her lips, she held her mouth closed as long as she could. His tongue slipped into her, circling slowly and rising. A quake of pleasure vibrated through her. "Maybe this wasn't a good idea."

Her mouth opened wide, a whine escaping when he tickled her clit with the tip of his tongue.

"Beautiful blossom," he whispered against her.

"There are too many people here for me to—" A yelp escaped when he slipped his fingers into her, his mouth still working on her clit. "Oh, God, Knox… Mmmm…"

"Like that?" he murmured against her, his voice a thick velvet betraying he knew exactly what he was doing to her. "Blossom?"

"I like it," she panted. "Yes, I like it. Don't stop! Don't… oh!" Teasing and playing, he got some kind of perverse pleasure from taking her to the edge and then pulling back. "Knox… I'm on the… We're protected, babe, please just…"

He surged up over her. "On the pill?"

"Mm hmm," she said, failing to focus on the blur he was over her with her eyes open just a sliver. "There's been no one… since we…"

"Ditto," he said, sliding himself into her.

Oh, life, love, liberty, all of it was right there in her center, in that part of her filled by him. That void inside her, the one that craved security, love, and devotion, it was finally satisfied. All her life she'd waited for him. For this man. This exact guy. He was The One.

When a tear slipped from her eye, concern hardened his expression. "Blossom—"

"I love you," she said, restraining a yelp. "All my life I've waited and… You're my dreams come true."

And with that revelation, she let go of the fear that held her back. She'd been so scared and hadn't known just how that reserve restrained her. She'd been terrified to surrender to her love in case she was disappointed again. Her optimism, her spirit, it wouldn't survive another blow.

His smile was easy, and he slowed to swipe away her tear with his thumb. "You're the forever every man dreams of. You're my forever."

Ensconced in their completion, they'd face their hurdles later, after appreciating what they'd found in each other for as long as their bodies held out.

THIRTY-EIGHT

AND IT WASN'T once. Or twice. Or even three times. They'd been making love all day and she'd lost count of how many times he'd brought her to climax. The sun was sinking in the sky, their bedroom door locked, something Knox took care of when Marty first knocked to ask if they needed anything.

"Will your brother be mad?"

"My brother?" he asked. "Cam? That I got to you first? Probably."

She laughed and sat up. "That he came all this way to see you and I've sequestered you the whole day."

"He was in Florida anyway, he didn't come that far. And, believe me, he understands."

"Roxie called him an anomaly."

His lips twisted like they were damming a laugh. "I guess you could call him that."

"What does that mean? Where does he live? Does he live in LA?"

"No," Knox said, trailing his fingers up and down her body. "He needed a clean break."

"I was thinking…" she said, wriggling closer to lay a hand on his chest. "We should stay in LA."

"We should?"

"Yes, you can't just walk away from your life overnight."

"You walked away from yours for Z and that was for less sex… At least I hope it was for less sex. Roxie does too, I'll bet."

Smiling at his tease, she lay down on him, careful to support her shoulder. "I walked away from Chicago for Roxie. And we don't have to decide everything overnight. You have your work in LA, your family, we should stay there, at first anyway. Prepare everyone for you leaving, get everything in order."

"Blossom, I spend little time in LA. We're a conglomerate, our work doesn't begin and end in California. I can work anywhere. Literally anywhere on the planet."

"And you don't think your mom wants a chance to adjust to the idea of you leaving? Won't she be hurt? Disappointed?"

He exhaled a laugh. "My mom spends almost as much time on the road as I do. Where do you think I get the wandering gene?"

"You think you'll always wander?"

"There may be reasons I have to travel for business, I can't tell you I'll never leave New York. But who's to say that wandering has to be business related? You like it here, right?"

She turned her head to lay her cheek against him. "I like it here," she murmured, running her palm up his torso. "Being with you like this."

"Wherever you are, that's where I want to be."

"So we go to LA, get whatever you need in order…"

"For how long?"

"A few days, a few weeks, months, whatever it takes. I won't be able to afford LA rents—"

"Don't worry about that," he said, finger-combing her hair. "You don't have to worry about bills ever again."

"I don't want to use you… I don't want to be one of those women."

"You don't have a job yet," he said. "You could work for CollCom… if you want."

"With you?"

"That's up to you," he said. "But we don't have to be on top of each other. There's so much to choose from. You can write your own ticket. Do whatever you want. Whatever makes you happy."

"Or I could work at Crimson."

"Or that."

"Not that I'd want to work there forever, but would it be okay to stay there? Crimson HQ? Live there… at least initially. When we're done in LA."

"Whatever you want, Blossom."

He made everything so easy. It wasn't that he didn't care, just that he'd really move heaven and earth for her.

Lifting her head again, she rested her chin on him. "What if I want to be a famous actress?" she said, slithering up his body. "What if I want an Oscar?"

"Then you better get yourself a pretty dress," he said, accepting her gentle kiss. "You'll need it in February."

She laughed and kissed him again, guiding his hand onto her breast, aching for the touch that enlivened her.

"I love you," she whispered, sliding her leg across him.

Their need grew with the fury of their kiss. He tried to turn her onto her back, but she resisted. With him, she could experiment. The freedom of him, of being with him, awoke all kinds of wondering.

Someone knocked on the door.

She heard it and Knox did too. When she tried to break the kiss, he caught the back of her head, holding her mouth to his. They'd neglected their friends, the doctor, all their responsibilities. Maybe Toria was heading to the beach for the cookout—

The knock came again. "Knox." That wasn't Marty's voice. It was far graver than the young assistant's. Knox released pressure to break the kiss. "It hit the wires."

His jaw clenched. Anger built behind his pursed lips. "Fuck," he hissed and eased her aside to get up. "Fuck!"

"What is it?" she asked as he put on his shorts. "What does that mean?"

He came back, stroking her hair down around her jaw to tip up her chin. "It's okay, Blossom," he said gently and kissed her. "I'll deal with it."

Deal with what? He marched to the door, and she pulled up the sheet to cover herself as he yanked it open.

"You didn't make the call?"

Was that his brother?

"You didn't?"

Their voices disappeared down the hall. Something had hit the press. She knew from experience with Roxie that could be a dangerous thing. On the island, they should be safe... shouldn't they?

Coiling the sheet around her, she held it tight with her good arm and went out after them. If something was happening, she had to be a part of it. This was her burden, not just Knox's. And if it was about Graham...

Those left were gathered in the living room watching the news on a wall-mounted TV.

"...confirmation is still pending, but witnesses claim the ceremony took place on the island earlier today..."

"Ceremony," she said, rushing closer. "What ceremony?"

Roxie put an arm around her waist.

"No one expected a wedding, much less a wedding like this..." the reporter on TV said.

With only a beach behind the woman on TV, it was difficult to place her location.

"A wedding?"

"This is bullshit," Ballard said.

Zairn raised a remote and the TV silenced.

"A wedding," she said again and gasped. "Oh my God, Rox, they think you and Zairn got married?" Knox came up next to Roxie and the two shared a look. "What? Oh, God, I'm sorry this is—"

"They don't think we got married," Roxie said, forcing a smile.

"They think we did," Knox said.

We? They? No one would—no one could... She staggered back a step. Knox grabbed her arm to keep her upright.

"Who would do something like this?" Toria asked.

"All arrivals today were canceled," Roxie said. "Anyone meant to come here today was diverted for a vacation somewhere else. Departures were allowed though; we can't hold people prisoner."

"It doesn't matter who," Cam said. "Pay someone enough you can get anyone to say anything. All they had to do was grab someone off the boat, put words in their mouth and money in their hand."

"You think it's because you came," Toria asked. "Knox's brother had to show up for a reason."

"It was Graham," Zairn said on a sigh, garnering everyone's attention. "You all know it, I'm just giving it a voice. A Collier shows up to warn him off, suddenly security is up his ass. His hopes, ideas for the future... finding out Jane was involved with someone else took all of that away from him."

"It's spite."

"What an asshole."

"Rourke already went in and deleted everything. Pictures, videos, emails, everything," Cam said. "The guy has no evidence of anything. This was the only way he knew how to hurt you. You hurt him, so he hurts you right back."

"On the plus side..." Toria said, peeking into her peripheral vision, "Graham's on a plane back to Europe right now."

The threat was gone, but the drama was just beginning.

"I have to call my mom," she said and laid a hand on Knox. "You should call yours too." Guilt ate her up. "I'm sorry, this is all my fault."

"Your fault? Why is anything your fault?"

"If I hadn't got involved with Graham in the first place—"

"You only got with him 'cause of Brendan," Toria said. "He tore you down so much—"

"That's no excuse," she said. "I should've known better."

"Honey, you've got to take a ticket in this room when it comes to making bad relationship choices. We've all done it. At some point or another," Roxie said and appealed to the others. "Right?"

"God, yes," Toria said, being the most vocal about it though the others were nice enough to nod and agree. "You are an angel compared to the rest of us. Remember that evangelist guy I went with?"

Breathing out, a smile found her lips. "Yes."

"How he preached all through sex? Screamed scripture at me? All damn night… What the hell was I thinking?"

"And my magician," Roxie said. "Remember him? He used to do tricks that involved money and valuables vanishing from our purses and apartment?"

"Smartest thing you ever did was make his number disappear from your phone," Toria said.

As her girls moved in, Knox eased back a step.

With a hand on her arm, Roxie was next to offer comfort. "Zairn dated a woman who got his face tattooed on her ass. Literally, his face, her ass."

A blub of laughter escaped.

"That is a true story," Ballard said.

"Knox dated a woman who would only eat white food," Cam said. "More than one actually. That's LA for you."

Knox nodded. "I did. Cam went out with a woman who took her clothes off everywhere they went."

"That is also true," Cam said.

"Everywhere they went…"

"Even in my mother's house… during dinner." All three women peered at him, but he just slipped his hands in his pockets, bobbing his head in a nod. "True story."

"Guess Ballard's the only smart one here," Toria said. "Maybe he can smell the crazy."

"Oh, no, he is not immune," Zairn said. "When he broke up with one of his exes, she handcuffed herself to him. The woman chained herself to him and swore she was carrying explosives. Threatened to blow him up. If she couldn't have him, no one could… Shut down four city blocks. Guy had to dictate his will to a lawyer on the phone." Ballard accepted Zairn's hand landing on his shoulder with a wince. Not of pain, of truth. "I was handed résumés. The guy was a goner."

"Yeah, okay, you get the crazy award," Roxie said. "Shit, Ballard, where did you find her?"

He and Zairn looked at each other. "Crimson."

"LA?" Roxie asked and they nodded. "There's something about that place, I swear to God."

"That's where you and Knox got together, right?" Toria asked.

It started with a restroom kiss, which wasn't exactly a romantic story. "We went back to his place from there, but…"

"Scroogey dumped me there," Roxie said, nodding backwards.

"You tell everyone that," Zairn said. "Everyone knows that, Lola. Everyone on the planet."

"I just like to remind you," she said, showing her girls a smile. "How close you came to losing the best thing that ever happened to you. If I hadn't saved your ass, you'd be all alone right now. Knox too, so, you know, you should both be grateful."

"Who got you in to make your big grand gesture?" Knox asked from behind Roxie. "And I'd be with Jane whether you two got back together or not."

Their kiss had happened the night of that breakup when Roxie vanished. Was he saying he'd have pursued her? Because if Roxie hadn't got back with Zairn, they'd never have been together in Crimson the night they went home together.

"I'd have figured out a way to get to him," Roxie said, "with or without your help. I'm a doer."

"Hate to be the one to tell you, Z," Knox said. "The crazy didn't go that far from your sex life."

"Oh, the sex is all kinds of crazy," Roxie said. "Gotta keep raising that bar."

Toria cleared her throat. "And we're not the ones who spent all day getting hot and sweaty in bed." Her cheeks warmed. "Are we hitting the beach?"

"If you want to."

"Uh…" Zairn started, but it was Roxie who tensed up.

"That's probably not a good idea."

"Why?"

Knox leaned past her girls. "Because the world thinks we got married."

"Right," she said as someone knocked on the door.

Ballard left the group to head over there.

"Five bucks it's Nigel," Knox said.

Roxie scowled, spinning to him. "When was the last time you saw a five-dollar bill? Shit, you're a Collier, the smallest you carry is probably a thousand-dollar bill… created just for your family's private use."

"I'm a Collier," Cam said, raising a feeble hand though amusement shimmered around him. "My power got shut off last month 'cause I didn't pay the bill."

Knox frowned at his brother. "Because you keep firing the Brooker assistants. That's an administrative error not a financial one. How much you making on your current project? Ten mill? Twenty?"

Still wasn't close to the rest of the wealth in the room. Cam was an oddity, Roxie was right about that.

Ballard came back over with the predicted guest.

"I assume you have a plan?" Nigel asked his cousin.

"Yeah," Knox said. "But I have to run it by my girl first."

Run it by her? Uh oh, that sounded ominous.

THIRTY-NINE

"NO, MOM. I'M not married," she said into the phone on the deck table the guys had been using earlier.

Roxie had put stools around it to sit with her and Toria. She needed the support for this conversation.

"This is that boy Roxie's mixed up with," her mom said from the phone. "Isn't it?"

Boy? Zairn was no kind of "*boy*" she'd ever known.

"No, this is nothing to do with him."

"He's a philanderer," her mom said. "Roxanna?"

"Yes, Momma S."

"He's a philanderer."

"Reformed," she said. "He doesn't philander anymore."

Her friend was at least accepting the insult as amusing. She didn't feel quite so relaxed about it.

"That is what they all say," her mom said. "You girls will get drawn into their debauched circle. It's temptation. All that money. They dazzle you."

Roxie picked invisible lint from her skirt. "He's less about dazzling me with money and more about dazzling me with his co—"

"Mom, you don't have to worry about us," she said, not appreciating where Roxie had been going. "Everyone's looking after each other."

"I'd never let anyone hurt Jane," Toria said. "She's fine. She's really great. Knox is great. They love each other."

"Then they should be married," her mom said. "You're not philandering with him, are you?"

That was a tough one to deny and she cringed against the truth. She'd been philandering all damn day. "He's a good man," she managed to squeak out. Her mom wouldn't miss that that wasn't a denial. "You have to give him a chance."

"To give him a chance, I have to meet him. Is he going to marry you? If he's going to marry you, he should meet your family. Have you met his family?"

"I've met his brother."

"Another philanderer?"

"No," Roxie said. "Cam's no philanderer."

"Maybe you should've considered that before tying yourself to this Knox," her mom said. "He'll tell you he loves you until he gets what he wants. And still no ring on your finger. You should know better."

She should. There was no denying that. Not that Knox was only after one thing, but the men from her past had taught her plenty of harsh lessons.

"He does love me," she said. "And I love him."

"And now your life is plastered all over the papers. Your private business."

"We didn't want that to happen."

"The world knows you're with a philanderer."

"Mom, he's not a philanderer."

"If he wasn't you'd know if he plans to marry you or not."

"He does." Came a deep voice she hadn't expected. Knox approached them from the beach. He'd been saying goodbye to Cam who wouldn't stay another night. "He does plan to marry her."

"Okay, well, Mom, this is Knox."

"Are you a philanderer?"

Oh, damn, she wanted the ground to swallow her whole.

"Not the last time I checked," Knox said.

Roxie laughed but stifled it into a kind of snort. "You have to see them together to know, they only have eyes for each other."

"Until he gets what he wants."

On an exhale, she sagged.

Knox was right there to hold her up, squeezing her shoulder at the same time. "What I want is to be with your daughter. Only your daughter. For the rest of our lives."

Silence lingered on the line for a few seconds. "I'll believe it when I see it," her mother said. "You plan to come up this way?"

Was that a question or a statement?

"We will," Knox said. "I look forward to meeting you in person."

"We'll see," her mom said again and the line disconnected.

She sighed. "I'm sorry about that. Everyone."

"We should've had Zairn out here," Toria said. "Charming the panties off her."

"I don't think that's possible in any reality."

"Who's hungry?" Zairn called as he stepped out of the house to cross the deck.

"The cookout is tonight," she said, putting a hand on Knox's.

"Nigel says we can go if we want."

"Seems strange though," Toria said. "You're kind of out of LIP. Now you're... out."

"I suppose we are."

Zairn came over and coiled both arms around Roxie from behind.

"Philanderer," her friend said in accusation, tipping her head back against his chest.

Confusion lit his frown. "Excuse me?"

"You're a corrupting philanderer," Roxie said, leaping off the stool and out of his embrace only to then turn and wrap her arms around him. "Thank you, Casanova."

"You're welcome," he said, gifting her a kiss.

Their whispering and kissing continued after she forced herself to look away. Seeing love in action still tickled her sentimentality.

"I am going to grab Astrid and go," Toria said, leaving her own stool. "Some of us are still in the market." She came around to give her a hug. "Call Merci. Invite her over. Do couples things." Toria kissed her cheek then went over to give Roxie a hug and kiss too before strutting her way back to the house across the deck. "Be safe or expect babies!"

Toria was so giving, so worthy, the most generous person she knew.

"Want to do couples things?" Roxie asked, still in her fiancé's arms. "We don't have car keys or a glass bowl."

"That's funny, Lola," Zairn said, tugging her with him as they retreated. "Philanderer."

"Uh, you're the one with the reputation, playboy… We never did have that threesome with Reid."

"Still thinking about that, huh?"

"Mostly just when we're having sex."

"Funny, me too."

As their voices faded, Knox came around to cup her face. "I love you."

"I know," she said, letting the weight of her head rest in his hands. "Roxie was kidding about the car keys." He probably knew that, but just in case. "She's not to everyone's taste, her humor, I mean, but she's a—"

He kissed her. "Do you want to go with Toria?"

"No, if she's with Astrid, she'll be fine. Ballard will keep an eye on them."

"People will take pictures."

"It's a beautiful island."

"Of us, Blossom. They'll take pictures of you… when we leave here."

Oh, she squirmed. "I don't know how I feel about that."

"Roxie's been through it, and I'll be with you, every step of the way. No one will hurt you."

"Did you mean what you said?" she asked. "About us getting married?"

"When we're ready, yes. You said it about LA. We don't have to do everything overnight. You can adjust to being with me, this life, my family, the scrutiny… Just don't freak and run out on me, okay? Whatever you need, you get."

"I want to meet your family."

"Okay."

"I want them to know I'm not… that this isn't about money."

"They know that."

She frowned. "How can they know?"

"Because I'm smarter than that. They trust me, which means they trust you."

She wasn't sure it was that easy. "I still want to meet them… I wish Cam had stayed."

"He's all about his work. It matters to him."

"You matter to me."

"Ditto," he said, helping her off her stool. "We missed the doc."

"I'll see him tomorrow," she said, smiling up at him. "It doesn't hurt."

"At all?"

She slid her good arm around him. "Not when I have you to lean on."

"Always," he said, bowing to kiss her. "You'll always have me to lean on."

And she believed him. Their courtship may not have matched her preconceived fantasy, but there was no doubt Knox Collier was it. Her forever guy. The One. From nowhere, the surprise of him was exactly what she needed. They'd proved they could weather storms, that they could heat the night, and still care in the morning.

Love. Her true love. Care wasn't a big enough word. She trusted him, needed him, and his certainty was just as powerful.

Her whole life she'd dreamed of her happily ever after and this man was it. He'd snuck up on her, but she wouldn't have it, or him, any other way.

FORTY

"WILL SHE BE SAFE?" Jane asked as she and Roxie left the golf cart that brought them home in the dark.

Two days had passed since her and Knox's relationship was broadcast to the world. Being on the island turned out to be a blessing. Yes, it was weird that people gawked and whispered whenever she walked by, but better a few than the entire world.

She and Roxie had joined their friend, and the other LIP members, for a drink at the club. But when she said she was ready to be home, Roxie didn't hesitate to say goodnight to the others.

"Toria is having the time of her life," her friend said. "The whole island is like her backyard. It's her playground. She'll be more than safe. You think I'd have left her there if she wouldn't be safe?"

"It's just strange…"

Roxie opened the bungalow door to go inside, slip off her shoes, and head for the bar. "To come home without her?"

"She's talking about staying on the island after we leave on Sunday."

"She can stay if she wants to," Roxie said, pulling bottles from the bar and glasses from the freezer.

She picked up her friend's shoes. Just because someone would tidy them didn't mean they should take that for granted. No need to be impolite or lazy. Though Roxie would've left her shoes lying around in their Chicago apartment without a second thought. It just so happened that these days, someone was employed to pick up after them.

"We'll all be apart again," she whined.

"Aww, honey," Roxie said, putting everything down to come over and hug her. "You just want everyone in one place."

"Don't you feel bad for her? I feel bad for her."

Roxie snagged her shoes to toss them aside and led her over to the bar to continue making drinks. "Why do you feel bad for her? She's having the time of her life."

"But she doesn't have that someone, you know?"

"Don't do that," Roxie said, opening a bag of mixed nuts to pour them into a bowl. "We're not going to be those women. The women who pity the single women."

"It makes a difference," she said, propping a hip on the bar to sugar the frozen glasses. "Getting into bed with Knox at night. It's safe."

"Toria's safe."

"Not that kind of safe, it's just…" Beyond the deck, striding up from the beach, Knox, Zairn, and Reid were side by side wearing towels around their hips. "Uh… do you see shorts?"

"Huh?" Roxie asked and presumably followed her line of sight. "Where's a camera when we need one?" Maybe they shouldn't have dropped Merci off at her bungalow. "Damn, those are some beautiful men though, right?" Her friend laughed and poured the drinks. "Which one do you want?"

She smiled. "The one at the end."

"Good. Bet I can get that middle one's number."

Roxie was a hoot.

She laughed. "You have his number."

"I do?" Roxie tossed her a quizzical look. "The middle one?"

"Yeah, that's his ring you're wearing."

"I work fast," Roxie said, admiring her ring. "Or he's just that easy."

"Who's that easy?" Zairn asked as the three men crossed the deck to come inside.

"You, I think," Roxie said, picking up the glasses to hand one over and raise hers in a toast before drinking. "What you wearing under that towel, Casanova?"

When he smirked and opened it up, she only saw a flash of flesh before Roxie's hand rose enroute to cover her eyes. It was unnecessary. She spun on the spot, sloshing her drink on the floor in her quick about-face.

"Oh my God!"

"Don't scar my friend," Roxie said. "Why are you naked with yours? Why were we barred from this nakey party?"

"It's too complicated for your female mind to comprehend," he said. "We're gonna take a shower."

"We like you and…"

"You and me," Zairn said. "Come on."

"Oh, we're going to take a shower."

Roxie handed over her drink and kissed her cheek before stage whispering. "You'll get the skinny if you give it up. We'll compare notes later."

Reid went down one hallway as Zairn and Roxie disappeared down the parallel one.

Her guy came up beside her. "You okay?"

Instead of answering, she gulped down her drink. Knox took the other, sipped it and put it down.

On her last swallow, she gasped and laid a hand on him. "I feel bad for Toria."

"You care about people," he said, taking her glass to set it aside before linking their fingers. "She's your friend."

"I don't want to abandon her," she said, following as he led. "I want to invite her to things. If we ever have things. She's my family."

They went into their bedroom. "I know. What's brought this on?"

"You."

"Me?"

Sitting on the bed, she bent over to unbuckle her sandals. "Is Caspian patient?"

"Casp? No. Definitely not patient."

"Is he a good man?" she asked, picking up her shoes to take them into the closet. "Does he value family and friends? Is he caring?" Spinning on the spot, her gorgeous guy was there in the closet doorway. "Why were you naked with Zairn and Reid?"

"Oh, you did notice? I wondered."

"Is it private?"

"Promise to a friend," he said, moseying over to gather her against him. "You don't want to set Toria up with Caspian."

"She's not his type?"

"He's not…" his head moved as he pondered, "wired that way."

"You have other friends."

"You want to set Toria up?" he asked. "Haven't we shown you, people find their own way in love, friends or not."

"The way you make me feel… Us, having this, being together… I want everyone I love to feel like this."

"Blossom, what we feel…" he said, curving both hands around the back of her neck. "A lot of people go their whole lives without feeling it."

"I still struggle to believe that I've been this lucky, to find you and I… I can't imagine ever walking away from you now. I'm sorry I pushed you away."

"I'm just grateful you welcomed me back," he said and dipped to kiss her. "We're going to be okay, Blossom."

"Even if we fly to Chicago to meet my mom on the way to our lives in LA?"

He snickered. "Yes. Trust me, babe, nothing will make this go away." He shrugged. "And we'll take Z, just in case. He and RK are coming back to LA with us anyway."

She laughed. "The philanderer might divert some of her judgment. Roxie handles it better than I do."

"No one can judge us because no one knows what we know."

"What do we know?"

Stooping lower, he kissed the end of her nose. "That we've found our own happily ever after."

Read more from the Roxiverse in *Nothing in Between: One...*

Thank you for reading this tale!
If you can, please take the time to review.

~

Ask your local library for more Scarlett Finn
novels!

~

For all things Scarlett Finn
check out:

www.scarlettfinn.com

Next in the Roxiverse:

SCARLETT FINN